Darkness in Ronda

Paul S. Bradley

Editor: Gary Smailes; www.bubblecow.com
Cover Illustration: Jill Carrott; www.virtue.es
Rear cover photo of Ronda Bullring by Paul Bradley.
Layout: Paul Bradley; Nerja, Spain.
Darkness in Ronda is the second volume of the
Andalusian Mystery Series.
Publisher: Paul Bradley, Nerja, Spain.
First Edition: March 2019.
Contact: info@paulbradley.eu
www.paulbradley.eu

Available in eBook and Print on Demand. See website
for details.

ISBN: 9788409199839

The Andalusian Mystery Series

Andalucía is wrapped in sunlight, packed with history and shrouded in legend. Her stunning landscapes, rich cuisine, friendly people and a vibrant lifestyle provide an idyllic setting for four mysteries linked by shared darkness. Whilst each book can be read on its own, the author strongly recommends reading them in numerical order.

Dedication

To AHI Travel Inc. Chicago, Illinois for giving me so many years of memorable travel directing experiences; one of which introduced me to Juan Ramon Romero, a retired bullfighter, and descendant of the highly respected Romero dynasty. His vibrant lectures on bullfighting at the Parador Hotels in Ronda and Antequera and my humble attempts to translate them inspired this book.

Acknowledgments

My heartfelt thanks to Gabriel Soll, Jill Carrott, Michael Kellough, Elizabeth Francis, Fran Poelman, Norman Millhouse, Renate Bradley and my editor Gary Smailes. The mistakes are all mine.

Paul S. Bradley

1

1986

"Ugh," screamed Leon Prado as a fierce black bull gored him in the groin with its right horn. The beast hoisted him above its head and tossed him five meters through the air as easily as a feather pillow. He landed on the arena sand with a heavy thump. The crowd gasped as attendants rushed to save him from more punishment by flapping their capes at the rampaging monster. Hopefully, they would distract it from finishing Prado off. He lay motionless, the pain was excruciating, and blood spurted everywhere. His blood.

He opened a bone-weary eye and blinked several times as the haunting nightmare faded, and reality started to bite. "Where the fuck am I?" he said to himself with a growing sense of unease as he sat up. "And why is my head thumping so badly?"

He looked around the traditionally decorated room,

searching for something familiar that might assuage his anxiety. The reflection of his twenty-year-old self in a large wardrobe mirror at the side of the bed startled him. "Not my usual pretty sight," he said, spotting his hazel bloodshot eyes and pallid round face. He ran the fingers of both hands through his close-cropped black hair and inspected his naked muscular torso for any damage. His stomach churned alarmingly. "OK, I was drunk," he admitted, as his foggy mind tried to make sense of the surroundings.

Opposite the end of the bed, he spied an old gilt-framed painting hanging on the wall above a bleached timber chest of drawers. He recognized the portrait instantly, as would nearly every Spaniard. It was of the famous Matador, Pedro Romero, painted by Francisco Goya back in the late eighteenth century.

The artist had captured Pedro at his best. A handsome man in his mid-forties with olive skin, long dark hair graying at his distinctive bushy sideburns. He was stylishly dressed in a black jacket lined with red silk, a gray waistcoat and a white shirt with a ruff collar. A pale rose-colored cloak was draped over his shoulders.

"Surely it's not the original," Prado mumbled as he staggered out of bed, guts lurching violently as he walked over to inspect it more closely. It was a high-quality print. Then the events of yesterday sprang back into his mind.

Prado was staying in the historic country mansion of distant descendants of the man in the portrait. The Romero family was one of the few remaining bullfighting dynasties in Spain. For three hundred years, each generation had produced several legendary heroes, still talked about among aficionados in the cafés and bars up and down the country. He'd been invited to a wedding by his best friend and work colleague, Juan Romero, whose elder brother Jaime was getting married to the daughter of yet another respected bullfighting family, Maria Ordoñez.

Leon groaned as he recalled the cause of his hangover. Knocking back that final orujo at last night's stag party had been a huge mistake. Then a sense of foreboding pricked his subconscious. Had he been goaded into something foolish in his inebriated state? The memory flooded back. A broken conversation, a challenge accepted. He smacked his forehead with his fist as he realized what he'd agreed to. Then instantly regretted it as a stab of pain behind the eyes reminded him of his delicate disposition. "You numbskull Prado, you dumb bastard. You allowed those Romero brothers to cajole you into fighting a bull. You're due in the bullring after breakfast."

As Prado showered and shaved, his heart thumped madly at the magnitude of his foolishness. He dressed in his favorite blue Levi jeans and white Real Madrid football shirt, ruminating over his dilemma, cursing as each detail of the morning's potentially fatal ordeal became clear.

This was not to be a mock bullfight wearing some stupid garish costume and an outsized sombrero against some timid breed of domestic cattle. He'd agreed to pit his wits against Toro de Lidia. Savage Iberian fighting bulls that had been maiming and killing capable bullfighters in arenas throughout Spain for centuries. This bad-tempered beast was renowned for its speed, strength, and agility; it feared nothing.

It was to be Prado alone in the bullring facing this killer. There would be a little training, admittedly from

Juan, himself an apprentice bullfighter, but even with that, he knew he stood no chance. The prize would not be an ear or a tail, just with luck; his survival and some salvaged pride.

Prado's pride.

He could back down, but then he would lose face, and he was far too stubborn to let that happen. Which just might be his saving grace. If he could somehow see this through, he would undoubtedly earn some degree of face, and despite his feeble condition and lack of skills, he was not about to miss it. He was going into that ring come hell or high water.

Afterward, ignoring the distinct possibility that he might not survive. He would have earned his cara, even some cojones, and would become mucho hombre, which was worth whatever degree of risk that might entail. Nothing could be said to deter him, and nobody would dare attempt to persuade him otherwise. Except, perhaps, his mother, who would be furious with her guapo niño at such macho nonsense, but she was miles away in Cordoba busy looking after his father and four younger sisters.

Prado and Juan had been granted a three-day furlough from their compulsory military service at the Spanish Legion base on the outskirts of the historic Andalusian mountain city of Ronda where they were both military cops. The wedding was being held at Ganaderia Romero, the family's bull breeding ranch. Over three hundred hectares of rolling hills, located in the Grazalema National Park to the west of Ronda. It was just off the snaking road to Jerez de la Frontera, the home of sherry, Flamenco and the Royal Spanish Riding School.

The ceremony would take place in the spacious

family chapel opposite the main hacienda, followed by a catered reception and live music in a large marquee erected on the manicured lawns to the rear of the property.

Prado posed fully dressed in front of the wardrobe mirror. The shower had marginally improved his headache, but his stomach was still complaining. "Let's hope it's pissing down," he said, going over to the window and drawing back the floral curtains.

As on most days in Andalucía, it was a crystal blue sky and not a cloud in sight.

"Fuck it," he said.

***

The central feature of the substantial granite-built Romero property was a circular tower with a pointed terracotta tiled roof and narrow barred windows. It was the original defensive structure constructed during the fifteenth century. Its purpose was to protect the occupants from marauding bandoleros or bandits that had plagued the area at that time. Today it formed the main entrance. A grand circular staircase wound its way around the inner perimeter of the tower providing access to the three floors. Over the centuries, several wings had been added to accommodate the expanding family and staff.

Leon closed his bedroom door and headed along the dimly lit stone corridor toward the tower. He stepped gingerly onto the staircase that curved around a massive crystal chandelier. All the way down, his eyes were drawn to the portraits of deceased Romero bullfighters dressed in their traditional sky-blue trajes de luz, or suits-of-light. They may have been heroes in their time, he thought, but they are all dead now and if I'm not careful, I could be joining them in about an hour. He clung tightly onto the well-worn timber handrail. His stomach still complaining. Nerves jangling worse than ever.

He found Juan in the elegant dining room that led off the main hallway on the ground floor. He was seated at one end of a long, highly polished wood dining table covered with white placemats and silver cutlery. The views through full-height windows to the rear of the house were of glorious landscaped gardens. Beyond those were luscious green meadows dotted with grazing cattle and a hazy outline of the distant mountains. A massive walk-in fireplace dominated the far end of the room. More family portraits lined the walls, this time including women and children.

Juan was laughing and joking with a dozen or so bleary-eyed stag party attendees. Cousins, friends, and Jaime the groom, who was serving his first full season on the circuit as a professional torero. Their eldest brother Pedro, who ran the family restaurant in Madrid was sitting at the head of the table next to the brother's father, Don Pedro Romero. A short, well-built balding man in his early fifties with silver hair. The eldest son in each generation was traditionally christened after their famous ancestor. The family resemblance to the portrait upstairs was incredible despite almost two hundred years between them. The only notable difference was progressive baldness and silver hair as each grew older. Otherwise, they were of athletic appearance, petite facial features, dark brown eyes, strong chins and a supreme aura of confidence. They all stopped talking and jeered at Prado's belated appearance.

Leon's stomach heaved at the sight of Juan's congealing dish of Serrano ham and fried eggs, sprinkled with crispy garlic. He preferred to consume nothing, but dutifully went over to the buffet table and poured himself a small glass of freshly squeezed orange juice. He took a seat next to Juan and sipped it cautiously, wrestling with his nausea.

"Not looking so good this morning, Leon," said Juan.

"Nonsense," said Prado. "Never felt better."

"A more robust sustenance might prepare you, better for this morning's entertainment," said Jaime. "Try the eggs, they're not too greasy."

"Never been one for large breakfasts," said Prado trying another tiny sip of his juice. "Hence my lean frame and superb fitness."

Everyone laughed, including Prado, who went back for some more juice and strong black coffee. He was starting to feel better.

They chatted generally over coffee until Jaime stood and said, "Everyone finished?" After a variety of nods and grunts of confirmation, he said. "Then shall we reconvene by the front door in ten minutes?"

Prado drank some water, then went outside through the massive oak entrance door. He felt improved, but far from perfect. His intestines were not behaving to his usual ox-like constitution. He stood in the warm sun admiring the old house, gardens and the family church opposite as he waited for the others. Birds were singing, and tractor engines humming as the ranch hands went about their daily tasks.

The spectators gradually assembled next to Prado. Some shook his hand, others slapped his shoulder and wished him luck. Then Romero senior and his wife

Marta, a petite, slender woman in her late forties with short graying hair arrived and they headed off.

The Romero practice bullring was located some four hundred meters from the main house, along an almond-tree-lined gravel track. Freshly painted white fencing on each side enclosed calves and their mothers grazing in rich green pastures.

The bullring was small in comparison to actual arenas but was still thirty meters in diameter and surrounded by sturdy railings of timber posts and beams. A whitewashed rustic outbuilding with a terracotta-tiled roof stood next to the ring. It housed hay, tackle, changing rooms, and more significantly for Prado, a fully equipped first aid station. Adjacent to the outbuilding was a row of pens, each large enough to accommodate one animal. They opened out onto a narrow passageway that once inside, an animal couldn't turn around; it could only go forward. There was a gate at both ends of the passage. The animals entered from the surrounding meadows through one, at the other, was the entrance to the bullring.

Prado spotted only one animal. He glanced at it as they passed. It seemed harmless enough as it chewed rhythmically on some fodder, ignoring him totally.

The audience took their places, leaning on the upper rail, waiting expectantly. A couple of farmhands stood by the outbuilding ready to help when needed. When Prado and Juan were done, they would herd the animal back to its grazing zone.

In practice bullfights of this nature, there is no possibility of the animal suffering any bloodletting or killing. The humans, however, were another matter. The ranch practice ring was where budding bullfighters learned their craft; serious injury was no rare event.

Following Juan's example, Prado climbed over the railings and jumped down. The pain in his head when his feet hit the hard, uneven sand jolted him back to his predicament. He knew this was the moment to back out. He swallowed.

"What's your blood group?" said one onlooker.

"Need some life insurance?" said another.

"At least he's having a go," said Juan.

Juan was also in jeans but sporting a Ganaderia Romero T-shirt bearing the family logo of a red rose in the center of a bunch of rosemary. He walked to the side of the ring and grabbed a rusting red bike that was leaning against the railing. It had a stuffed bull's head, mounted onto the handlebars. Prado touched the unevenly curved horns. They were gargantuan and deadly sharp. Juan climbed aboard and circled around the ring. The squeaking pedals set Prado's nerves even more on edge.

"The head is the same height as most of the bulls we fight," shouted Juan riding towards him throwing him a shabby gold and magenta capote, or cape that had been lying neatly folded on the bike's saddle.

Prado caught it and was surprised how heavy it was.

"Have you ever been to a bullfight?" said Juan.

"Never, my parents were against it," said Prado.

"Then hold the capote, with its collar at the top with both hands in front of you, and then spread your arms so that the collar is just below chest height," shouted Juan as he pedaled in circles around the ring, picking up a little speed.

Prado lifted the cape as instructed. "Why does it have to be these awful gaudy colors?" he said.

"The cape is a replica of those used by noblemen during the sixteenth century," said Juan as he pedaled faster and faster around the ring. "Man has been chasing bulls for thousands of years. The Romans used to pit them against Christians in their stadiums. Bullfighting in Spain evolved from Spanish Royalty seeking some light entertainment. Wild bulls were rounded up and the King surrounded by his noblemen chased them on horseback around town squares trying to stab the bull in the back with lances. Noblemen took off their brightly colored capes and waved them at the bull to distract it if it came too near his Majesty. In those days bright clothes signified wealth and position. We're just following that tradition plus it makes it easier for the audience to appreciate our passes."

"If I find these colors garish, they must drive the bull bananas," said Prado deliberately deepening his voice "Have you anything more masculine?"

The spectators howled.

"Bulls are color blind Leon," said Juan. "It's the movement of the cape that attracts their attention. So, don't shake it until you are mentally prepared for it to charge."

"OK. Why is it so heavy?" said Prado.

"Nothing but complaints this morning my friend," said Juan. "The weight of the cape is deliberate. It prevents uncontrolled movement in the event of strong winds."

"I see," said Prado.

"Now shake it," said Juan. "Show us what you can do."

Prado feebly waved the cape.

"You'll need to do better than that Leon," said Juan.

Prado shook it as hard as he could.

"Better. With your sharp inquisitive mind, you've probably noticed that cattle have eyes in the sides of their heads."

"Actually, I hadn't. The nearest I usually get to cattle is attacking their grilled insides with a knife and fork. Is it important?"

"It gives them better peripheral vision. Which means they must turn their head to look where they are going. For example, if they look to the left, then they are going that way. It's why we look the bull in the eye all the time, they are the mirror of their intent."

"You'll be expecting me to say good morning to the damn thing next," said Prado to more laughter from the crowd."

"Ha, ha," said Juan. "There's one more point and then we can make a start with a few passes. It's crucial to stand behind the cape and always keep it close to your body. Then all what the bull sees is a single entity. I'll explain why later."

"OK. When the beast is thundering toward me, what should I do with the cape?" said Prado.

"Throw it over the horns and leg it," said a helpful onlooker.

"Ignore him, Leon. Stand your ground until the last moment, then as the bull approaches stand perfectly still and guide it around you with a sweep of the cape. Take care never to touch its horns and don't have the cape too far in front of its eyes. You must be close enough to block its vision but far enough away for it appear tantalizing. Then, when the bull has passed, quickly turn, reset the cape and prepare for the animal to spin round and charge you again. Then keep repeating that until it starts to tire. Now I'm going to charge you several times on this bike until you feel comfortable enough to have a go with a real animal. Are you ready?"

"As ever I can be," muttered Prado turning to face Juan as he accelerated toward him.

"I'm traveling at about twenty kilometers an hour," said Juan. "Which is a similar speed to the animal, but be wary, they can go faster, much faster. Watch their eyes as they approach. As I said, If the animal is going to swerve their eyes will look where they intend to go. It will give you advance warning to step away."

Juan approached, the bike squeaking loudly. Prado swung the cape at the bull's head, but it was too close. The cape snagged on the horns. The bike stopped dead, causing Juan to somersault off and land in a heap on the sand.

Juan picked himself up and dusted down his jeans. He didn't look happy, but untangled the cape, gave it back to Prado and remounted the bike.

"The cape needs to be higher," he shouted as he circled around the arena and steered straight at Prado. At the last minute, Prado stepped nimbly out of the way, but forgot to sweep the cape. Juan kept on going around, and this time told Prado when to sweep the cape. Everyone applauded as Prado completed his first pass adequately. They persevered and by the sixth attempt, Prado swept the cape as perfectly as he was ever going to.

Everyone cheered. Prado began to feel better. Momentarily.

"Miguel," shouted Juan to one of the farmhands. "Can you let the animal in now, please?"

Two minutes later, the gate to the arena opened with an ominous creak. Prado stood fifteen meters from it, cape held in front of him, even though his arm muscles were already burning from the practice.

The animal trotted into the arena and stopped just

inside the door looking curiously around. It was a magnificent example of its kind; jet-black, except for a white sock on its left foreleg, finely muscled, only two years old, but fully grown and weighed at least four hundred and fifty kilos.

Prado shook the cape. It made a loud swooshing noise. The movement attracted the animal's attention and it regarded Prado through black obsidian eyes, but it wasn't the cold, menacing stare that concerned him. Above the eyes were two massive, curved, sharply pointed, cream and black speckled horns aiming straight at him.

He watched them like a hawk, intestines rumbling, legs trembling, and throbbing head about to explode. Realization dawned on Prado instantly. This was not a practice bike, nor the stuffed dummy he was accustomed to during bayonet or unarmed combat exercises. It was a massive lump of fearless muscle that could smash a hole through a brick wall, or more significantly kill him stone dead with one thrust of those lethal weapons.

The animal trotted toward him, then accelerated into a gallop lowering its head and horns to aim directly at Prado's groin.

The nightmare flashed into his mind; all he could see was his blood spurting.

His mind stopped functioning. He could move nothing as if he was frozen to the spot, then his guts liquidized. He prayed; perhaps something he should have done more of, for a hole to open below him, but nothing happened.

The beast was only meters away. Prado's mind went blank as he prepared to meet his maker. All the maneuvers and side steps he'd almost mastered with

Juan had been wiped from his mind.

"Move now," yelled Juan. "Remember, sweep the cape in front of its face, just in front of the horns. Pretend it's me on the bike."

The beast lowered its head further.

Why won't my legs move? Prado said to himself, as collision seemed imminent. "Goodbye Mum," he whispered as his sphincter finally lost control.

Juan barged Prado out of the way, grabbed the cape, span round, and presented it to the charging beast, managing to guide it around his body with consummate flair and elegance. He finished with a final flourish, twirling the cape above his head mimicking rotating helicopter blades.

This was just one of his extensive range of passes or *veronicas*, reputedly named after Saint Veronica who, according to Christian legend, wiped Christ's brow with a cloth as he passed by on his way to Golgotha.

Juan kept the beast occupied with more passes while Prado scraped himself up off the sand. Then he skulked off to the washroom, disgusted with himself and distraught about his shameful performance, but more importantly his favorite jeans.

2

As Prado came out of the shower, Juan was opening one of the wooden lockers opposite. "Thanks," said Prado feeling totally depressed. "For saving my life. I'm sorry for my pathetic behavior and that mess." He indicated the steaming jeans on the changing room floor. "To say I'm embarrassed would be an understatement. I hope I haven't offended your family."

"Leon, dear friend, please forget it," said Juan opening a cupboard drawer and sorting through a pile of clean, folded clothes. He selected a pair of jockey shorts, a cream T-shirt, dark blue pants and socks. "You were not the first, neither will you be the last. Leave the jeans, etc., where they are. The staff will attend to them. They are used to it."

"Are you sure?"

"Please do not concern yourself with anything Leon, you have no cause to be embarrassed and my family's only concern is that you are alive, well and will forgive them for badgering you into the ring when you were full of orujo. Bullfighting is about managing fear, and it's a perfectly normal human function to evacuate your bowels when terrified. At some stage in our apprenticeship, it happens to us all. Here, try these," said Juan handing over the clean clothes and grinning amiably. "You're taller than me so you'll have a half-mast problem."

"It all seemed so easy with the bike and the stuffed head," said Prado shaking his head. "But that combination didn't want to kill me. The way that beast stared at me was deeply disturbing, and I couldn't move my legs. Sorry amigo, but I'm obviously not cut out for this line of work and thank you again for intervening. I'm forever in your debt."

"You owe me nothing Leon," said Juan. "At least you tried, most can't enter the ring, even with the bike."

"Well, if that is how horrifying it is with a young bull, I can't imagine how it would be with a fully grown one," said Prado slipping into the boxer shorts.

"Leon," Juan laughed. "That was a cow."

"A cow? Fuck you. Thanks, amigo, you know how to boost my self-esteem. But why cows? I thought you were here to train against bulls?"

"We practice with cows and steers, but not with bulls that are destined for the ring. They are deliberately kept away from human contact."

"Really, why?"

"The Toro de Lidia is substantially different from domestic cattle because it has been selectively bred under tightly controlled conditions for centuries. It has a thirty percent more developed fight reflex, is incredibly intelligent and learns quickly. If it becomes too familiar with humans, it will recognize their smell and shape in the ring. Our capes would be rendered useless, and we wouldn't stand a chance. The bull would kill us instantly."

"I hadn't realized that capes played such a major role."

"Without them, we could never get close enough. Bulls behave instinctively in the ring, just as they do in the wild. His role, aside from fathering the next generation, is protection. He's naturally wired to clear any space of potential threats to the herd.

"What he sees, when he enters a bullring is a lot going on. This is deliberate to disorientate him. For example, a man will pop out from behind the barrier, and then almost as quickly disappear. At the same time, the bullfighter's team spreads out in a fan before him, each standing behind their spread-open cape, shaking them at him and goading him with taunts of Toro. With so much going on, he chases everything at full speed twisting and turning like a boxer. It saps his energy extremely quickly because he's not built for such varied movement, only short sprints preferably in a straight line.

"After his initial expenditure of energy, he realizes that he hasn't caught anything. He slows down and re-examines what is in front of him more closely. However, all he can see is a shape. We know that it's a man holding a cape, but to him, it's a single entity. It's the same on an African Safari. All an elephant sees is the large shape of a Landrover, therefore he won't see the passengers in it and will leave it alone. However, as soon as a person climbs out of the vehicle, the elephant sees a smaller moving object, which he is more likely to attack. It's why I stressed that one should never wave the cape around separately from the body, always keep them as one entity otherwise the bull will spot the smaller moving man and go for that.

"Anyway, after his closer inspection in the bullring, the bull decides that the moving cape is the threat and it has to go. However, every time he charges, the cape keeps escaping him. Gradually, he becomes more and more enraged with this elusive prey and that anger converts into an obsession. He must kill the cape, to the exclusion of everything else. This is what the bullfighter watches for, the point when the bull has reached the peak of its obsession, it's when it can be killed reasonably safely.

"Obviously, there's more to it, but it's the cape-work that will lead the animal to his death. It's why we put in thousands of hours practicing our Veronicas with live animals. The more bruises we accrue, the more experienced we become, and can stand closer to the bull, the objective being that its horns almost kiss our suits as it passes. We call it dancing with bulls. You need to see a fight to really understand."

"Love to. Perhaps you could take me to the next one in Ronda. When is that?"

"The Pedro Romero Festival is the first two weeks of September. I have three relatives appearing this year, so we can get family tickets. The penultimate day is the best. We call it La Goyesca. I'll try and get seats."

"Great, thanks, though I still don't understand why you practice with cows. Surely, they are smaller and more timid, except for that monster earlier."

"Ranchers need to identify the bravest and most aggressive females from their herds. The fiercest is then mated with those few exceptionally brave bulls that are pardoned in the ring. The combination produces fearless killers, facing them is terrifying."

"I would have thought it safer to fight meeker bulls, why have you deliberately taken on the nastiest possible?"

"We are entertainers Leon; we want to put on the finest of credible performances in the prestigious Plazas de Toros of Spain. The crowd must believe that we face bulls that are as determined to kill us, as we are them. The crowd adores bulls, we toreros love bulls with a passion, the fiercer the better. Bullfighting wouldn't have lasted for centuries if we used wimpy or drugged animals. The most rewarding accolade a torero can receive is when the crowd is so delighted with the courage, stamina, and determination of the bull, they demand that he's pardoned. Nothing gives us greater pleasure than not to kill the bull, so it can go home to a life of green pastures and an endless supply of fine females such as your protagonist today. She's called Melinda by the way."

"Dear Melinda, she may be a big ugly brute, but I will never forget her. Anyway, thanks for explaining all this. In the future, I'll learn about bullfighting as an observer. Meanwhile, I'd like to practice more with the two-legged variety. If I could find one."

"Well, you might be in luck at the reception tonight? My new sister-in-law has some rather delectable and available siblings. One might suit you?"

"That would be erm..."

"Yes, wouldn't it. Meanwhile, let's grab a couple of horses and I'll show you around. We'll be back in time for lunch if you can stomach it."

"I'm OK now, but no more cow confrontations?"

"No more orujo either," Juan laughed.

Prado slipped the T-shirt over his head, threaded

his belt from his jeans and slipped into the blue pants. He buckled up, chuckled at the six-centimeter gap between his shoes and trouser legs, and then followed Juan off to the stables.

"Adios," he said to his stained Levi's on the way out. "I suppose I'll have to save up for a new pair now."

***

Prado was impressed by the luxury cars as they disgorged their finely dressed passengers outside the church that evening. This was not a world to which he was accustomed, but it didn't worry him. Spain is more egalitarian than elitist, and everyone welcomed him warmly.

The wedding guests were restricted to immediate family and friends, which still added up to two hundred people. The marriage was not founded just on romantic love between the couple, but was also a merger of bullfighting interests to expand both parties as a major force in the industry.

He and Juan stood by the church door both wearing their smartly pressed Legionnaire dress uniforms and highly polished boots. Juan whispered who was who, as each new arrival filed into the church.

"These are the bride's sisters," said Juan digging Prado in the ribs as a white Range Rover pulled up to the church. Three young women ranging from mid to late teens exited the rear door. They were all stunningly pretty with long dark hair, wearing elegant gowns. They whispered among themselves, pointed at the two handsome soldiers and giggled, as they waited for the driver to assist their wizened chaperone out of the front passenger seat.

"Buenas tardes, Doña Ordoñez," said Juan.

"Hola Juan," wheezed the girl's grandmother. "And is this your new friend from the Legion?"

"Leon Prado, ma'am," said Juan.

The grand old lady ran her eyes over Prado, nodded approvingly and said, "Will you both be out here until everyone's inside?"

"Si señora," said Juan.

"Then make sure that you pay particular attention to my grandson Fredo when the bride's party arrives. He's always banging on about soldiers. Show him your medals or something. I presume you have some?"

"Er… yes," said Juan, who did not.

"And one more thing. I expect you and young Leon here to be on your best behavior with my granddaughters."

"As always, señora," said Juan, grinning.

"Girls, you watch these two soldiers. They might look pretty, but you can't trust them an inch. They'll have your knickers off faster than you can blink."

The girls squealed and blushed.

Doña Ordoñez appraised her granddaughters, eyebrows raised. They quietened instantly and filed obediently into the church in line behind her. As the middle one passed Prado, she looked at him with twinkling eyes, then smiled at him demurely before following her sister into the church.

Prado was gobsmacked. His pulse raced.

"That's Inma," whispered Juan. "You could be alright there."

3

2018

"Frankly, Señor Crown," said Detective Inspector Leon Prado in Spanish. "I've had enough of you." They were sitting opposite each other in the interview room of the Central Comisaría in Málaga. There were no windows, but on one wall was a large mirror that provided one-way visual access from a small adjoining room. Prado's boss and his assistant were standing over the engineer operating the video equipment.

"We arrested you at the villa in Torrox Park over three weeks ago," said Prado rubbing his earlobe. "Thankfully for the victims, we were just in time to stop your partner in crime from raping a young man and two girls. Luckily, he was killed trying to escape leaving you with all his responsibilities. You chose to decline a solicitor but have not given us any reason as to why you might be innocent. We, therefore, have no choice but to charge you with people trafficking, abduction, imprisoning persons against their will and torture. You are not obliged to say anything unless you wish to do so, but what you say may be put into writing and given in evidence. I will ask one more time. Who are the people financing your criminal enterprise?"

Crown stared blankly back at Prado and said nothing.

"Do you realize," said Prado. "That the seriousness of these offenses will guarantee a lifetime prison sentence?"

Crown looked away from Prado's relentless eye contact but remained silent.

"In that case, you give me no choice," said Prado. "You will be taken to Alhaurin prison where you will be held without any chance of bail until the courts can find an available date for your trial. I should warn you that Spanish jails are packed with disturbed minds from all nationalities and religions. One of the common characteristics among your future cellmates is a distinct hatred of sex offenders, especially foreign sex offenders. Initially, your life inside will be in total solitary confinement to protect you, but there will come a time after the trial when you will be accommodated among these desolate souls. To put it mildly, your life will be in extreme danger."

Crown said nothing.

Prado stood up, collected his gray suit jacket from the back of the gray chair and put it back on over his crumpled white shirt. He glanced at the mirror and nodded. A few seconds later the door opened and in stepped a tall, tanned, athletic-looking man in his early forties with steel-blue eyes, and shaggy blond hair dressed in black chinos and a short-sleeved light blue shirt.

"Señor Crown," said Prado. "You may remember Mr. Phillip Armitage, my English translator from previous interviews. I'm going to leave you alone with him for a few minutes before the officers outside take you up to the prison. If you have any domestic arrangements that need attention, let him know."

Phillip waited until Prado left the room before sitting down at the table opposite Crown. He looked him directly in the eyes and smiled warmly.

Crown ignored him.

Crown was forty-seven years old. A short, skinny, effeminate man with slender hands, blue-gray eyes, and greasy dark hair. Even though he kept his head down, eyes averted and left leg twitching furiously, he still managed to project an evil presence. As if the devil himself was lurking inside his body.

"Where are your parents now?" said Phillip.

Crown frowned, shifted in his chair and said, "What the fuck has those bastards to do with this?"

"I just thought they might want to know where you are?" said Phillip. Even after several interviews with Crown, he was still surprised at the man's upper crust English accent. It was so incongruous with his appearance. "I could call them on your behalf."

"Difficult, they are dead."

"Any siblings?"

Crown glared at him with a hateful expression. Phillip was amazed. After three weeks of hardly a word, finally, a reaction. Not much, but at least a change from the usual blank mask.

"A sister, perhaps?" said Phillip.

Crown put his head in his hands and shuddered momentarily. When he looked back at Phillip, the mask had returned.

"Malcolm," said Phillip quietly. "The microphone is off now. Is there anyone that you would like me to inform about your circumstances? Any personal effects that you may wish for your long sojourn behind bars?"

No reaction from Crown.

"It is obvious that whomever you are protecting has a relentless hold over you. It's the only logical justification for you not talking. Prado wasn't bullshitting you about the dangers facing you in a Spanish prison. Not just from the weirdos, but also from the person or persons you are protecting. They will be concerned that at some time in the future, you may give them up to the police. It's more than conceivable that they have contacts inside who will come after you?"

"I know that," said Crown, lifting his head and returning Phillip's gaze through watery eyes. "I doubt I'll last twenty-four hours."

"I've been authorized to offer you protection in return for your giving us the names Prado asked for. A safe house and a new identity, a chance for a fresh start. But you have to give me the information immediately."

Crown thought for a moment. Then he looked Phillip in the eye and shook his head.

"But, if we can guarantee your safety, I don't understand why you would choose to die."

Crown's eyes watered more heavily, he reached up and wiped his eyes with his shirtsleeve.

"Is there anything?" said Phillip. "That you can tell us. At least then your death would not have been in vain?"

Crown stood up, stretched his legs and made the sign of writing. Phillip passed him the pen and notepad lying on the table. Crown walked over to it, picked up the pen, scribbled something quickly and threw down the pen. Phillip picked up the notepad and tried to read the almost illegible script. All he could make out was what seemed to say 'look in the darkness'. Phillip ripped the note out of the pad and slipped it into his pocket, then stood, walked to the door and rapped on it. Prado entered with two uniformed officers who took Crown away.

"Did he say anything?" said Prado.

"Nothing we can use," said Phillip holding his ear while looking at Prado directly in the eyes. "I fancy some fresh air,"

"Then may I suggest a coffee?" said Prado.

They stepped out of the Comisaría, walked over the quiet street to the café opposite and took a seat on a terrace table under a green awning. Prado ordered their usual.

"He did write something down," said Phillip as they waited for their drinks.

"I saw that. What?"

Phillip took the note out of his pocket and gave it to Prado. He read it and shrugged.

"It says, 'look in the darkness'," said Phillip.

"What's that supposed to mean?" said Prado.

"Darkness can be nighttime, a place without light or somewhere, where bad things are going down physically or mentally. The word in Spanish would be Infierno."

"What's he's trying to tell us?"

"I can only assume that he means to look in the dark or deep web. It's where we found his Peepers website."

"Without more information, that's worse than looking for a needle in a haystack."

"Yes, but at least we know where the haystack is."

"That's one hell of a haystack. Wasn't it you that told me the deep web is at least four hundred times bigger than the pages searchable by Google? And, it's unlikely to be in Spanish, so can I leave that with you?"

"Fine. Any progress in Gibraltar? We could really use the detail of the CVS bank accounts and a court order for their lawyer's files."

The waiter delivered their coffee. They sipped them quietly, each lost in thought about Crown.

"You're right," said Prado. "However, it's a lot of work fathoming the Rock's bureaucracy then chasing after them. They are deliberately elusive and evasive to requests from the Spanish police. So, while we ought to press them, I'm not sure it will bring us anything extra. As it stands, we have more than enough to put Crown away, and I think we're going to have to be satisfied with that. Unless you can find anything in this damned darkness web thingy."

"I can only try."

"I'll talk to the boss about Gibraltar," said Prado. "Maybe he has connections that might work better than mine."

"Good idea. Any luck with the Sanchez brothers, Crown's Málaga lawyers?"

"Some idiot granted them bail and unsurprisingly, they have vanished.

"What happened to Crown's victims?"

"Angelika is having some counseling so should pull through. Juliet, you know about. Lars has gone back to Sweden. The illegal migrants have been transferred from Las Claras Convent to a detention center near Antequera."

"How are they?" said Phillip.

"Angry at everything," said Prado.

"Hardly surprising," said Phillip. "They left their homes and suffered brutal treatment on their journey to Spain, with only their dream of a better life to keep them going. Then they are captured by the Guardia Civil, sold off by corrupt officials to a sexual slavery ring where they are tortured into abusing each other, then locked up pending deportation back to the horrors that they escaped from in the first place. I'd be apoplectic."

"Me too, but they should have known all that before they started out on their journey. It's not our problem, but my country is expected to pay for all this when we have enough problems of our own. The UN should be addressing global immigration with some urgency, otherwise, this will blow up into a massive explosion of violence all around the northern Mediterranean coastline. Meanwhile, our job is to round them up and send them back."

"Only to be replaced by the next relentless batch of new arrivals."

"Of which, we intercept about ten percent."

"Given your limited resources," said Phillip. "That's not so bad and don't forget, in your first major case, you tracked down twelve abductions, over a dozen missing migrants and closed down a sexual slavery ring and a corrupt network of civil servants profiting from this grim trade. That's a good result."

"Which we couldn't have achieved without you and Amanda. Are you two er?"

Phillip paused, a loving expression lighting up his face. "Er, wonderful," Phillip said. "But what about you? We've never discussed your life outside of the police. Are you married?"

"It's complicated," said Prado. "I married a beautiful, fiery, but stubborn girl from just outside Sevilla. Inma Ordoñez, she's related to the famous bullfighter, Antonio. We met when I was twenty at a wedding in Ronda while I was doing my two years National Military Service. After that, I joined the National Police in Málaga and worked my way up to my current position. We have two fine sons now in their early twenties. However, until recently, we've lived apart for some fifteen years."

"That's sad," said Phillip.

"Not really, it was by mutual agreement. We own and still do, a lovely house in Ronda from where I used to commute to wherever I was working. However, when I was promoted to run the Málaga Serious Crime Squad, it meant that I was away most of the time and failed to perform my paternal duties. To us Spaniards, that is a capital offense. However, now that I've been moved into the foreigner's department, I have more free time and we're making some serious attempts at reconciliation."

"That's great news. I hope it works out."

"So do I. Long nights alone in my studio apartment here in Málaga with a bottle of Scotch, does not bode well for a happy retirement in about three years' time."

"But you're still young?"

"Fifty-two is old in this business, especially after thirty years on the job."

"What about management?"

"I'm a nuts and bolts copper, Phillip. I love solving crimes and locking up bad people. It takes a special breed to even think of becoming a manager and that is not me. Anyway, we have a rundown smallholding on the edge of Ronda that I want to develop."

"Farming?"

"Goats. We want to make cheese."

"You and Inma?"

"Hopefully."

"Are you on your own tonight?"

"Yes, why?"

"Care to join Amanda and me for a tapa. She wants to hear all about Crown's case."

"Love to, where?"

"Cortijo de Pepe, on Plaza de la Merced."

"I know it. I have a few things in the office to tidy up. See you there in half an hour?"

"Perfect."

They finished their coffee, Prado left some coins on the table and headed back to the Comisaría. Phillip headed off to Plaza de la Merced, extracted his phone from his pocket and called Amanda.

"How did it go with Crown?" she said.

"Yes, I'm fine thanks, had a good day?"

"Sorry, no, still stuck on this bloody editing for the foie-gras man."

"What you need is a drink. We're due to meet Prado in half an hour at Cortijo de Pepe. He can tell you all about Crown. Interested?"

"On my way."

Phillip walked the few hundred meters along attractive narrow streets of elegant townhouses and modern apartment buildings to Plaza de la Merced, one of Málaga's prettiest tree-lined squares. It was a balmy June evening, with a clear blue sky. The traditional tapas bar was on a corner overlooking the former medieval marketplace. In the center stood an obelisk constructed in 1842 to celebrate the life of General Torrijos, a liberal Spanish soldier renowned for his slogans of freedom and justice. According to legend, the doves that used this memorial as an evening perch had a major influence on the young Pablo Picasso, who was born in a house on the northeast corner of the plaza. There was a statue of him seated on a bench outside the house.

On arriving at Cortijo de Pepe, Phillip sat down at a table on the terrace under a shady awning, stretched his legs and enjoyed people watching until the waiter popped outside to collect his order.

"Una copa de Verdejo," said Phillip to the waiter's request several minutes later.

"Una tapita?"

"Jamon Serrano por favor."

A group of blonde-haired girls walked by carrying textbooks and chatting loudly in what sounded like Swedish. Phillip assumed that they were students at one of Málaga's nearby language schools. Three smartly dressed seniors hobbled by Phillip leaning heavily on elegant walking sticks and deep in conversation. They stopped to watch the girls, nodding in approval. Phillip overheard one say, "The day I stop appreciating a pretty girl, is the day they carry me out in a wooden box."

"Mentally, I could still ravish that lot," said another.

"Physically, you would need rather a lot of blue pills for that," said the third.

Phillip laughed aloud as the waiter delivered his order. He picked up the chilled glass and was about to take a sip of the delicious fruity white wine from Rueda in northern Spain when someone snatched the drink from his hands. A petite olive-skinned woman with an appealing elfin face, curvy figure and long silky raven hair sat down at the table, sipped his wine and smiled lovingly at him. The golden flecks in her light-brown eyes sparkled. They melted his heart every time he gazed into them. He reached out and stroked her cheek. She kissed his hand. In the background, the seniors gave him a thumbs-up.

"Hi, Amanda," he said.

The waiter delivered Phillip's ham.

"Una copa de Verdejo más y una tapa de Manchego por favor," said Phillip.

"Por supuesto, Caballero."

"What's the problem with the edit?" said Phillip.

"I'll show you at home later," she said. "I need a break from it now. When's Prado coming?"

"Ten minutes or so?"

***

Prado was in his office tidying up a few loose ends on the Crown paperwork when his mobile phone rang. It was his old friend retired bullfighter, Juan Romero.

"I hear you are getting back with Inma?" said Juan.

"Ronda rumor mill hard at it again?" said Prado.

"No, seriously, a friend bumped into her in the town center, they had coffee. Inma was most insistent that she wanted you back home."

"Well, we are probably heading in that direction. Is this why you called me? Nothing better to do than listen to gossip?"

"Actually, there is something I wanted to chat through with you. You remember I told you that the family is concerned about the state of bullfighting and is trying to do something about it. Well, we've not achieved a damned thing. However, what we have discovered is a rather alarming stance taken by the

Royal Taurino Society. The old farts on the committee are not listening to the people or to us."

"Bullfighting business still bad then?"

"It's falling off a cliff, but there is a ray of hope. My young nephew Diego, you remember, my brother Jaime's son, has developed a cunning plan to turn it around. I can't tell you over the phone, but I recall you saying that you are working with a couple of foreign translators, who make documentaries and broadcast them on their own website."

"That's right. Why?"

"We need a series of hard-hitting videos for social media and a full-length documentary explaining our vision for the future of bullfighting. Would they be the sort of people that could help us?"

"Why don't you use your own contacts in the Spanish media? With your radio and TV commentating, you are practically the voice of bullfighting?"

"You know how well connected the Society's committee are, they'll bring pressure on the Spanish media to squash our campaign. Foreigners should be independent of all that."

"Good thinking. Listen, Juan, I think their videos are brilliant, but look for yourself on their website, it's at www.Nuestra-España.com. I have some stuff here I must finish, call me back in a few minutes."

Prado rattled off his final emails. Juan rang just as he was turning off his machine.

"You're right," said Juan. "They are good. Listen, amigo, can you help persuade them to work with us?"

"I'll try. Is it urgent?"

"Desperately. If possible, I need them in Madrid tomorrow. We will pay whatever it takes."

"That's just as well mate," said Prado. "These two insist on doing things properly. May I suggest that you send them two first-class tickets on the AVE, book a fancy hotel room and a gourmet restaurant? I'll persuade them to come, but the rest is up to you."

"So how do we do this?"

"I'm seeing them shortly for a tapa. I'll confirm if they are happy to come to Madrid. If so, I'll send you their email addresses for the tickets afterward. If not, then you'll have to look elsewhere. OK?"

"Perfect, mi amigo. Thank you."

Prado turned off his laptop, tidied his desk and headed off to Cortijo de Pepe.

***

Prado bent to kiss Amanda on both cheeks, pulled up a chair from a nearby table, sat down and ordered his customary glass of San Miguel from the hovering waiter. He looked out across the square. "I love it here," he said.

"Me too," said Amanda.

The waiter returned, placing a small paper table mat on the table upon which he carefully positioned the frosty glass of beer.

"Anything more with Crown?" said Phillip.

"Crown no," Prado paused. "But there is something else, and it involves you two."

4

Phillip and Amanda walked the short distance from her apartment opposite the impressive Moorish entranceway of the Mercado Central Atarazanas to the María Zambrano central train station on Avenida Ingeniero José María Garnica.

Over the last twenty years, Málaga has blossomed from a poorly maintained industrial port into a bustling, dynamic modern city of some six hundred thousand residents and nearly two million annual visitors. The City Council has ensured an intelligent blend of new architecture with the vast array of ancient Phoenician, Roman and Arab monuments. A revitalized port has attracted most of the world's cruise liners, there are several first-class museums, excellent language schools, and an outstanding cultural calendar.

Rolling a small suitcase each, Phillip and Amanda were headed to Madrid to meet the mysterious Juan Romero and listen to his proposal briefly outlined by Prado the previous evening.

They settled into comfortable and spacious seats in the first-class carriage of the AVE, Spain's awesome bullet train service and exchanged excited glances as they pulled out at eight o'clock precisely. They covered the five-hundred and twenty-five kilometers to central Madrid, in well under three hours.

Madrid is the capital and largest city in Spain by a long way. With a population of well over three million, it is substantially bigger than the second, Barcelona. It's been occupied since the Stone Age but only began to gather credence in 1560 when Philip the Second moved his court there from Toledo. Its tree-lined avenues, green areas and a magnificent mix of classic and modern architecture combine to form an extremely fine city much grander than Málaga.

The taxi rank at the Puerta de Atocha station lies between the refurbished red brick building built in 1892 which now contains the ticket hall, an impressive tropical garden, shops, cafés, and a night club, and the new modern glass, steel, and concrete extension constructed in 1992 which houses the platforms.

Phillip and Amanda sat in the back of their cab listening to the driver rattle on about that evening's football match between Madrid and Barcelona, the old rivals forever battling the top positions in La Liga. They passed the famous Prado Museum, home to many of the world's most famous old masters, including major paintings by Velasquez, El Greco, Rubens, Goya, and Hieronymus Bosch.

The traffic was light and five minutes later they were dropped outside the five-star Hotel Wellington on Calle de Velasquez in the elegant Salamanca district, which bordered the northern perimeter of Retiro Park, the former Royal Gardens. They checked their cases with the concierge then caught a Metro train to the city center aiming for lunch at the stylish Mercado de San Miguel, a refurbished market just off the Plaza Mayor, Madrid's central square with excellent tapas stalls and live classical music.

After lunch, they'd planned some shopping before meeting Juan in the hotel lobby at five. However, as the creaky escalator transported them relentlessly upwards, out of the depths of the Madrid Metro system, they heard a rhythmic screeching growing louder as they approached ground level, it sounded alarmingly aggressive. Amanda reached behind her and grabbed Phillip's hand.

They stepped off the moving staircase, pressed by the people coming up behind and constrained by those in front. There was no escape, even if they wanted one and were inevitably shoved gently out from under the whale-shaped glazed roof covering the Metro exit, and into the vast pedestrianized square of Puerta del Sol, basking under the burning heat of the June midday sun and into the middle of a noisy demonstration.

They stood on the fringe of the chanting crowd assembled in the renowned plaza, home to kilometer zero and the gateway to the elegant city's principal shopping and entertainment. Both were accustomed to mass displays of Spanish citizen's dissatisfaction at something or other, but not quite along these lines.

These protesters were all young, naked above the waist, and splattered in fake blood. 'Ban bullfighting', was painted over each torso in bright red letters. Never seen so many topless people, thought Phillip, and all those tattoos make it look like an open-air, seething mass of body-art.

Many   were   waving   makeshift   placards

communicating their fervent messages supporting animals and a vegan lifestyle.

"What do we want?" screeched a woman into a megaphone.

"Ban bullfighting now," responded the masses.

"Do you think that this might be something to do with why we are here," said Phillip.

"Could be, but why protest here?" said Amanda. "I would have thought outside the bullring would be more effective."

Phillip expected more comments from her, but when he looked, he saw that someone among the protesters had distracted her. He massaged her neck while he waited for her to tell him. In the meantime, he surveyed the crowd. Their average age must have been early twenties, their expressions were serious and passionate, but they appeared good-natured and represented many Spanish cities, skin colors and nationalities. He could hear several languages and many of the obvious couples were interracial, oblivious to the differences that continued to divide many of the world's communities. Phillip admired that they had crossed the old boundaries, were completely comfortable with each other, and in twenty to thirty years' time would be the new leaders of the world. He hoped their egalitarian principles would make for a vast improvement over the current incumbents.

Amanda turned to him. "I think I recognize some of the organizers, can you lift me up so I can take a better look?"

"My pleasure," he said, bending down, putting his arms under hers and gently raising her up so her face was level with his. He nuzzled her ear. She reached back and rubbed his shaggy hair between her thumb and forefinger.

"Yes, it's definitely them," she said. "I met them in Pamplona when I was filming my running with the bulls' video a couple of years ago. They protest there every year and I interviewed them. It seems their empire has expanded."

"It still doesn't answer your question. The main bullring is four kilometers away."

"Should I go and find out?"

"Wouldn't we be better for knowing?"

"You're right, probably best that you wait here."

"I'll be at the Apple store. Text me if you need rescuing."

Phillip turned, threaded his way through the many leering men enjoying the spectacle and went into the popular device shop. He never missed an opportunity to go ogle an Apple. He had an impressive collection in his study at home and tried to add to it when he could. Unusually, the store was deserted. A few male staff gathered near the main door filming the protesters on a variety of machines. They compared each other's footage accompanied by lots of pointing fingers and excited exclamations.

Perhaps they're also anti-bullfighting? Wondered Phillip but then shook his head. These geeks world revolved around technology. They would be comparing pixel-depths and color densities. Bulls and naked women would be well down their list of priorities. He left them to it and enjoyed being alone to peruse the latest models without some well-meaning idiot interrupting, asking if they could help.

He was playing with a new tablet when his phone buzzed. He dug it out of his trouser pocket and read the text message. 'I've joined in. Will see you back at the hotel around three. I'm sure there's something fishy going on. xx.'

Phillip frowned. He loved Amanda's spunky impulsiveness, but the something fishy worried him, especially after the warning from Prado. He went outside and was impressed that the protester numbers had swelled significantly during his brief technology update.

He rose on his tiptoes and caught a brief glimpse of Amanda chatting earnestly with three women as they brushed her pert, shapely naked breasts with powder paint and smeared the protest message on her stomach. He smiled, decided to leave her to it and walk the two kilometers back to the hotel. Their planned lunch would have to wait for another day.

5

Diego Romero, Spain's top torero, bullfighter, walked alone along the timber-paneled corridor of The Royal Taurino Society's offices in Puerta del Sol. He was on his way to the inner sanctuary, the committee room of bullfighting's watchdog, where the decisions of eight men defined and controlled all aspects of Spain's national tradition. He was twenty-six years old, of average height with film star looks, a chiseled physique, long dark hair tidied into a ponytail and penetrating brown eyes that missed nothing. He'd dressed in his trademark white linen suit, white open-necked shirt, and brown brogue shoes. A small backpack contained his phone, laptop, chargers, and water bottle. His footsteps echoed on the rose-pink marble tiling.

Mounted on both walls were illuminated framed paintings of varying dimensions. They were portraits of famous toreros going back over the centuries. His distant ancestor, Pedro Romero was there, his late father Jaime and Uncle Juan, along with El Cordobes,

Juan Belmonte, and Antonio Ordoñez. Further along were the recently gored Victor Barrio and poor Ivan Fandiño, who only the previous year had the misfortune to trip on his cape at the Corrida des Fetes in Aire-sur-l'Adour, France. The bull had been merciless.

"One day I will join them," he whispered to himself. "But God willing, not just yet."

He took a seat on a row of wooden chairs lined up outside the imposing committee room door, feeling humbled by the exalted display of his predecessors.

Then his mind returned to the purpose of today's appearance before the powers that be, and the acid churned in his stomach. He swallowed, grimaced and tapped his fingers on the back of the chair.

After a moment, he stood up to look out of the single window to Puerta del Sol four floors below. He smiled wryly to himself. The participants in the semi-naked demonstration had swelled to more than he could have possibly envisaged.

He sat back down, pulse racing, thoughts all over the place. Initially, the committee had refused his request to make a presentation about the state of bullfighting and some suggestions to modernize it.

They were already familiar with his ideas from the bullfighting media, strongly disagreed with them and were reluctant to waste time discussing the subject.

Diego concluded that they preferred to bury their heads in the sand rather than acknowledge the groundswell of public opinion against their art.

In the end, he'd had to threaten them with his resignation. He'd known that the Society's finances were in dire straits and that his withdrawal from the bullring would open the floodgates to even more sponsors pulling the plug.

They'd finally agreed to give him fifteen minutes.

The door opened and a hand beckoned him inside. Diego rose and strode purposefully into the room. Eight elegantly dressed, elderly distinguished men sat in a row behind a rectangular table covered with a white tablecloth, jugs of water, glasses, notepads, and pens. No phones or devices were anywhere in sight.

Behind them, on the timber-paneled wall hung a huge painting of the Spanish Monarch mounted in an ornate gilt frame. Diego looked at each man and nodded as he went along the line. In his mind, he reeled off their individual businesses: Escobedo; Olive oil, Dorantes; wine, Lorenzo; fashion, Agustin; shipping, Bosque; hotels, Zambrano; wind-turbines, Quintanilla; solar-energy, Pizarro; international engineering. Their combined worth was almost greater than most of the Spanish population.

Diego's father had known them all well before he died of old chest wounds the previous year. The Chairman of the Society, Pablo Bosque, owner of Grupo de Hoteles, Bosque y Lagos – the largest hotel owner in Spain was married to Diego's fiancée's aunt, the Duquesa de Aragon. His own fiancée was the Condesa de Aragon. Both smart, beautiful women with fearsome reputations for their passionate support of good causes.

Much to the Romero family's disdain, both the Duquesa and Condesa were vehemently opposed to bullfighting. The Condesa had only accepted Diego's marriage proposal, on the basis that until he retired from the ring, there would be no wedding or physical relations.

The world of slaughtering noble beasts in public,

maybe an incestuous business in which Diego was well connected and highly favored, but in this room, that would cut no ice. This small group of powerful and ruthless men totally controlled bullfighting.

"Buenos días señores," said Diego as he walked toward them slipping off his backpack and placing it by the solitary chair facing the men.

Not one of them acknowledged Diego's greeting. Cold, inscrutable faces were staring hard at him as if he was nothing.

"Please take a seat, Diego," said the chairman. "I'm sure there's no need to remind you of the time limit. However, I must warn you that should we become displeased with what you are saying, we will cut you short. Do you understand?"

"Yes, Don Bosque. However, I prefer to stand."

"As you wish. Please begin."

"I have no desire to appear arrogant or disrespectful," said Diego, feeling more confident now that he was talking. "However, I am one of the best toreros in Spain and my appearance at any bullring guarantees a backside on every seat and that sponsorship income is maximized. The point being, that I have the right to stand before you and speak about the state of our beloved national tradition."

He paused to measure the effect of his words. Not a frown or grunt, just eight inscrutable gazes staring straight at him.

"On the face of it," he said. "Bullfighting appears to be booming. When I talk to my colleagues, they all say how well they are doing. Ranchers and Restaurateurs gush volubly about their successful businesses. When I read the Spanish press, their articles describe a wonderful world that is so far away from reality, I wonder if I'm on the same planet. Gentlemen, you and I know that bullfighting is practically dead in the water."

Diego walked around the room as he talked, waving his arms to emphasize his points.

"This is the twenty-first century. The age of fairness and equal opportunity for all, regardless of age, color, gender, or sexual orientation. So, señores, where are the female bullfighters? Unsurprisingly, they are still barred from qualifying. Cast an eye around this splendid old room. What do you see? Old men using bullfighting to further their business interests. As far as you're concerned," Diego strode quickly over to the window and pointed down to the square. "Those brave bare-breasted whippersnappers out there who are the future of our country whether we like it or not can go fuck themselves."

Diego paused to gauge their reaction, worried that he was overdoing it. He sensed the tension rising. Teeth, no matter whether gold, ceramic or real, were being sucked.

"If you compare the technology in today's car," he said. "With those from even ten years ago, it is unrecognizable as we head towards carbon-free vehicles. My grandmother refuses to use a mobile phone preferring the traditional landline models with a circular dial on the front. Most of her grandchildren think it is just another of her many quaint antiques.

And that is where we are with bullfighting. Our national tradition remains the same today, as it was twenty, even thirty years ago. Nothing has changed while the rest of the world is transforming itself so quickly that the technology, we learn at university is already out of date by the time we leave.

"What is wrong with that? I hear you ask yourselves.

"Gentlemen, I ask you to consider this. Nobody under the age of forty-five goes to or shows any interest in bullfighting. Apart from attendance at my own performances, spectator numbers have fallen by fifty-two percent since 2007, the forecast is that the trend will continue dramatically downwards.

"TV stations no longer broadcast bullfights; advertising revenue has vanished. Red-meat consumers are disappearing faster than lemmings over a cliff, despite our feeble efforts to eliminate hormones and factory farming. As our rivers and oceans are poisoned or choked by a growing mountain of plastic, a vegan world dominated by animal lovers and green disciples is rapidly approaching. Already, traditional bullfighting restaurants are closing, and cattle-ranches are going bankrupt.

"Attracting new talent to bullfighting schools has become almost impossible. There are less than three students in classes of what used to be thirty. The schools must rely on Government grants to stay open.

"This, esteemed sirs, is the current state of our beloved industry and these are not my statistics. A recent poll found that only twenty-nine percent of the Spanish population support bullfighting and three-quarters have not attended a fight during the previous five years.

"Señores, at this rate, bullfighting will be dead in ten years. I repeat. In ten years, this Society will no longer be necessary. Your revered committee room will become surplus to requirements. Those portraits of our heroes in the corridor outside will be condemned to a dusty museum shelf somewhere. Our bullrings are likely to become venues for pop-concerts or, perish the thought, be converted into another architectural monstrosity, such as the shopping mall in Barcelona. Gentlemen, our country's national culture would have disappeared. Over five hundred years of tradition; gone, whoosh, vanished like a puff of smoke.

"You can imagine how affronted my ancestors would feel after centuries of putting our bodies on the line, especially the many who lost their lives building this industry. Your old friend and fellow committee member, my father Jaime Romero, included.

"There are two choices. Carry on as we are and fade into the annals of history or modernize and stay relevant to a rapidly changing world."

"And your proposal is?" said the chairman.

"Or your fiancée's?" muttered Dorantes.

Diego ignored the remark. "The single biggest objection among the young is that we are killing animals for fun. This association with animal cruelty is finishing us off. I respectfully suggest that we take the blood out of the equation. No more picadores stabbing the bull with a lance or banderilleros sticking darts in its back, and, more crucially we must stop killing the bull in the ring. The spectator should remember a brave beast for its noble performance, not its death rattles."

"Young fellow, I should not need to remind you," interrupted Pizarro shouting and banging the table with his fist. "That we are talking about bullfighting. The objective is, and has been for hundreds of years, to kill the damn animal. Without blood, there can be no killing and no purpose. That's why people go. To see death in the afternoon. Or, is it your intention to convert our national heritage into a circus act? Can you imagine discerning fans flocking to see wrestling with bulls? Are we to copy the Portuguese cavalieros and forcados? For me, they behave like clowns and show no respect for the bull. If that is your argument, then I'm out. I refuse to listen further."

6

Phillip decided to walk back to the hotel and see what he could find to eat on the way. He paused at a café overlooking the Puerta de Alcala, to enjoy a beer with a toasted ham and cheese sandwich and admired the colorful display of flowers in the beds surrounding the old gateway into the city as he ate. It now formed the centerpiece of a giant traffic roundabout; the ancient city walls were demolished in 1561.

He arrived at the hotel and was welcomed warmly by the uniformed doorman standing in front of a giant blue cow dressed in a bullfighter outfit. He explained that it was an impulse purchase by the owner, a serious fan of bullfighting.

Phillip refrained from commenting and walked through the revolving glass door, checked in and went up to their traditionally furnished spacious room. He lay down on the king-size bed for a siesta. He worried about Amanda momentarily, but dismissed his concerns within seconds. If she was capable enough to run with the bulls in Pamplona, then she could handle anything that may arise during a semi-naked protest. As he lay propped up on the soft pillows, staring at the ceiling, his mind meandered over the events of the last few weeks.

When he, Prado and Amanda had met earlier in May, all three of them were suffering from mild depression. Working together on the Darkness in Málaga case had not only rescued the missing victims, but also helped each lost soul to discover some new direction. It had made them realize that what was important in life was helping others, not being obsessed with their own insecurities. All three felt better for knowing each other.

A gentle knocking on the door roused Phillip from his light doze. He slid off the bed and opened the door to admit a rather straggled Amanda, her face still covered in red powder paint. They hugged.

"Shower?" said Phillip, knowing that she would want to be rid of the street dirt and the rather poorly applied body-art as soon as possible. He picked her up, carried her into the bathroom and helped remove her stained clothing. She turned on the water, climbed under the powerful spray and began washing. Phillip leaned against the sink opposite and watched her tiny but shapely, figure move behind the translucent shower curtain. She stuck her pretty face out between the gap with eyebrows raised, and flannel in hand.

"Can you do my back?" she said.

Being the gentleman that he is, he was happy to oblige, dried her off afterward and carried her through to the bed.

Later, they lay naked and intertwined, relaxed and chatting.

"So how did you fare with your old friends?" said Phillip.

"They were extremely suspicious of me and close-mouthed at first," she said. "They remembered that I made films and were concerned about my motivations. I explained that I was there by a freak coincidence and was curious as to why they were demonstrating in Puerta del Sol and not the bullring. After I'd stripped off and subjected myself to their rather over-zealous application of paint to my boobs, they opened up a bit. Apparently, there's an anonymous whistle-blower inside the Royal Taurino Society. They'd warned them of a big meeting in their headquarters office at noon today. It's on the top floor of the building opposite the Metro Station."

"So that's why they weren't outside the bullring, but how did a few girls from Pamplona organize such a massive demonstration in Madrid?"

"They had no idea. All they'd done was announce it to their Facebook group a few days before. They came down on the train this morning and were staggered by the response, not just from women but also hundreds of men. All the TV news channels were there, so as demonstrations go, it was hugely successful."

"Will they be demonstrating outside the bullring this evening?"

"They said not. But when I asked them when they were returning to Pamplona, they informed me that they were attending an event this evening then traveling back tomorrow."

"That's strange. Why come all this way, not to demonstrate outside the largest and busiest bullring in the country at one of the most prestigious fights of the season. Did they say where they were staying?"

"With friends."

"Well done my little Mata Hari," said Phillip. "I guess if they're not going to the bullring you won't have to worry about them seeing you there in your best frock tonight. They may have taken umbrage about you deceiving them."

"No, they wouldn't. I told them I was doing a video about bullfighting, and in order to film an effective story, I needed to learn how it worked from the inside. We exchanged contact details and will stay in touch, but do you know what their parting words were?"

"Go on."

"Make sure that you take your camera tonight."

7

Diego looked long and hard, but patiently at the apoplectic speaker whose nose seemed to have doubled in size as his blood vessels swelled almost to a point of explosion. He waited until Pizarro had recovered his composure.

"I hope you feel better for getting that off your chest Caballero, but I have no intention of becoming a circus performer for anyone. As you know, they call me El Bailerin, the Dancer. My performances sell out because of the chemistry I build between the bull and me. They say that the way we move together is as hypnotic as the best of tango partners. That is what my fans come to see, not a bloody execution. That is something you oblige me to do to keep my license. I do it well because I want the bull to die quickly, not because I enjoy it."

"So, you are resolved that we should stop killing bulls?" said Bosque.

"We should, but not to replace it with wrestling or

similar absurdities."

"The bull will be far more dangerous without being bloodied," said Zambrano, the man next to the Chairman.

"I agree, and therefore a more enthralling entertainment," said Diego. "Imagine the wild, raging animal charging about randomly just as it does now, but instead of killing it, we tire and tame the beast by dancing with it. The goal is to earn its respect, stand before it and take a bow as it watches us, unmoving, before being haltered and meekly led out."

"Sort of ballet with bulls?" said Bosque, earning laughter from the others.

"Preposterous," said Dorantes.

"Sport for bloody poofs," said Lorenzo.

"We'll become a laughingstock," said Pizarro. "Why should we subject ourselves to such mockery?"

"Because it will attract the younger generation," said Diego. "Without whom there will be no future for bullfighting. I'm sure that you have noticed outside, the lengths that today's youth are prepared to go, to force the debate for change. Their movement is expanding rapidly."

"It seems an incredible coincidence," said Bosque. "That this demonstration is taking place opposite our office at precisely the same time as this meeting. As very few people know about us being here, I suspect your hand was involved in arranging it. Is that so?"

"No, but both your wife and my fiancée knew I was coming, and you are all familiar with their anti-bullfighting stance. I might not agree with their tactics, but they are determined to change the way we do things. They, along with the groundswell of public opinion would prefer to ban it totally but would be happy to accept my proposals as a compromise. As the Condesa reminds me, when the older people die off, these young voters will replace them. Their different views will force politicians to respond or be thrown out of office. Their electoral power has already been proven in Catalonia and the Balearic and Canary Islands where bullfighting has now been banned."

"No Diego, that is incorrect," said Bosque. "It has not been banned. The Madrid Government and Constitutional Court have introduced legislation to prevent banning a common national heritage anywhere in Spain. It's the politicians in our autonomous communities that have made it unviable. They've excluded the use of sharp instruments in the ring, prohibited the sale of alcohol, limited fights to ten minutes, restricted the transport of live animals and introduced onerous veterinary scrutiny. I could go on, but bullfighting has not been banned anywhere."

"I understand," said Diego. "That this committee wields enormous influence over our Madrid politicians, but in the regions, you are powerless to intervene. There the Society is a toothless tiger.

"Gentlemen, please, this is not a personal crusade against you. I am just the mouth person communicating to you the consequences of doing nothing. I want the Society to sustain its position and influence, just as it has for centuries. But unless you make some urgent modifications and announce a plan of transition recognizing and respecting the will of today's young people, then I fear that events will overtake you."

The room fell silent. The men looked at each other clearly harassed. Now their faces betrayed their true emotions and they regarded Diego as if some obnoxious odor had appeared in front of them.

"Thank you," said Bosque eventually in clipped tones. "We may be ancient, but we are neither blind nor deaf. We see and hear what is going on as clearly as you do. To that end, we have taken a survey among your colleagues. We have also held workshops with the ranchers, restaurant owners, and the like to hear their suggestions for modernization.

"You may be surprised to learn that most of them want to keep killing the bull but recognize that we need to change young people's perceptions so that they support what we do, not protest against us. To this end, we have appointed marketing consultants and briefed them to develop a hard-hitting campaign pointing out the benefits of what bullfighting has done for the nation, and the role it can continue to play going forward. Their messages will address the following criteria.

"Bullfighting is an art-form and should be compared with paintings, music, and theater. It is an ancient tradition since beyond Roman times that reminds us of the human struggle for survival. It is the only remaining example of man against beast, where each has a chance of winning and is a role model for bravery, grace, and courtesy. As Marlene Dietrich once said, 'Courage and grace is a formidable mixture, the only place it can be seen is in the bullring'."

Bosque paused and took a deep breath before continuing more quietly.

"The majority of today's youngsters enjoy a hamburger, yet they have no idea how the meat is produced, or how it gets to the table. If they could be bothered to visit an abattoir and compare how animals are slaughtered as against what they see in the bullring, they would probably be more supportive. Abattoirs are dreadful places. Terrified animals are crammed into a truck for long journeys without food or water. On arrival, they are lined up for hours waiting to meet their maker, while listening to the death squeals of their friends only meters away. Yes, they may stun the animals before cutting their throats, but the person doing the stunning often gets it wrong. Halal slaughterhouses don't even bother to stun. They rely on prayer, not to assuage any pain the animal might feel, but to ensure that meat preparation is according to the rituals of their religion. At least killing bulls in the ring is more honest and open. We're going to focus on this with hard-hitting articles and documentaries on social media.

"We are also going to remind everyone about the social and neighborly interaction that bullfighting festivals bring to communities. People come to see and be seen, at what are the nerve centers of our ancient cities. In short, Spain without bullfighting is like the North Pole without snow. We are confident that this promotion aimed at the young and ignorant will more than stop the decline in attendance numbers and fill our stadiums better than ever before."

"Don Bosque," said Diego. "Your plan sounds excellent. However, I would point out that abattoirs have improved substantially from the days of the stun gun. I don't know when you last visited one, but today most use carbon dioxide to render the animals painlessly unconscious before cutting their throats.

"However, even those days could be over in the next decade or so. New technology, currently under development in the USA, is likely to replace animal cultivation almost completely. Synthetic meat, indistinguishable from the real thing, can now be manufactured in laboratories from chicken feathers or bull's hair. Furthermore, unless we dramatically reduce global warming, the prospect of snow-free Polar Regions is a distinct possibility. Several of you have accepted that change and are already playing your part by providing clean energy. Why could you not accept that bullfighting also needs to respond to a changing environment?

"Now, regarding your marketing campaign. The demonstrator's downstairs, whose attitudes toward bullfighting are typical of today's younger generation, don't want to go to bullfights. Irrespective of history and tradition, they are as steadfastly against it, as you are for it.

"They understand completely why the Romans stopped holding gladiatorial contests in their stadiums centuries ago, yet in Spain, we choose to ignore the civilized example of even ancient societies. The world has moved on from archaic, barbaric practices. To paraphrase the animal liberator Peter Singer; to protest about bullfighting in Spain, the eating of dogs in South Korea, or the slaughter of baby seals in Canada, while continuing to eat eggs from battery hens or the meat of factory-reared calves, equates to denouncing apartheid in South Africa, while asking neighbors not to sell their houses to blacks. These kids understand that. They want clean, un-doctored food produced fairly, and organically. By the way, you will be staggered how many of them prefer veggie-burgers and fruit, not meat."

The old men paused and looked at each other unsure of themselves.

The chairman nodded. "Diego, we need to discuss

this. Would you mind stepping outside for a moment? We'll confirm our conclusions to you directly."

Diego nodded, turned, closed the door behind him and walked back along the corridor of fame to the restroom by the elevator. As he stood in front of the urinal, he regurgitated the past ten minutes in his mind. He zipped up, satisfied that he couldn't have made his arguments more strongly, but in his heart, he knew he might as well have been talking to the wall. As he returned to the committee room, he took a longer look at the portraits recalling the contributions of some of his heroes. While his ancestors Frederico and Pedro stood out among them as the instigators of change, he conceded that Juan Belmonte was the greatest of them all. As a cripple with a gammy leg, he was unable to run. He was the first to stand still and steer the bull around him with the cape. On many an occasion, he had been injured, but his example was the inspiration to all that followed.

"Now, here stand I," muttered Diego. "Yet another Romero fighting to change things. Will we ever learn?"

Diego looked out of the window. The protest below had swollen even more. It must be well into the thousands, he thought. However, he doubted their presence would sway anybody on the other side of the imposing door. It opened. Pablo Bosque frowned at him and gestured for him to enter. Bosque went behind the table and took his seat before them. He felt like a naughty schoolboy about to be reprimanded by the headmaster.

Diego looked at each old man calmly and deliberately but again, they ignored him. Whatever, they were about to say, he was prepared and knew exactly what he would do next.

Don Bosque cleared his throat. "Diego. Thank you for your no holds barred presentation. We respect you and your talents and would relish your continued involvement in this Society helping us resolve the urgent challenges that we all face. I've told you what we are doing to rebuild our brand, which is the wish of us all behind this table, and of your colleagues out in the field.

"However, we need to know if you are with us, or against us. If you do wish to support our cause, you will need to stop talking publicly about this dancing with bulls' nonsense and start making positive noises about why we will continue to kill bulls in the ring. If you are against us, then you should be honest with us and yourself, and resign immediately."

Diego stood up disappointed, but unsurprised. He walked over to the window and looked out, leaning his strong arms on the windowsill. He turned, smiled at the chairman and at each one of the committee members. "Very well, gentlemen, thank you for your patience. I'm sorry if my words disturbed you, but my only concern is the future of bullfighting and making it appealing to the next generation.

"Nearly three hundred years ago, my ancestor, Frederico, faced a similar challenge. He stood before your predecessors and persuaded them that for audiences to return to the empty arenas, they should stop going around in circles chasing bulls on horseback with lances and face them on foot with a cape and a sword. As you know that committee approved his proposal and it saved the day. It was the end of the Jerez method of bullfighting and the beginning of what we know today. Without that change, bullfighting would have died out back then and none of us would be here now.

"Today, I stand on an identical threshold. The circumstances are different, but the challenge is the same, we must save bullfighting.

"I look forward to evaluating the new marketing plan and pray that it is the redeeming feature that you all want it to be. Meanwhile, let me reassure you that my commitment to our national tradition and this Society is as always, resolute."

A look of relief came over the members who smiled and nodded at each other. Bosque stood up, came around to the front of the table, grasped Diego's hand and shook it. "Thank you, Diego," he said. "My warmest regards to the Condesa."

Diego bowed, turned, walked out, past the portraits and summoned the elevator. As soon as the doors slid shut, he took out his phone and pressed a well-thumbed contact. When his uncle Juan Romero answered, he whispered, "Plan B."

8

Later that afternoon, just before five, Amanda and Phillip stepped out of the elevator and into the hotel lobby. Amanda looked stunning in a short, figure-hugging, sleeveless, royal-blue dress, matching high-heeled shoes and purse. Phillip wore a brand-new blazer that he'd purchased on the way back to Amanda's apartment after meeting with Prado the previous evening at Cortijo de Pepe. The blue serge complemented his beige chinos and light blue shirt.

The elevator door slid closed behind them and they walked into the lobby toward a short passageway that led down into the lounge where a grand piano was being played expertly in the far corner. The notes echoed hauntingly around the spacious, well-lit room furnished with clusters of elegant sofas, armchairs, and glass-topped coffee tables. Several executive types were huddled around the low tables talking quietly. A few pensioners were enjoying afternoon tea and scones. An attractive young couple was engrossed with a laptop sharing a headphone each. They exchanged tender glances as they watched the screen pointing at it and giggling from time to time.

At the top of the lounge steps, stood a man in his early fifties, below average height, but solidly built wearing a Panama hat and beige suit. He took off his hat to reveal a thinning head of gray hair, stepped forward and extended his hand to Phillip.

"Señor Armitage?" he said in Spanish. "I'm Juan Romero. It's a pleasure to meet you both this afternoon." He exchanged cheek kisses with Amanda. "I'm not sure if you are aware, but the garish blue cow outside the front of this hotel is not just a whim of the owner, or to advertise that he is a supporter of bullfighting, it's far more than that. It's to celebrate that the toreros always stay at this hotel when appearing at the Las Ventas bullring here in Madrid. It's part of their ritual and has been for decades. They'll be ready to leave for tonight's performance shortly. You can meet all three of them. Look, here they are now."

Amanda extracted her tiny GoPro video camera from her purse and aimed it at three men wearing the classic bullfighter attire, amazingly extravagant trajes de luz, who had exited the elevator and were walking towards them carrying their monteras, black hats.

A group of men in business suits swarmed around them, but the bullfighters shrugged them off and headed towards Juan. Two of the fighters held back in deference to an incredibly handsome young man in a tailored sky-blue outfit covered in ornate patterns of gold sequins and dark-blue braid. His long hair tied back in a ponytail.

Juan introduced Diego Romero and the other two bullfighters to Amanda and Phillip. Superficially, all three fighters smiled, shook hands and said the right words, but they were quiet and reserved, the pall of their imminent challenge hanging over them like a death sentence. A small group of excited, elderly American women wearing rusty-orange Texas Longhorn baseball caps surrounded them clamoring for photo opportunities. The bullfighters obliged for a few minutes before the suits pressed around them consulting timepieces and urging them to leave. They were ushered downstairs into reception, out through the revolving door, and together with their entourage, climbed into a black stretch limousine. The doorman did his traffic control bit and the vehicle sped off up Calle de Velasquez on their way to the Las Ventas bullring. Phillip wondered if it would bring all three of them back again afterward.

"I assume that you are related to Diego?" said Amanda, returning her camera back into her purse as the passageway cleared, and they were left alone.

"He is my nephew. My late brother Jaime was his father."

"And we're meeting him for dinner later?" said Amanda.

"Yes," said Juan.

"Do we have to wait until then to learn what all this is about?" said Phillip. "And how much time might be involved. We do have a business to run."

"No, we can discuss it as we go along," said Juan. "May I ask how much you know about bullfighting?"

"I ran with the bulls in Pamplona," said Amanda. "But apart from scaring myself shitless, I didn't learn much."

Juan raised his eyebrows at Phillip, who shook his head.

"Do either of you have any entrenched opinions about it?" said Juan.

"Frankly, we wouldn't choose to go to a fight," said Amanda, "but on the other hand, we are completely ignorant about it and as it's the national tradition of our adopted country, feel that we shouldn't dismiss it. So, we've agreed to watch, listen, and then make a more informed decision."

"That's better than I expected," said Juan.

"You should also know," said Amanda, "that I joined the protest in Puerta del Sol earlier. According to the organizers, there was a top-level meeting at the Royal Taurino Society offices today. Would you know anything about that?"

"Yes, Diego was giving a presentation at their offices around that time. Some of our supporters helped promote that protest. Why?"

"We couldn't understand why it wasn't outside the bullring," said Amanda. "The meeting explains why."

"I'm glad that you were at the demonstration," said Juan. "Now you've seen how passionate the anti-bullfighting lobby is, and I can assure you that their ranks are swelling rapidly. Nevertheless, it will still be an uphill battle to persuade the Royal Taurino Society to accept change."

"There seemed to be a massive media presence," said Amanda.

"Yes, but hardly anything will actually be broadcast or published," said Juan. "The Society control most of the Spanish media."

"So, the protesters were wasting their time?" said Phillip.

"Not at all, there will be enormous coverage on social media, although as yet quite amateur material.

That's where you guys come in. To tell our story professionally."

"And what story would you like that to be?" said Amanda.

"I'm sure Leon mentioned that bullfighting is dying out rapidly. Spectator numbers are shrinking fast. We estimate that bullrings will go bankrupt in about ten years, followed by our family business shortly after. The Romero and Ordoñez clans have been at the core of bullfighting for centuries, I've lost count of how many lives we've lost in the arena. Only last year my dear brother Jaime died of old chest wounds from a major goring during his fighting days. With so much of our blood in the sand, we cannot sit here doing nothing and watch our historic contribution fade away into oblivion."

"How do you propose to stop the rot?" said Phillip.

"We have to make it more appealing to the younger generation. That means stopping the killing and focus on the creative and artistic elements. We refer to it as, dancing with bulls. It will be more dangerous for the bullfighters, but the added drama should improve its allure as acceptable entertainment. The Society's proposal is a massive media campaign to promote bullfighting's traditional bloodletting values and why we should continue doing so. In our view, this will only hasten its demise. To counter their efforts, we want to launch our own campaign.

"However, my reason for asking how much you know about bullfighting is that for you to stand any chance of producing a meaningful campaign that will squash the Society's, you need to know the basics. Would you be happy to learn them and then help us? It will mean several trips to our ranch near Ronda."

Amanda and Phillip exchanged excited glances. "This is a fantastic opportunity to substantially increase the exposure of our business," said Phillip. "But why all the hush-hush? From what you've just told us, it seems a straightforward campaign to settle differences of opinion."

"You don't know these men that we are up against. They not only control the Society but practically everything in Madrid. They are incredibly wealthy, ruthless, and love traditional bullfighting with a deep passion. We are certain that they will try to use their power to prevent us from publishing our suggestions for change. As to what lengths they will go, we are unsure. Our obscure warnings via my dear friend Leon were to prepare you for an exciting, but challenging project. We didn't want you to think that this is going to be a walk in the park."

"Are you implying that we might be in danger?" said Amanda.

"Physical danger, unlikely, but they may put pressure on some of your advertisers, hotels particularly and probably supermarkets. If you have any debts, they may interfere with your lenders. There could also be a tax inspection, or you may suffer some disruption to your network of advertising agents, writers, and creative providers."

"I don't think that our partners will be happy if we jeopardize our business," said Phillip.

"That I understand," said Juan. "However, we do have an attractive proposition if your revenues are damaged as a result of working with us. Diego will explain it over dinner later."

"Forgive us, but we need to talk privately for a minute," said Phillip.

"May I suggest that you have a drink in the bar," said Juan. "I have a few calls to make and will join you shortly."

Amanda and Phillip walked down the steps into the lounge, through to a timber-paneled and mirrored bar that resembled an old London pub. They ordered a glass of dry sherry each and when the waiter delivered the drinks along with some roasted almonds, they sipped from their glasses at a corner table, sitting in comfortable brown leather armchairs.

"We should discuss this with our business partners Richard and Ingrid," said Amanda. "These Society people don't sound particularly pleasant."

"I agree," said Phillip. "However, we are uniquely poised not to be unduly worried. We have no debts, landlords, or suppliers. Our product is knowledge that we have already paid for. Nobody can take down our website. Furthermore, if we stopped earning tomorrow, would it really matter? For us personally, no. The only people likely to suffer would be our agents and content providers, but only temporarily. They are all freelancers and are used to reinventing themselves."

"You're right, and if everything works with this project, it should mean even more work for them. I suggest that we learn the whole picture first. Let's see the night through, sleep on it, then discuss it with our partners in the morning."

Phillip reached over and picked up Amanda's hand and held it in both of his. He looked into her eyes. "Look, my love. We don't have to do this. If at any time you feel uncomfortable or frightened by anything, we stop immediately."

"Are you kidding me? After all these years, this is

the nearest I've ever been to have some real influence on anything Spanish. All I've done so far could be called clowning around with a few of their crazy customs but this? This is major league news material, foreigners influencing the politics of a nation-state. Imagine the furor if the Russians interfered with elections or immigrant Mexicans tried to stop American rodeos or change the rules of baseball."

"Hmm… Hadn't thought of it like that. OK, then we'll tell Juan that subject to a satisfactory negotiation with Diego later, we are happy to proceed to learn more about their campaign and what they expect from us."

Amanda nodded.

"I'll take that as a positive sign," said Juan coming across to them from the bar entrance. "You'll help us then?"

"For now, yes," said Phillip. "However, we will need the go-ahead from our partners in Nerja. We'll call them in the morning after we've heard your proposals."

"Fair enough," said Juan. "Then shall we go to the bullring?"

They followed him out through the revolving door. The door attendant summoned a cab from the rank opposite. They all squeezed in the back and followed the route of the torero's limousine to the bullring.

"Can you tell us more about your families?" said Amanda.

"There are many of us involved in this industry," said Juan. "As I've said, Diego is the most prominent and commands a huge following among the fans. We need to use his popularity to re-educate them into accepting a new way of doing things. Altogether, ten of us are still fighting, seventy-odd run the family ranches, five have restaurants and many more are in associated bullfighting businesses such as slaughterhouses, transport, veterinary services, gift shops, etc. I commentate on the radio and on cable TV. I also lecture, give presentations to tourists and teach new bullfighters. OK, we are not impoverished and could easily fund the study to acquire new skills. Some of us will have to, but we prefer not to let bullfighting fade away. We've given so much and are dedicated to keeping a more modern and accepted version alive for the next generations. Remember, we redesigned it in the eighteenth century and can do so again."

"A worthy project?" said Amanda, as the cab turned off Velasquez, and onto Jorge Juan.

"Thank you," said Juan.

Amanda, Phillip, and Juan exited the taxi onto the crowded square in front of the Las Ventas bullring. In front of them was an imposing three-tiered neo-Mudejar styled circular building in terracotta hand-painted brick with rows of different sized Arab archways on each floor. The red and yellow Spanish flag was flying from the top of the entrance tower.

"The original architect was José Espeliú," said Juan as he led them toward a quieter side entrance. "He was a friend of the famous torero Joselito. They started building in 1921 but he died during construction. It wasn't completed until nearly ten years later and they held the inauguration in May 1931. It's the largest bullring in Spain with capacity for 23,798 spectators, but the ring itself is only sixty meters in diameter, which is relatively small when compared to the ring in Ronda. I have killed many bulls in all the great arenas around the world, but it was here in Las Ventas that I was severely gored in the gut. Thankfully, I recovered but have never fought in the ring since."

That must have been terrible," said Amanda.

"It was, but far worse for my wife and children," said Juan. "They were why I stopped fighting, and it was then that I resolved to change our national tradition into something more appropriate for the modern world."

Juan escorted them through the entrance for VIP's waving his pass at the security guards and exchanging a few friendly words. They stepped through a large archway and onto a wide circular stone corridor with people scurrying backward and forwards as they jostled to find their seats. Every twenty meters they passed a walkway that provided access down into the terraces where many had already taken their seats. Some were standing and talking, some looking at mobile devices, others opening picnic baskets and settling down for the duration which is usually between two and three hours of entertainment.

"Here is the lift up to The Royal box," said Juan as they passed a stainless-steel doorway guarded by two armed sentries. It has its own bar and toilet. We're going up to the VIP lounge."

They climbed two flights of stairs and onto a quieter circular corridor, walked around it for a hundred meters and entered the VIP cocktail lounge reserved exclusively for season-ticket holders and special guests. Full height windows opened out onto a terrace which overlooked the arena below that had been recently swept and was ready for action.

They sat down in comfortable sofas surrounding a coffee table on the terrace. A gorgeous server, they were all pretty and female, brought glasses of cava then placed a china dish of olives on the table.

"Salud," said Juan raising his glass.

They chinked copas and took a sip of the fine sparkling wine.

"Tell me about your Pamplona experience, Amanda," said Juan.

"Not much to say really, I trailed after an experienced runner with a chest camera and did as I was instructed."

"Fernando, by any chance?"

"Yes, do you know him?"

"He's another cousin, we have them everywhere. While you were in Pamplona, did you see your fellow American Ernest Hemingway's statue standing at the bar in Café Iruña?"

"Of course, why?"

"Because before I start boring you with bullfighting snippets, I want to refer to some of the immortal words from his book, *Death in the Afternoon*, which in my opinion remains one of the finest and technically correct non-fictional tomes about our national heritage, although nowadays somewhat dated. On the first page, he writes something along the lines of, it is easy to be sickened by bullfighting without ever having been to one, but it is only possible to truly make a judgment having seen one and learned what personal reactions would actually be. He then went on to advise new attendees to learn about the spectacle first, in order to understand what was going on, and qualify them to make a more informed appraisal. Otherwise, all they would see is a wretched animal being chased around a ring and slaughtered. That wise counsel is still relevant today, and I hope to impart to you a greater understanding of what is unraveling before you, so you may appreciate the nuances and reasoning behind why it has been so popular in Spain for so long.

"Tonight, you will watch three top-level toreros fight six magnificent bulls. Everything will proceed just as it has for centuries. It will be a perfect introduction, and if all goes well, a starting point for our project.

"It will also be Diego's final fight until September. We want to work with you over the summer to educate you about bullfighting and the industry so that you understand the big picture from all viewpoints.

"In September, we hold our family event in Ronda. It's known as the Pedro Romero Festival. On the last of the three days, there is the finest and most elegant bullfight of the season, La Goyesca. We are going to use that day to announce our plans. Now, it's time to watch Diego. Shall we take our seats?"

The interior of Las Ventas consisted of the ring itself covered with raked sand, which was surrounded by a burgundy painted fence just under two meters high containing several doorways through which the bulls and bullfighters entered and departed. Parallel to the outer wall was an inner wall providing a narrow corridor for officials, media, and medics to quickly move around the ring without exposing themselves to any danger. Above this inner wall were two tiers of open-air concrete terraces. These were the lower-cost seats starting at around fifty Euros. Above, were two further tiers of covered terraces supported by narrow steel columns, under a roof of terracotta tiles. Seats in these shady areas were from ninety Euros but could be much higher when famous bullfighters such as Diego Romero were appearing.

One of two uniformed ushers pointed out their seats situated at the back of the President's box which was a square-shaped area on the lower covered tier surrounded by a waist-high wall that separated them from the crowd. They went up, took their seats and looked around them at the magnificent arena. It was filling up rapidly.

The picnickers were packing away their stuff. Many men stood around chatting and pointing at their device screens.

"Can't they leave their phones at home?" said Amanda.

"They are comparing the latest odds from the online bookies," said Juan. "Betting in bullfights is usually limited to what awards any of the bullfighters might win such as an ear, who is likely to be the best fighter of the afternoon, or will the bull, be pardoned? There are also a few sites operating on the dark-web offering odds on whether the torero will survive uninjured, gored or dead. Apparently, it's hugely popular, to me, it's disturbing."

"Do you know the names of any of these sites," said Phillip.

"I haven't seen any myself," said Juan as they sat down at the back of the small box in what were surprisingly comfortable chairs for stadium seating, but we can find out if you want to take a look.

A uniformed brass band sporting colorful tassels and sparkling sequins entered the arena and marched around playing raucous marching music. Phillip thought the trumpet blasts were painful to the ear, but the locals cheered loudly when they played the Pasadoble especially written for Las Ventas. Somehow, the crowd managed to carry on chatting with each other, even though it was impossible to hear anything above the musical discord.

The president arrived with his two assistants, one of which was a veterinarian who walked with a slight limp and had a built-up shoe, the other a technical bullfighting advisor. They said a cursory good evening and sat down in the front row talking among themselves.

"The vet is Fredo Ordoñez," whispered Juan, indicating the short, slender, handsome man in his mid-forties with a full head of silver hair and brown eyes. "My wife is his sister. Sorry, yet another family member; you'll get used to it. He's retained by the Royal Taurino Society as their expert on fighting bulls and is well respected by everyone in the industry. He's also our whistle-blower."

At that moment, Fredo looked back at Juan, smiled and winked. Juan nodded. The crowd applauded as the president waved at everyone.

"The president," said Juan. "Is usually a senior policeman or local government delegate accustomed to officiating at bullfights. Presidents equate to football referees, the most experienced are selected for the top-quality matches.

"While Spain could be accused of having more politicians, civil servants and police per head than any other country, it has yielded some benefits. Our robust control of olive-oil production, wine, hams, meats and dairy guarantees a superb quality from trusted sources. These same practices also apply to bullfighting. Every element is closely monitored and expected to meet demanding standards. The breeding and nurturing of bulls, ranch facilities, and personnel training, transport, veterinary inspections through to every element of the fight itself are subject to a set of strict rules defined by the Society, and rigorously policed.

"I have to say that over the centuries the Society has done a splendid job. The members are well respected and it's only natural that they are resistant to change. Unfortunately, they are not getting any younger, their views are well entrenched and that's making them deaf and blind to what is happening on the street. Thankfully, though, they don't interfere with the management of the actual bullfights because the bullrings are usually multi-purpose buildings owned and managed by the local council as concert venues, exhibition centers, and specialist markets.

"In the bullring, it's the president's job to supervise and ensure compliance with the regulations that govern the normal course of a fight. The vet and technical advisor assist him, but the President always has the final word. However, the three normally strike an accord. Today the president is Guardia-Civil Captain Jorge Benitez."

The president was a short man with a slender figure, greasy dark hair, and a ruddy complexion, but he was dressed impeccably in a dark gray suit, white shirt, and red tie. He carried a small leather pouch, which he zipped open, and extracted five perfectly ironed different color handkerchiefs placing them on the shelf in front of him.

"The handkerchiefs," said Juan. "Are the president's communication tools, a tradition going back centuries. Rather than bore you for what each one is used; I'll tell you as it happens."

Down in the arena, the band changed its music to another pasadoble. Everyone stood up to applaud as the paseillo, the parade began.

Three separate groups of bullfighters entered the ring on foot, gold and magenta capes draped around their shoulders, hats on, waving and bowing to the cheering crowd as they strutted around the freshly raked sand. This is a traditional ritual. The oldest torero and his team would be on the left, the youngest in the middle. For his first appearance in a ring, a torero would carry his hat. Diego was on the right; all three toreros wore their hats.

"Today," said Juan. "The three cuadrillas, teams, will face six bulls, two each. Being the most high-profile fighter, Diego will go first and fourth. The teams consist of at least five but at this level, usually six men. The torero or matador is the man that kills the bull. He is assisted by a picador, who rides a blindfolded horse protected from the bull's horns by a peto, a heavily padded covering. The objective of the picador is to blood the bull with a lance in the morrillo, the massive lump of muscle on the bull's back behind the shoulder. It encourages the bull to charge in a straight line and hold his head lower. A particularly lively and aggressive bull may need two or three stabs to make it focus on attacking the torero, rather than charge around madly. Then come the three banderilleros. They are acrobatic, fleet-footed men who each plant a pair of darts on either side of the morrillo. The other attendant is a mozo de espoca, sword assistant, who will keep Diego equipped with the right equipment as the fight unwinds.

"When the bulls arrive at the bullring and are encouraged out of their luxury transporter by the herdsmen, they are held one-by-one in a small corral at the back of the stadium. The toreros receive five minutes to inspect each animal. The idea is to glean as much as they can about the animal's characteristics, such as agility, which horn does it favor, is it nervous or intelligent, heavy and slow, or lean and fast? This will help them determine the aggression, turning speed, and stopping capability of each animal.

"Lots are then drawn, and the animals allocated to each torero. The bulls then wait in straw-lined accommodations until their turn in the ring.

"All through this process, the animals are kept at a distance from humans, as they were back on the ranch. Their movement from transporter to stall and eventually into the ring, are controlled from platforms, several meters above the narrow passageways used by the bulls. Look, now the parade is ending."

The crowd applauded.

Diego's team remained in the arena. The others retired to the cuadrilla marshaling area outside the gate. Diego's men took up their positions and prepared themselves mentally. At a nod from Diego, they turned as one to face the gate where the bull would enter.

9

Amanda sat riveted, watching the preparations down in the arena. Occasionally, she would film something that caught her attention. She zoomed in on the handsome Diego Romero as he stood under the burning late afternoon sun attending to his final preparations.

"These rituals," she said still filming. "Do they actually work?"

"It's a similar process to a golfer," said Juan. "The waggle of the club and the visualization of the shot are all about managing the mindset. Sometimes, it doesn't work, like a golfer missing the fairway. Nowadays, a torero is rarely gored, and death is practically unheard of. However, not to prepare is not an option. Diego must collect his thoughts; his mind must be in the right balance of concentration and alertness but sufficiently relaxed. These rituals facilitate that. We all know they are superstitious nonsense, but so far they've blessed Diego with good fortune."

They watched as Diego adjusted his montera to ensure that it fitted snugly on his head, then accepted the heavy magenta and gold capote from his sword assistant. He swirled the cape high above his head in his right hand with an artistic flourish. Then bowed to the cheering crowd before turning to face the maroon-painted door where the bull would enter the arena.

The gold sequins on his clothing sparkled in the sunlight.

"Does Diego wear any protection built into the suit?" said Amanda.

"None whatsoever. It would restrict his freedom of movement, which is far more likely to get him killed. However, the suit is made from seven layers of polyester-mix. It's resilient enough for light contact with the bull's horns but wouldn't stop a direct thrust. The assistants also wear the same clothing, but in a different color to Diego, it aids spectators to identify who is who in the arena."

"I couldn't help but notice when we saw them in the hotel," said Phillip, "that all three appeared apprehensive about their forthcoming ordeal."

"Wouldn't you be?" said Juan. "They are about to put their life on the line. Even though it's something they do on a regular basis, they can't afford to become laissez-faire. That would be the fastest route to meeting their maker. All bullfighters suffer from fear, which is beneficial as it sharpens their reflexes and that helps keep them alive. Three days before a fight, fear will start to build. Each torero has their own system of dealing with it. Some withdraw totally from company, others need a priest, and a few prefer to be with their team.

"Over the years Diego, despite not being much of a

believer, spends ten minutes in the arena chapel for some solitary contemplation before each fight. He kneels before the small altar and looks intensely at a statue of Jesus Christ set in the wall behind it. He finds the spirituality of the experience inspiring and relaxing. It doesn't stop the fear, but it boosts his total focus on the task before him. It cleanses all the peripheral elements out of his usual brain clutter, leaving a clean sheet with just him, the bull, and what must be done. It enables them to put fear in perspective until the bull enters the ring. After that, they're too busy to worry about it."

***

Diego stretched his chiseled physique in final preparation for the danger ahead. He regarded each of his team members imparting a look of encouragement. Despite the inner turmoil each had endured during the build-up to the fight, they looked good. They were brave and confident men with whom he had shared sandy arenas around the world for the last five years, his trust in them was steadfast. They would cover his back no matter what, because tonight, they were about to make history. Nobody had ever achieved what they were about to attempt.

Diego heard the bullfighters' entrance gate close behind him with a solid chunk. His men jogged to their opening positions behind the protection of the burladeros; the narrow timber upstands around the perimeter of the ring that would protect them from the early, savage, terrifying rushes of the bull. This was it. There was no going back. Withdrawing was impossible. For the next twenty minutes, nobody was leaving this corral whatever the excuse. Unless of course, the bull was too clever for him and tossed him aside like a papier-mâché figure. It had happened to him before, but just the once, and he'd been lucky to escape with a few bruises. Diego took a last look to confirm his men were in position, looked up at the president standing in his box at the top of the upper tier and nodded.

The president draped his white handkerchief over the top of the wall at the front of his box. A trumpet blast sounded to herald the start of the first of three thirds of the fight referred to as tercio de varas – third of pikes. Everyone's attention was on the innocuous gate. A bolt was drawn, the gate opened and in trotted a massive, jet-black wild bull, snorting, tail swishing, and horns bristling. He looked around him curiously; alert and confident. This savage beast was five years old, weighed over four hundred and eighty kilos, finely muscled, fit and with incredible acceleration, he was afraid of nothing. His name was Miura.

As Miura trotted toward the center to take command of his new domain, a sudden movement distracted him to the right. He immediately put his head down and sprinted toward it, only to find that whatever it was disappeared at the last minute.

Good, concluded Diego to himself, satisfied with his first sight of the bull in action. There had been not a moment's hesitation to attack. We have a brave animal here who deserves his reward. The crowd will instinctively like him. My job is to make them adore him.

"Hola Toro, ven aquí," said one of Diego's men.

The bull turned towards the voice. He turned around and spotted more movement. Without any hesitation, he charged.

For the first few minutes, Miura rushed around the ring expending enormous energy chasing ghosts that never materialized. He stopped to rest and stood in the center of the ring breathing hard. Diego had been watching the bull like a hawk, as he hurtled after his men.

Diego approached the bull, cape in front of him, arms spread either side. He shook the cape as he drew near the panting beast. He'd noted from his initial appraisals and as the bull dashed around that he favored his left horn. This crucial piece of information would determine the tactics that followed, just as if a boxer was entering the ring to fight a left-hander.

"Venga toro," he called looking the bull directly in its dark brown eyes. They were the mirror into its soul and read carefully, would forecast its next movement. The bull lowered his head and headed straight for him.

Diego stood his ground, raised himself on tiptoe and guided Miura past his right side with an elegant sweep of the cape, the bull's right horn only millimeters from his chest. He twisted round only seconds faster than the bull and repeated the sweep. Each movement ended with a different flourish, demonstrating a comprehensive range of Veronicas executed to perfection. The crowd yelled 'Ole' with each pass and applauded the demonstration of sublime cape work. While the bull was preoccupied with ending Diego's existence, the arena gate opened and a man on a horse entered, carrying a long-pointed lance. The gate shut behind him. The horse cantered about inviting the bull to charge. This time the bull did not turn to attack Diego but went straight at this new threat.

The picador's horsemanship was brilliant. He

pranced, dodged and galloped out of the bull's way anticipating his every move, tiring the bull and edging him closer to the arena wall. He wanted to trap Miura between the horse and the wall to deliver his thrust to the bull's morillo.

The picador repeated this twice. Diego deemed it enough.

Miura behaved differently after the picador left. Blood started to drip down his side and he held his head lower. From now Miura would be more focused on a single target, rather than charging randomly at anything that moved. He was learning fast, now he was considerably more dangerous.

The president waved the white handkerchief and replaced it over the wall. The trumpet sounded and the second third of the fight began – tercio de banderillas – third of little harpoons. It was time for the acrobatic banderilleros to stab the bull near the wound caused by the picador with three pairs of darts. Each dart was about a meter long and wrapped in a variety of colors. Diego favored two sets of sky blue and red, the other to match the red and yellow of the Spanish flag.

The banderilleros approached the bull one at a time with darts in hand while the rest of the team stood nearby, capes in hand ready to distract the bull if needed. These men were incredibly athletic and agile. They could turn and withdraw much faster than the lumbering animal.

With the three sets of darts delivered accurately and now dangling from Miura's shoulders, the trumpet blasted again. It was time for el tercio de muerte – the third of death.

10

Prado leaned back in his chair, span it around and looked out of his office window. The view of the laundry drying on the back of the apartments opposite rarely changed, but today it seemed that the lady of the house had invested in some new sexy red underwear. Prado wished her luck and tapped the dialing icon on his mobile phone.

"British Consulate," said a female voice in English.

"Hola, this is DI Prado from the Central Málaga Comisaría," he said in Spanish. "I want to trace a British citizen?"

"One moment please, I'll connect you with the assistant consulate," she said in Spanish.

Their extension was busy. In a futile attempt to keep Prado sweet while he waited, Spanish guitar music played, interrupted every thirty seconds by an irritating message, in both English and Spanish, explaining that a person would attend them shortly.

Prado tapped his thumbs cursing occasionally at the

negative influences of modern communications. He much preferred the days of switchboards and direct contact with real people.

Five minutes later, a woman said in Spanish, "Hola, inspector, how may I help you?"

"You may have read in the press," said Prado. "That we arrested a British sex offender called Malcolm Crown some weeks ago?"

"Yes, one of our staff has just been visiting him in Alhaurin Prison."

"How was he?"

"He's a lot happier, now that he's seen a doctor and is safely tucked up in solitary confinement."

"Has someone had a go at him?"

"He said he had an argument with a door, but yes he had been roughed up pretty badly."

"For sex offenders, only to be expected I'm afraid. Listen, our inquiries into Crown's background have hit a brick wall, and we need your help. We have his UK criminal and prison records, but know nothing about his history, family members or contacts. Could you contact your appropriate offices and see what you can find? Ideally, we need an address for his parents or any siblings?"

"Of course, but it will take a few days."

"I understand, as fast as possible please."

"The information will all be in English, do you have a translator there?"

"Yes, thanks, we do."

Prado clicked end call, took one more look at the skimpy knickers, turned back to his desk, put his feet up on the edge, arms behind his head, and closed his eyes. His door clicked open. Prado opened one eye. It was his chief. Jefe Superior, Provincia de Málaga:

Francisco Gonzalez Ruiz, a short, slight, man in his early forties, with thin black hair swept straight back from his forehead. Chiseled features, a Roman nose, and cold dark brown eyes that lent him a hard, imposing disposition.

"Another stressful day at the office Leon?"

"Good morning, sir," said Prado putting his feet down and standing up. "Just thinking, sir, I find my head works better in a relaxed mode."

"And to what little gems have such a treasured repose inspired you?"

"I've just been onto the British Consul to begin a search for Crown's relatives."

"I see. Excellent, keep me posted," said Gonzalez. "Meanwhile, I've drawn up a consultancy agreement for Phillip and Amanda. As they are not officially qualified interpreters, their testimonies regarding any translations would not be admissible. However, as our official consultants, they become, to all intents and purposes, members of staff and can attend court and give evidence. Could you have them sign on each page the next time you see them?"

"Certainly, sir."

"Where are they anyway?"

"In Madrid, sir, at the Hotel Wellington. I believe they are making a film about bullfighting."

"The Wellington? A fine establishment. How the other half live Prado?"

"Indeed. Will that be all, sir?"

"Yes, thank you. Carry on Leon. Carry on."

With a classical leadership wave, el jefe turned and swept out of the room, leaving Prado's door wide open. Prado closed it and returned to his former state of contemplation. Crown's case was temporarily out of his hands, and he had no other cases to concern him. This was just fine; the lesser workload was why he preferred this position.

Inevitably, his thoughts drifted to Inma and his sons. With the family back in his life, his well-being and state of mind had improved substantially, but was he ready to move back into the family home? Did he want to recommence the tedious daily commute back and forth to Ronda? But wait a minute. He thought. Surely with the latest technology, I don't need to be based in Málaga every day. I could view my caseboard in digital format, interview suspects and colleagues over Skype, and do much of my job from anywhere. But would his chief be able to accept that?

His mind whirred as he kicked around the possibilities. After a while, he decided to let things evolve. Eventually, such heavy thinking drained his energy level and he succumbed to the pressure of Spain's finest legacy to the world. He took a Siesta.

11

Miura stood panting in the center of the arena, blood dripping steadily down both shoulders, collecting in small pools on the sand. The weary bull watched the activities of the strange shapes moving around him girding himself to charge.

Diego removed his hat, passed it with the magenta and gold cape to his sword assistant, and exchanged it for a muleta, a smaller red felt cape used with a short stick. It was red because there would be a lot of close-up work, and the blood from the bull's wounds would smear the cape. The short stick, which he would hold in his right hand was to extend the reach of the cape. A concept invented two hundred and eighty years previously by Diego's ancestor Pedro.

A sword of tempered steel would later replace the stick. Until then, the lighter weight facilitated more precisely controlled Veronicas and precision was vital for his safety.

He now had a maximum of fifteen minutes to kill

the bull. The objective was to build on Miura's cape obsession. To wear him down with pass after consecutive pass. This was Diego's moment to demonstrate to the crowd why he was the best in Spain. With the end of the cape draped over the stick, he could place the position of the cape precisely where he wanted directing the bull to exactly where he wanted him.

It is largely unknown, even by discerning bullfight fans that an object placed directly near a bull's eye, will instinctively cause the bull to turn towards it. To make it keep left, all Diego had to do was position the cape directly over the left eye, not touching, but just a few centimeters away and holding it at that distance as the bull moved forward and turned around him. It had taken him years of practice to maintain the cape in the correct position. It required enormous upper body strength, fluid hand-eye coordination and nerves of steel to stand stock-still and trust the bull to follow the cape.

Miura charged. Diego positioned the cape accurately over his left eye. Miura followed, but immediately realized that he'd been duped, turned and without pausing, charged again.

Diego was relentless. Not once did he fail to anticipate each of the massive animal's moves. On each pass, the horns deliberately almost kissed Diego's chest as he, in effect, danced with the bull. The nearer the horns, the greater the danger, the higher the appreciation.

The knowledgeable crowd rose to their feet applauding feverishly in favor of what they were seeing. One of the finest displays of man and animal performing together in harmony.

Inevitably, Miura began to tire.

There were three minutes left for Diego to kill him. He stood directly before Miura, some five meters away, taunting, goading him with shakes of the cape and cries of 'come on toro'. However, Miura had had enough.

Diego recognized that the time had come.

He turned his back on the bull, cape dangling in his right hand and raised his arm to the crowd, confident that Miura wouldn't charge him. The crowd applauded as he turned through 360 degrees to wave at them all.

His attendant exchanged the stick for the sword. Diego glanced at the president who waved his white handkerchief granting permission to kill the bull.

Diego walked towards Miura, the cape in front of him. He bowed slightly at the waist, lowered the cape to the sand and waggled it in front of the bull's eyes. It would tempt the bull to look down which dropped its head. It presented a more accessible and safer position to lunge over his horns with the sword.

This was the most lethal moment of the fight. In order to lunge, he had to break eye contact and would no longer be able to read the bull's intentions. While he was in mid-maneuver, the bull could lift his head or turn a horn. This was the moment when most bullfighters were gored.

Having survived that, he could still hit bone. This was his one and only allowable attempt. All the good work done up to this point could be ruined by a bad aim. If he failed, the bull would be killed by cutting the spinal cord with another sword called a Verdugo. It was drawn out, messy and painful for the bull. And, he would be booed by the crowd.

Diego lined up his sword, over the horns and into the small killing zone between the shoulder blades that provided unimpeded access to the heart.

Ideally, one thrust down into the aorta would be enough. Miura would die slowly but painlessly. The mules would then enter and tow out his corpse ready for the butcher's knives. However, if the crowd made enough noise, and the president had been impressed enough by the bull's bravery, he would place the blue handkerchief over the wall. This signified that the corpse was to be dragged once around the ring, a final opportunity for the crowd to acknowledge the poor animal's courage before the butcher's knives sliced him apart.

As Diego lined up his sword, he kept one eye on the president waiting for the go-ahead to kill the bull. It was at this moment that Diego usually prayed, wished and hoped fervently that his sword would hit the exact target on the bull's back with the first thrust, but tonight, he wanted none of these.

If their family plan to force the Society to change the destiny of bullfighting, what happened next was a critical ingredient to their success.

He waited on tenterhooks, listening to the crowd, keeping one eye on Miura, the other on the president. Then it started. Quietly at first.

***

Juan asked Amanda to point her camera around the crowd and then at Diego and the bull. Everyone was on the edge of their seat gripped by the tense moments unraveling in the ring below. Thousands of eyes flicked constantly between Diego poised to kill and the president pondering his decision. Was the bull to be killed? Or might something else be possible?

She zoomed in on Diego's face, which was a total look of concentration. The bull stood stock still, panting hard looking at Diego as if he was wondering what was going to happen next.

Phillip couldn't make out what some of the crowd was shouting at first, but then, as the remainder took up the call, it became clear.

"Indulto, indulto, indulto."

Then they waved their white handkerchiefs.

At first by the hundred, then the thousand and eventually without exception, everyone was standing, waving their handkerchiefs frantically and shouting 'indulto' – pardon, with a passion unheard of, especially in Las Ventas which had a reputation for not being generous toward the bull.

The president consulted with his advisors. There was hardly any discussion between them.

Diego looked straight into the bull's eyes, and waited, unmoving, sword ready to strike. The bull stared straight back at him panting, blood dripping, resigned to his destiny. The president reached for his array of handkerchiefs.

12

Prado stood by the large case-board mounted on the sidewall of his office. Colorful magnetic pins held up all the forensic materials, photos and reports gathered during the Darkness in Málaga case. Even though it was over three weeks since the arrests had been made, additional evidence was still coming in and the case-board was practically full. He made a note to discuss with el jefe when Interpol intended to take the case over. Until then he remained responsible for it and was the only officer with a comprehensive understanding of the detail, and that worried him.

Other than the victims, the villa in Torrox Park had yielded little in the way of detail about Crown and his now-deceased partner Rick Duffy. They'd found thousands of Euros in cash in a safe, but no details about personal bank accounts, car ownership, passports, insurances or domestic bills. Sanchez and Sanchez, the CVS lawyers based in Málaga had taken care of all the administrative matters and nothing was in Crown's name. He'd been operating completely under the radar, and nothing could be traced to him, or connected with him.

When the police had raided the Sanchez brother's offices, they had found little incriminating evidence. Their computers had been sabotaged and everything wiped clean. The brothers had been released on bail despite police appeals to the contrary at the highest levels. Unsurprisingly, they had disappeared.

Whilst the Syrian immigrants had been cooperative, they knew little of consequence.

The victims had provided detailed information about their abuse, how they came to be abducted off the streets or acquired by Crown from the corrupt official at the immigration center in Algeciras. However, nothing they had said pointed to involvement by others. Crown appeared to be the only boss. Duffy had been nothing more than a giant lackey to add muscle and to terrify the victims.

The Spanish lady working in the villa as cook, cleaner and general assistant to Crown, had suffered a stroke. She was in hospital with her memory totally confused. It was dead ends everywhere.

He rubbed his earlobe in deep thought as he cast his eye over the photos of the parties involved, statements and forensic reports.

"We must be missing something," he said out loud.

His phone rang. An unknown number snapped him back to reality.

"Prado," he said.

"It's Barraclough from the British Consul," said a man's voice in Spanish. "I'm the assistant Consul's assistant. We have that information on Crown."

"Tell me," said Prado.

"His parents John and Gillian Crown are recently deceased."

"When?"

"You may well recall an explosion at a farm outside Ronda, about a year ago. What little of their remains were found in the burned-out wreckage of an outbuilding packed with computers. The police report concluded that it was some sort of accident after a power surge. Apparently, they were trying to put the fire out. There wasn't much left of them, so the coroner had little choice other than to record a verdict of accidental death. I'll email you the report."

"I vaguely remember something about the fire. Thanks. Anything else?"

"There are two other siblings. An elder sister, Georgina Crown and her twin brother George."

"Any address?"

"Their last known location was in the UK. Just outside Bournemouth, to be precise. They applied to renew their passports from there only last year. We've also discovered that the Crown family lived in Marbella until Malcolm was fourteen. All three children attended an international school there. Unfortunately, the school closed years ago. However, when they returned to the UK, the Crown's had to present their Spanish school records to their new school near Bournemouth. We've managed to obtain a copy of these records. Apparently, all three children were expelled midterm for severe disruption and abusive behavior to other pupils. The school psychologist wrote a report at the time suspecting that their parents had sexually abused all three children. It was shortly after this that the whole family returned to the UK."

"Any reports of further abusive behavior?"

"No, they stayed off the police and social services radar. After school, the twins gained scholarships to Cambridge in computer sciences. Malcolm followed them. Oddly enough, he was considered by his teachers as being the family tech genius. After collecting a top-notch Ph.D., he walked straight into a high-level job as an IT consultant based in Warwick. A few years later he was caught abusing young boys in a local park."

"How long were the parents living at the farm in Ronda?"

"Sorry, you'll have to find that out yourself."

"Do you have copies of all their passports?"

"Included with my email."

"Where are the twins working now?"

"Last year's tax returns have them down as self-employed IT consultants operating from their home in Bournemouth."

"Would you describe them as high earners?"

"Yes, but not like footballers."

"Thank you."

Prado sat back down at his desk, checked his emails from the consulate and forwarded the twins' passports to Border Control.

He searched the Property Register for the farm in Ronda. It was still owned by the twins and had been purchased by them sixteen years previously. There was no mortgage. The farm had been expanded considerably since. All legally and above board with proper planning permissions being granted and building licenses paid. Most of the expansion, however, had been into outbuildings and machine rooms to run a communications center. There was no mention of growing anything. As he read the registry documents, something was nagging him, but he couldn't put his finger on it.

Then it struck him. The name of the farm. In Spanish, it was Cortijo Infierno. He typed that into Google translate and it was as Phillip had said. Hell, Inferno, underworld, Hades, pit or darkness. He stood, went over to the case board and looked at the note written by Crown to Phillip.

"Look in the darkness," it said.

13

The president picked up the orange handkerchief and waved it to the crowd. The bull was pardoned and free to return to the ranch, but the show was not over yet.

The audience was ecstatic and as one burst into song, "Ole, ole, ole, ole. Ole. Ole."

Diego lowered his sword and passed it with the bloodied cape to his assistant. The arena clearance team entered cautiously, wary of any rapid movement that might attract the eye of this still lethal beast.

Diego remained standing stock-still in front of Miura.

A young man from the arena team walked up to Diego eyeing the bull attentively. He handed Diego a thick leather halter attached to several lengths of sturdy rope.

Diego walked up to Miura looking him in the eye for any signs of intended movement. He saw none. He uncoupled the ropes from the halter and dropped them one-by-one to the ground. The crowd gasped as they grasped his intention. Diego reached out a hand and stroked Miura under the chin. Miura shook his head and snorted. Diego stretched his arm to Miura's back and one by one extracted the darts, throwing them onto the sand. Miura didn't flinch, they were only irritating pricks in his massive thick-skinned shoulders.

Diego slipped the halter over Miura's head and buckled it. He tucked his hand into the chin strap and led the massive wild animal, on a lap of honor. Pardoning a bull was a rare event among Madrileños. Yet tonight, they cheered, some even wept at the sight of Diego alongside his protagonist.

They both walked slowly around the arena, and out through the exit gate to the stables, to tumultuous applause and passionate cries of 'viva toro'.

Miura would be hosed down, have his wounds attended then after a hearty meal and drink would re-enter the luxury transport that had brought him here the previous day. Later that night, he would lumber down its ramp and trot back out to the green pastures of his ranch outside Segovia to a rosy future involving large numbers of young cows' keen for his attention.

***

"Is the pardon part of your plan?" whispered Phillip into Juan's ear.

Juan looked at Phillip, nodded and put his finger to his lips. "We'll discuss it over dinner," he said.

"How many bulls are pardoned per year?" said Amanda.

"Hardly any," said Juan. "I'll give you the big picture for 2015. 5,316 bulls were killed in Spanish bullrings in 1,736 bullfights by 175 toreros. During the whole year,

104

only eighteen were pardoned. However, in 2017 there were twenty-two pardoned with fewer fights. The press labeled it as a year of indultitis and severely criticized this sentimental trend. You can guess who was behind that?"

The President and his two advisers stood and left the box. On his way by, Fredo stopped by Juan. They man-hugged then Juan introduced him to Phillip and Amanda.

Fredo was a short, slender man dressed smartly in a light gray suit, white shirt, and tie. His thick black hair fell into a mop over his handsome face, which he continually brushed away with his right hand, dark brown eyes darted around ceaselessly.

"I look forward to seeing your work," said Fredo and limped off after his colleagues.

"He was born with the leg if you're wondering," said Juan. "As he was the only son, his father Alfredo, the brother of the famous Antonio, was initially saddened that family appearances in the ring would die out with him, but Fredo surprised us all with his determination to make something of himself. He was Spain's youngest ever vet and is the recognized expert on Toro de Lidia. The Society uses him as their animal advisor. Our family is extremely proud of him.

"My wife Maribel is Fredo's sister. My late brother Jaime married another sister Maria who is Diego's mother. And, it might surprise you to learn that Leon's wife Inma, is yet another sister. Although they have lived separately for ages."

"You've known Leon for long?" said Phillip.

"We did our National Service together in Ronda over thirty years ago. I actually introduced him to Inma," said Juan. "And was devastated when they separated. We are all great friends and those two were soul mates from almost the first kiss, but they were both stubborn buggers. He was determined to be a top cop whatever the cost. He may have succeeded, but at a hell of a price, and for what? Without each other, they've both been lonely and depressed for years. I pray that they can sort out their differences."

"Let's hope so," said Phillip.

They both turned back to the arena as fresh applause rippled around the audience. Amanda was still filming, and she panned towards the source. Having escorted Miura out of the arena, Diego had returned. He bowed, and then crossed over the sand to the bullfighter's gate where the next cuadrilla was marshaling.

Diego chatted briefly with them then disappeared through the gate into the depths of the bullring. It was time to brief the team for the next bull before adjourning to the arena chapel for his ritual preparation.

14

Amanda returned from the restroom to see that the next fight had begun. She took her seat and said. "Is the atmosphere different or is it me?"

"You're right it is," said Juan. "Even for a normal fight day, Diego is a tough act to follow. After a pardon, it's impossible. I can assure you that Sammi Bettencourt, the torero fighting now, is first class, but no matter what he does, he will struggle to compete for the crowd's attention. They are too busy debating the possibility of Diego achieving two pardons in a row."

Sammi ended with a clean kill. The President waved his blue handkerchief awarding the bull's corpse a lap of honor. A team of mules towed it around the sand and out through the stable gate. Some of the spectators noticed, stood and applauded, but most continued their debates.

"What had the bull done to deserve the lap of honor?" said Phillip.

"Fighting on the same program with Diego ensures

that the bravest and fiercest bulls are put up against all three toreros. Sammi's bull was no exception. It didn't hesitate to charge, was relentless and focused in his pursuit of Sammi and the two danced well together.

"On his own, Sammi would receive a standing ovation from the crowd, but not tonight. However, it won't bother Sammi, both he and the next fighter are part of our group trying to change bullfighting. They know that the most important event of the night is coming up shortly. If Diego can win his second pardon, it would be the first back to back by the same torero in history. The world's media will be hankering for the story. And that is where you guys come in. To package, control and drip feed our group's objectives out there so that it is noticed globally, not just here in Spain. We want international pressure to help us seduce Spanish politicians and bullfighting fans to our way of thinking."

In the arena below, the third torero and his team entered.

"Who is this?" said Phillip.

"Manolo Cienfuegos," said Juan. "Or Macca as we call him. Diego often shares the program with Sammi and Macca, so they are used to fighting in his shadow. When Macca fights without Diego, he is normally the lead for the night, but he prefers to fight with Diego as the bulls are better and the crowds are bigger. Let's watch his performance and you'll see an exemplary display of classic bullfighting. It's exactly the style that The Royal Taurino Society wants to sustain.

"The problem is that fans who appreciate such fine performances are a dying breed. Look around the crowd and you'll see what I mean. Their average age is well over fifty. We estimate that in ten years' time the crowds would have dwindled to below the level of commercial sustainably. Tonight, the seats are all sold out. They always are when Diego appears. The fans here in Madrid are among the most knowledgeable supporters. They are more than capable of appreciating his unique talents. Especially when the horns pass only a fraction of a millimeter away from his body. Believe me, there has never been anyone as good as Diego."

"Then tell us why he and you want to change bullfighting," said Amanda. "At this level, it clearly works well and makes sense to continue as it is."

"A logical assumption," said Juan. "However, it's a question of scale. Throughout Spain, land equivalent to the size of Málaga province is given over to breeding and nurturing Toro de Lidia animals. There are currently over two hundred thousand people gainfully employed in the business of bullfighting. The ranches, and ranch hands. Then there are Veterinarians, transporters, meat industry, leather, milk, restaurants, and bars. Bullrings are prime real estate in hundreds of Spain's historic town and city centers. They are also used for concerts and sporting events such as tennis or basketball. Every citizen enjoys the role that the bullring plays in society as a meeting point. So much so that bullrings are as much as an integral part of the Spanish way of life as a bus or train station or an airport. And let's not forget the torero schools, the toreros and their teams, event managers, advertisers, printers, sign makers, clothing makers, I could go on. When these aging audiences disappear, there is nobody to replace them. All those jobs will disappear, and the bullrings will be knocked down to become hotels, offices or apartment blocks."

"Is that what the protesters this morning are

demanding?" said Phillip.

"Yes. The younger generation thinks that we are barbaric in our practices and want it banned or modified to protect the animals. As the future of bullfighting depends on their support, we have no choice but to transition our national tradition into something more caring and appropriate for the future. If we don't, there won't be one."

Macca, a tall, elegant man gave an excellent display and his dead bull followed that of Sammi's out through the stable door.

Then the volume of the crowd increased.

An air of expectation sprang out of nowhere. It was almost possible to hear the electricity buzzing around Las Ventas as Diego and his team entered the ring.

While all eyes were on him, only a few noticed what was happening in the president's box. One of the ushers escorted a distinguished man with silver hair, smartly dressed in a dark gray suit to the front row of seats. The man squeezed into the only vacant seat, which was next to Fredo. The three officials turned to see who it was, and automatically stood deferentially to shake hands, but the man waved at them to sit. "Don't make a fuss." Phillip overheard him say.

The man leaned forward, urging the officials nearer to him and spoke to them earnestly, but in hushed tones and briefly. When he'd finished, the three officials seemed tight-lipped and mildly disgusted, as if they'd been asked to consider something distasteful.

"Fuck," said Juan. "That's Pablo Bosque, the chairman of the Royal Taurino Society. I bet he saw Diego's pardon on a cable network and has come down personally to try and influence the decision on any possible second."

"Can he do that?" said Phillip.

"In theory no," said Juan. "He has no power in the ring unless the code of good bullfighting is being abused, or any of the Society's procedures are infringed, which of course they aren't. However, by the look of the officials' faces, he may have threatened them with something. He knows what a second pardon will do to elevate Diego's status in the industry and is probably paranoid that it shouldn't happen."

"Were you expecting this?" said Amanda.

"Something like it, yes," said Juan. "However, we were more worried that they would find some excuse to cancel the tournament, but that's too late now. Irrespective of any interference by Bosque, there are still a few barriers that could prevent a second pardon from happening. Diego could be injured or perform badly. Unlikely, but possible. The one thing that really concerns me is the next bull. You'll see why shortly."

Amanda turned her camera away from Don Bosque and back to the bullfighting. In the arena, the innocuous gate opened, and in trotted the largest bull any of them had ever seen.

The audience gasped in unison as the giant animal trotted into the center of the ring totally ignoring the distractions of Diego's team. Hands went to mouths as seven hundred and ninety kilos of solid muscle stopped in the center and surveyed his surroundings. He snorted and sniffed the air as he looked about disdainfully trying to pinpoint his principal enemy among this new and noisy environment. Within seconds he'd spotted Diego and lowered his head. Huge curved horns aimed straight at him.

"That's Islero," said Juan. "I've never seen anything so huge. Normally, we don't worry too much about size, but this guy is also quick and can turn on a dime. Over twenty meters, his acceleration is faster than a Lamborghini."

"Some challenge for Diego," said Phillip.

"Definitely the most lethal adversary in his whole career with only one thing on his mind?" said Juan, grimacing. "To kill Diego."

***

Diego looked at each of his men one by one. They nodded their readiness and held up their capes as one. Diego shook his cape.

Islero hurled himself straight at Diego.

His Veronica was sublime.

However, the bull stopped dead, span round immediately and almost caught Diego with his right horn. But he leaped back, and the bull missed him by a millimeter.

The crowd gasped.

It was incredible to watch the determined bull and the evasive Diego as they danced around in the center of the ring. Every time the bull's horn almost grazed Diego's chest, the crowd gasped in admiration. Diego's team attempted to intervene and draw Islero away from attacking just Diego, but the bull ignored them instinctively, knowing that his true enemy was Diego. The others were irrelevant.

In came the picador.

The bull ignored him and continued laying siege to Diego, ceaselessly attacking, with unfailing stamina. Diego concentrated on the bull's eyes. Islero was totally ignoring the obvious movements of the horse. For the first time in Diego's career, the picador had to come for the bull.

The skilled equestrian guided the blindfolded horse alongside Islero, took aim with the lance and stabbed down into his morillo. Islero ignored it and continued to focus on Diego. It gave the picador no chance to bear down and maximize the bloodletting.

"Leave it," shouted Diego.

The picador galloped off to the exit. The speedy horse's acceleration distracted the bull momentarily. The trumpet blasted ending the first third and launching the next.

Diego used the few seconds to back off to make room for the banderilleros move between him and the incredibly focused bull. The first placed his darts perfectly. The blood began to flow down the bull's shoulders.

The second slipped at the last second and stumbled under the bull's hooves, dropping his darts. The crowd moaned as the bull attempted to trample him. The team rushed in with their capes to blind the bull from the sight of his victim.

Thankfully, the banderillero was only shaken and slightly bruised. He scrambled to his feet, picked up his darts and persevered with his task to tumultuous applause.

With all three sets of darts dangling from Islero's back, the trumpet blasted and the third of death began. Diego exchanged his cape for the red muleta and stick.

"Fuck me," Diego whispered staring at Islero. "You are one mean son of a bitch."

He draped the cape over the stick and walked towards the bull appraising the large animal's cold eyes.

"Venga, toro," he said, shaking the cape.

Islero charged, turned and charged again. Each time

Diego parried his attack with superb cape work, his body on the line with each pass as Islero's horns brushed his chest. Mot bulls would have been exhausted after such intense and sustained energy expenditure, but not this one. It took another thirteen minutes of relentless twisting and turning before Islero ground to a halt. He stood before Diego in the center of the ring, panting heavily, blood streaming down his back.

Diego looked him in the eyes and saw it. That hint of resignation. Diego turned his back on Islero and waved to the crowd. Their cheers were deafening.

He exchanged the stick for the sword and lined himself up for the kill. Cape low, sword aimed straight at the killing zone on the wrong side of those deadly horns.

Then it began. Not quietly, as with Miura, but as one, the crowd started shouting in unison.

"Indulto, indulto, indulto."

The volume was deafening.

***

Bosque and the president were staring hard at each other. Neither was giving way.

"We have to grant this," said the President. "It was the finest display ever by both bull and torero."

"We have no choice," said Fredo.

"I agree," said the technician.

Bosque listened carefully to the officials' arguments, but his expression was easy to read. It was obvious that he didn't concur with any of their justifications.

"Everything has been according to The Society's regulations and guidelines," said the President.

Bosque looked around at the mass of cheering spectators, frantically waving handkerchiefs. If anything, the volume of their demands was increasing. Normally, he would be delighted at the spectacle, but there was far more at stake here than the wishes of the crowd. The future of bullfighting was in jeopardy, or at least his committee's preferred version of it.

"Gentlemen," said Bosque. "Before you make your final decision, I remind you that your appointments are controlled by my committee. If you pardon this bull, I will guarantee that you will not be re-elected."

"Don Bosque," said Fredo. "While we respect your wishes, the decision-makers tonight are not you, or us. They are the audience. You weren't here for the first indulto, but I can assure you that every person was clamoring for it. The bull's bravery and performance were outstanding and more than exceeded the committee's guidelines for a pardon. We, therefore, had no choice but to grant the bull's freedom. If you were in our position, you would have come to the same conclusion. With the second bull, it is even more so. That had to be the best single bullfight ever and must be rewarded with the highest possible accolade.

"Many of these spectators have been coming here for decades. They place their trust in us to make the correct decisions. By instructing us to go against your own guidelines, you are telling us to break that bond. Once broken, it will never be repairable and will surely damage any chances of success for your new marketing campaign. Tonight, here in this hallowed place; right must prevail."

"Absolutely," said the President.

"It's the only option," said the technician.

"I insist," said Bosque glaring hard at each one

consecutively.

The president turned away from Bosque, picked up his orange handkerchief and waved it at the crowd.

The noise went off the decibel scale as Diego gave up his sword and approached Islero unarmed, open-armed and vulnerable to any attack.

Diego smiled warmly at the bull, talking to him calmly as he neared those lethal horns. He watched his eyes like a hawk but saw no anger or warning of movement. He took the halter from his assistant and slipped it over Islero's head. His team joined him, all petting the bull's back lovingly as they removed the darts. Together they walked around the ring leading the bull on a lap of honor. The crowd was ecstatic.

Pablo Bosque said nothing, turned and left the box, ignoring Juan totally, but unable to disguise his emotions, his face flushed with anger.

As he barged his way past the ushers, Bosque reflected on the situation. He was bitterly disappointed that his authority had been challenged by mere officials. On a normal night, Diego would have killed both bulls. They had been good, but not that special. Something was afoot. These pardons had obviously been contrived somehow. After their meeting earlier this morning at the Society's office, it was too much of a coincidence not to be. Clearly, Diego had lied to them. He and his blasted family had no intention of supporting the Society's marketing campaign. They obviously had a plan to counter it, and this evening had been the first demonstration of their intent.

"What will he do next?" he said to the uniformed chauffeur as he climbed into his Rolls Royce at the VIP car park. As they drove off into the light traffic, he started dialing his committee members. Within seconds, he had a group call with more than half of them. They too had been watching the evening's dramatic events on cable TV, the remainder had been busy with their businesses.

"Suggestions?" said Bosque.

"We'll have to remove his license," said Lorenzo.

"Slight problem with that," said Bosque. "The man's a hero in the eyes of the spectators. Technically, he's committed no offenses, so we have no grounds. All it would do is play into their hands. Look, gentlemen, irrespective of our anger at Diego, we have just witnessed one of the most historic moments in bullfighting. Two pardons back to back are an incredibly good advert for our national tradition and we should exploit it as best we can. In normal circumstances, we'd be giving him a medal."

"Then we should revert to the old adage," said Escobedo. "Keep your friends close, but your enemies closer. Let's give Diego a medal and hang his photo in the Society corridor, but at the same time start cutting his fights. Eventually, he will fade away and we can return to business as usual."

"The wise old sage strikes again," said Bosque. "Good counsel my friend, we'll do exactly that starting with his next appearance in Ronda."

"That would be too obvious," said Escobedo. "Also, it's his home patch. There would be a riot. I propose we start slowly here in Madrid. From October, we squeeze him out progressively. The timing also fits well with the beginning of our marketing campaign in which we should now include an additional new component."

"Which is?" said Bosque.

"A section on why pardoning too many bulls is

extremely damaging for the industry," said Escobedo. "Stud prices will tumble, which will be devastating for the ranchers."

"Fair point. I'll brief the marketing agency," said Bosque. "I also suggest that we bring the launch date of our campaign forward. We should start at the end of August just before the Ronda Festival. It should spoil whatever plans Diego may have in mind for La Goyesca. Are we all agreed?"

No one spoke.

"Good," said Bosque. "Then so be it."

15

Restaurante-Braseria El Rancho del Romero was located only a few hundred meters north-west of the Hotel Wellington, halfway along a narrow tree-lined one-way street with vehicles parked on both sides. Juan instructed the cab driver to stop outside the entrance and they clambered out.

The restaurant was on the ground floor of an ornate residential apartment block. Its facade was a large window displaying various cuts of beef hanging on stainless steel hooks from a sturdy rail, in what appeared to be a refrigerator. Some were still on the bone, others prepared for roasting.

"Is that meat from the bulls killed in the ring?" said Amanda.

"No," said Juan, pausing outside the window.

"Then enlighten us please?" said Phillip.

"The majority of beef for human consumption is from castrated bulls known as steers. They are slaughtered in a stress-free environment at two years old and then ideally hung in a fridge for a month or more."

"Why castrate them?" said Phillip.

"It's a combination of reasons. Too much testosterone loose in the pastures can cause chaos. The bulls kill each other, damage fences and are constantly at the cows. Castration solves all that. It calms them down and the resulting relaxed lifestyle produces tender, tasty meat with marbled fat, ideal for good cooking."

"Does that mean we shouldn't eat the meat from uncastrated bulls?" said Phillip.

"You can, but it's an acquired taste. The flesh of uncastrated bulls is recognizable by its tainted odor. The testosterone racing around their systems lends it an unpalatable flavor like meat that has gone off."

"Even the ones killed in the ring?" said Amanda.

"They're even worse," said Juan. "The bulls killed in the ring are at least four years old, meaning that the meat is already tough. The enormous stress levels they endure charging around tightens their meat even more. Tough and tainted meat is a difficult ingredient for chefs to prepare something half-decent. We're trying to change that perception in our family restaurant here.

"What you see in the window is meat from Toro de Lidia steers nurtured on our ranches. We're attempting to build the Toro de Lidia breed as an alternative gastronomic experience to Angus or Waygu.

"The Italians say a true Bolognese sauce is based on ground uncastrated bull's meat. Many Americans swear that an uncastrated bull meat burger is the best there is. The fact remains though that until recently, the meat of the Toro de Lidia breed has only been used for pet-food. Chefs haven't learned to do much with it except for when the tail is made available shortly after a fight when it's stewed slowly in red wine to make Rabo de Toro. Because of this, it's incredibly cheap, even when compared with low-grade supermarket cuts from factory farms.

"However, modern thinking among gourmet chefs is that the Toro de Lidia is one of the purest meats available. It's nurtured exclusively on natural wild grasses and ranges free all its life without hormone injections and antibiotics. The fat content is much lower, the meat darker and when combined with the right culinary skills can produce succulent burgers and superlative stews. Some of Spain's top chefs are experimenting with various marinades to nullify the gamey taste of larger cuts even from bulls killed in the ring."

"What happened to the bulls killed at tonight's fight?" said Amanda.

"They will be at the slaughterhouse by now for the rest of their blood to be drained, and the butchers to do their work. The best cuts will be auctioned off to the highest bidder in the morning. The remainder sold for pet food. What I will recommend tonight is dry-aged fillet Toro de Lidia steak from our best steers. It's been hanging in these bacteria-free cabinets at a constant two degrees centigrade for six months. The flavor is unique. Intensely beefy, some would say a little gamey and it needs some chewing, so I hope your dentures are firmly attached."

"Ha, ha," said Phillip. "By the way, we forgot to tell you that we're vegetarians."

"Que?" said Juan with a serious face.

"Of course not," said Amanda smiling and shaking her head. "Don't worry Juan, we eat everything and especially love steak."

"Only if we wash it down with at least one bottle of Arzuaga," said Phillip.

"That's a relief," said Juan smiling. "And I'm sure when Diego arrives, we'll be sinking more than just the one. He goes a little wild after surviving an evening in the ring and loves his red wine, especially the top end Ribera del Duero.

"A man of taste," said Phillip.

"Indeed," said Juan. "On a more serious note, this evening will conclude the first phase of our plan to change bullfighting. Those two pardons may have been the first ever back to back by the same bullfighter, in the same ring, on the same night, but they were no accident. We've been working up to this for some time, so tonight we intend to celebrate as well as discussing our business together. Shall we go in?"

They climbed a couple of steps, went through a glazed door and along a passage lined with carcass filled fridges on the right. Opposite were the kitchens where just one uniformed chef was cooking meat and vegetables over what looked like giant kettle barbecues, their lids open. Smoke disappeared fast through a powerful extraction system above.

A stocky man in a dark gray suit with thinning hair with a familiar look about him walked towards them. He and Juan hugged.

"My eldest brother," said Juan. "Pedro, meet Phillip and Amanda. Our filmmakers."

"It is an honor," said Pedro shaking hands with Phillip and exchanging cheek kisses with Amanda. "Welcome to the Romero family restaurant. I hope you like beef. It's all we do."

"Are those?" Phillip was about to ask, pointing at

unusual equipment in the kitchen.

"Weber grills?" said Pedro.

"How did you know I was about to ask?" said Phillip.

"Most grill fans recognize them as larger versions of what they have at home," said Pedro. "After tasting the incredible steak cooked at the Weber Grill restaurant in Chicago, we just had to have them. There's also a wood-burning oven for the larger cuts. Shall we find you a table?"

Pedro led them through into a surprising half-empty restaurant.

"We do most of our trade at midday," said Pedro. "As I'm sure you're aware, we Spaniards prefer to linger over lunch. The evening clientele is mainly foreigners, or from out of town."

Pedro led them to a circular corner table laid with a white tablecloth, silver cutlery, crystal glasses, and green serviettes. A red rose head nestling on a base of rosemary formed the center decoration.

"The family motive," said Juan, noticing Amanda admiring them. "The herb rosemary, or Romero in Spanish, isn't reserved solely for culinary usage. It's also tucked into pilgrims' hats to ward off evil spirits and is a common Spanish surname."

Amanda excused herself to the restroom while Pedro poured Cava from Bodega Juves y Camps. Reserva de la Familia noted Phillip.

This promises to be a good evening, he thought to himself. However, I better hold back on the alcohol until we've resolved how our involvement in this project isn't going to ruin our business.

Amanda arrived back at the table at the same time as Diego. He was dressed in his customary white linen suit, but with his hair loose. He was alone.

"May I suggest," said Diego in between sipping his Cava. "That we finalize our business discussions before we start with the red wine. Otherwise, I'll probably end up giving you everything I have."

"Not before me agreeing to work for nothing," said Phillip. "But before we talk about money, can you clarify what your plans are, and what you require us to do?"

"I'm reluctant to reveal everything at this stage," said Diego, "just in case we fall out, but what I will say, and forgive me if Juan has already been over this, but to put it simply, bullfighting has to change or die. Most young people understand and accept that, however, the Royal Taurino Society that controls everything is determined that it should continue as it is. They are launching a campaign in October to increase awareness of why killing bulls is a good thing and why we should carry on doing so. The main problem with the Society is that they are all too old to understand the younger generation's views. They assume today's youth are just ignorant about history and tradition. Apparently, all they need is some good old education and they will dash down to the next fight injected with passion and enthusiasm to continue the slaughter. They envisage that somehow bullring attendances will magically increase to the levels of the former golden age of the 1980s. This will be the thrust of their campaign.

"Personally, I think that it will only remind youngsters as to why they don't want to watch a bullfight. Meanwhile, what we need are a series of short, sharp adverts that derogate killing and introduce the thrills of our new version of bullfighting."

"Can you give us more detail?" said Phillip.

"It's really quite simple. We use the same wild bulls nurtured with identical methods. In the ring, we keep the same team structure and cape-work, but add in more drama with the interplay between the picadors' horses and the bull. The banderilleros will replace their darts with rosettes in the owner's colors and increase their daring antics in pinning them to the bull's neck. The objective being to goad the bull into charging madly around, then artistically twist and turn it enough until it is so exhausted, it stops moving. The performance will end pretty much as this evening with the stroking under the chin routine with Miura and Islero.

"To get the ball rolling, we'd like a short film that celebrates the two pardons. Once we're all happy with the footage, we want to broadcast it on social media and have viewers vote on supporting our version or staying with the old. It will give us some rapid feedback that we're hopefully doing the right thing."

"Brilliant idea," said Amanda, eyes shining at the concept. "Regretfully, my camera may have been too small for good close-up shots."

"Don't worry about that," said Juan. "We had a professional team with other cameras and a drone with a superzoom recording everything. If we give you all the footage, could you edit it into something?"

"We'll take a look," said Amanda. "What other films did you envisage?"

"We have a couple in mind," said Diego. "We want Fredo to talk about Toro de Lidia, their history, upbringing, selective breeding, natural instincts in the wild, and what they physically experience in the ring. He speaks excellent English and French, but we will take your advice on his suitability in front of the camera.

"The other film is to be about the Pedro Romero Festival in Ronda. Particularly, the penultimate day of the Corrida de La Goyesca when I intend to reveal the final stage of our plan. Finally, when we know the full extent of the Society's media campaign, we would like a full-length documentary on the state of bullfighting, why it needs to change and more detail about our new version. What sort of time do you need to produce the first film?"

"That depends on the quality of the footage you're giving us," said Amanda. "If it's good, we would need at least two or three weeks."

"Can you estimate how much the films will cost?" said Juan.

"We base our costs on a menu of services," said Phillip. "Such as actual filming, editing, voice-overs, soundtrack, subtitles in other languages, and distribution to traditional broadcasters, social media and on the Nuestra-España website. We'll be able to quote you more accurately after we've seen your footage, etc., meanwhile, I'll send you a price list."

Diego and Juan exchanged glances and nodded at each other.

"That sounds good," said Diego. "But before we get too far down the line, I think we should do the first film, and see how it goes. Now then, Juan mentioned that you have some concerns about the risk to your business if the committee members act against you because of your relationship with us. For example, Pablo Bosque may use his power to persuade your hotel advertisers to cease working with you."

"Exactly," said Phillip. "So, my question is, how can we protect against that?"

"Hopefully," said Diego. "There won't be any problems, but we're dealing with powerful men with massive egos, renowned for their determination to win at everything they touch. Therefore, our offer is this. On the off chance that your business loses revenue as a consequence of making this film for us, we will reimburse you for those losses in a mix of cash and stock in our family empire, which is a successful public company quoted on IBEX. You will have to justify your costs, but it is our intention that you or your business shall not suffer in any way. Our company lawyers have drawn up a contract that describes how all this can work. I suggest that they communicate directly with your lawyers to finalize matters. How does that sound to you?"

"Fine with me," said Phillip.

"Me too," said Amanda.

"Do you envisage any difficulties with your business partners?" said Juan.

"We've already discussed what offers you might make," said Phillip. "And this was one among the options that we agreed to accept, so no, I don't expect any problems."

"Then we'll need Pedro to open the red wine," said Diego.

16

"I want you to move back in," whispered Inma, as they lay in bed, naked, wrapped in each other's arms.

"Are you sure my love?" said Prado sitting up and leaning back against the padded headboard. "Because I still have to work for at least the next three years."

"I know, but not so hard as before," said Inma gazing adoringly into his eyes.

He looked down at her. It seemed incredible that she was in her early fifties. She was almost the same as that first day they'd exchanged glances back at Jaime's wedding over thirty years ago. Yes, her dark hair was shorter, with a hint of gray and a few lines around her eyes, but to him, she was just as beautiful and sexy.

"Looking back on our long separation," she said. "It seems so futile now. We wasted our best years because of mutual stubbornness. You were determined to make a name for yourself, and I needed you here. As soon as you'd moved out, I knew it was wrong, but was too proud to say so. I've missed you so much, especially here in bed where it has always been so good."

"And still is," he said. "Listen, I'm trying to pluck up the courage to ask the boss to let me telework from home on occasion. It means I wouldn't have to be in Málaga every day."

"That would be awesome, but look darling, we're older and more relaxed now. I understand that sometimes you'll be too tired to drive back up to Ronda. That's OK. I'm not asking you to quit your apartment, and I won't be complaining about your absences."

"You could come down, have a night on the town."

"That would be fun."

"OK. Let's give it a try," said Prado.

"Wonderful, I love you," she said.

***

The next morning, on his way to Cortijo Infierno, Prado drove over the new bridge that traversed El Tajo, Ronda's dramatic gorge, then past the Parador Hotel and the bullring. He glanced at the statue of Antonio Ordoñez standing proudly outside the front. He had been Inma's uncle and had died in 1998.

Caffeine was a crucial ingredient to feed Prado's mental stability. In the mornings he wasn't worth a damn until he'd consumed at least one cup of coffee, he'd stop at the first café en route.

Driving along the narrow Ronda streets reminded him of his first history lesson about the ancient city during his National Service all those years ago. The teacher's droning voice came back to him now. "The Celts named it Arunda over 2,600 years ago. Which, with the subsequent influences of Phoenician, Roman,

Visigoth and the Moor evolved into Ronda. It perches on top of a dramatic limestone gorge that divides the old from the new town and is surrounded by a circle of mountains referred to as the Serrania de Ronda. At over 739 meters above sea level, the winters can be chilly, the rainfall, high, and the summers searing hot; a climate well suited for producing excellent wines, olive oils, and cheeses. Nuts, cereals, citrus fruits, and vegetables also thrive in the nutrient-rich soil."

Prado always had and would continue to abhor the principle of takeaway coffee. The concept of traveling to work with a plastic cup of tepid watery liquid in one hand, taking an occasional sip through a plastic straw with one eye on the clock was his idea of Armageddon. "They'll be asking me to wear a nametag next," he laughed out loud.

Two kilometers out of town was a gas station with a quality-dining establishment attached to it. The traditionally decorated bar was packed with truck drivers, many of whom he knew. Twenty-odd hams were suspended from a rail over the bar. Conical plastic cups stuck in the ends, collected the occasional drip of fat as the succulent meat continued to cure.

Prado took a seat at a window table, exchanged greetings with old friends as they departed and new ones arrived. They respected that he wasn't one for small talk, so didn't linger to exchange opinions on the latest soccer team performances, or politics. The waiter brought his customary café con leche and a toasted mollete. He drizzled some extra virgin olive oil from Ronda on the warm bread roll, sprinkled on some salt, took a bite and reflected on his visit with Inma. Until now, he hadn't been sure if moving back in was the right course of action, but after their wonderful night together and her fantastic cooking, he was warming to the idea. After the visit to the Cortijo, he'd drive on down to Málaga and discuss the possibility of some teleworking with el jefe. He smiled to himself.

At last, he thought. An enjoyable but only mildly stressful job, along with a rejuvenated relationship with a happy and relaxed Inma, was the life-work balance he'd always dreamed of, and a belated chance to become a proper father to his sons.

The extensive parcel of land and buildings that made up Cortijo Infierno were located next to Urbanization Los Merinos, a massive golf, and housing project that had been proposed during the 1980s despite there being no obvious source of water. During 2015, the Supreme Court declared the project illegal. Not that the developers had bothered to wait for planning consent. They'd already ripped up thousands of ancient oak trees from what was a UNESCO protected site and carved the foundations out of the grassland for the roads. Prado passed the sad-looking entrance, abandoned construction signs and equipment. He shook his head at the desolation and ruin of a once stunningly beautiful area.

"Fucking idiots," he said aloud in anger at the corruption of some local councilors, conspiring with shady Swiss financiers and their mafia-like tactics. The land was now owned by a bank. It would likely sit there unattended for decades.

Prado wondered about Cortijo Infierno and why the Crown's had bought such an isolated property in the first place? The ground was hilly, rocky and only good for oak trees; as agricultural land, it was useless. Fifteen years ago, the project next door seemed more than probable. Did they hope to profit from the increased land values? It also seemed a remote place to install a data center. Back then, mobile phone and internet coverage up here were practically nonexistent. Another thing that puzzled him was that the late parents were well into their seventies. Hardly the profile of appropriate candidates to maintain such a modern facility.

He shook his head and drove through a shabby wooden gate onto an overgrown bumpy track that hadn't seen much traffic for a while. Three hundred meters later, after several curves, and a mild descent down into a valley hidden from the main road, the farmhouse appeared.

He'd arranged for the lawyer representing Crown's siblings to meet him at the Cortijo along with the local police who would bring the case file with them.

Their vehicles were parked on an old circular stone threshing platform located outside the front door. The name of the farm was arranged in white pebbles set into the gray stone. Two uniformed local officers were chatting with a passably attractive, but over made-up, slender, middle-aged woman with dyed blonde hair. She wore a smart beige trouser suit. Prado parked by their vehicles and clambered out.

Seb and Tobalo were the two local lads, some ten years younger than himself. He'd known them for years. Trustworthy, but not the sharpest knives in the draw.

"Buenos dias, señores," he said to the officers. They mumbled an acknowledgment. "Señora?"

"I'm Bibi Gomez," said the lady, shaking hands and passing him her card.

Prado glanced at it. Her office was in Marbella.

"How long have you represented the Crowns',

Señora Gomez?"

"Over seventeen years, inspector, their Danish bank in Fuengirola introduced us. I helped them find and acquire this property. I've had power of attorney over their affairs since the beginning."

"Just out of curiosity, did its adjacency to Los Merinos have any bearing on their purchasing decision?"

"Their ideal property was to be up in the mountains and in an isolated location, inspector, something to do with less interference with their satellite traffic, but they were not stupid. There were also a couple of other options. They chose this because of its resale potential in the long term. Regretfully, that won't happen now, and they will struggle to attract a buyer."

"Thank you. Forgive me if I'm stating the obvious," said Prado. "But I can't see any burnt buildings here, just the farmhouse."

"They were knocked down a few weeks ago, inspector," said Gomez.

"May I ask why?" he said.

"The Crowns want to sell. Their estate agent advised that the data center ruin would be a negative feature, so I arranged for a local builder to bulldoze it and dispose of the rubbish."

"I assume that the Town Hall provided all the proper licenses?"

"Of course, I have them in my car if you...,"

"No, that's fine," said Prado. "At least, may I inspect the remaining buildings?"

"There's just the house and garage block remaining," said Gomez fumbling in her bag, extracting a set of keys and heading towards the substantial timber front door. A thriving grapevine meandered over a pergola providing shade to the entrance area.

"Does anyone maintain the house?" said Prado.

"Not anyone in particular," said Gomez. "But I've contracted a local service who comes every three months to clean inside and out, keep the plants around the house in order and check for squatters. However, as the house isn't visible from the road, there haven't been any problems. Not that there is anything of value inside. Basic furnishings only. The Crown's had everything cleared out just after their parent's died."

"Did you meet the twins?" said Prado.

"Just twice," said Gomez. "For the initial purchase and then last year, when they came out to collect their parent's ashes and sort the house."

"What did you think of them?"

"They were pleasant enough, but I thought them cold. They showed neither emotion at their parent's demise or annoyance at the damage the fire had done to their data center. The only smile I saw was when I dropped them at the airport as if they were glad to see the back of the place."

"Or their parents," said Prado recalling the school psychologist's report. "Run me through the day of the fire?" said Prado.

"I have all the photos and coroner's report here, sir," said Seb offering Prado a thick file.

"A summary will do," said Prado.

"A passing driver spotted thick smoke wafting over the horizon," said Seb. She called the emergency services. By the time the fire truck arrived from Ronda, there wasn't much left of the outbuilding."

"I was the initial contact in the event of emergencies," said Gomez. "The local police called me to ask about any residents. I called the Crowns in the UK. They returned my call within the hour to confirm that their parents were staying at the property on a permanent basis."

"Forgive me," said Prado. "The parents seemed a little long in the teeth to be manning such a hi-tech enterprise."

"On the contrary," said Gomez. "Data centers were their area of expertise. They told me that they'd set them up all over the world."

"Did you meet them, señora?"

"Yes, when they needed some help translating for the power hookup."

"How were they?"

"She was eccentric, to say the least, and drank a lot. He was an old letch and couldn't keep his hands off me. I was glad to escape intact."

"Did they mention their children in your conversations?"

"Never."

"No references to another younger son called Malcolm?"

"No, and I never saw any photos of relatives. Other than a painting of snow-covered mountains, they didn't personalize the house at all."

"What was left of the machinery?"

"Take a look at this, inspector," said Tobalo passing over a photo from the file. "As you can see not much."

"So, none of the hard drives survived?"

"None, sir, they'd all melted," said Tobalo.

"Are there any cellars, or other outbuildings on the estate?"

"None," said Gomez.

"Do they own any other properties in Spain?"

"Not that I'm aware of."

"What about vehicles?"

"I helped them purchase a second-hand Jeep that the parents used for shopping. I sold it for them straight after the funeral."

"What about money?"

"They made regular transfers of cash from their British bank to the Bank in Fuengirola. I'm also a signatory for that account and prepare their annual returns. They insisted that everything was above board."

"Mmm…," said Prado thinking for a bit and rubbing his earlobe. "I'd like the contact details please of both banks."

"I'll email you everything when I return to the office."

"Fine, the officers will let you know where to send it. How was the data center financed?"

"The building work was paid for in the same way as the property purchase, as was the demolition work after the fire, but I had nothing to do with the machinery. I think they did that through their company. Anyway, it was all brought here in a large truck and installed by their own engineers."

"Who was here for the power hookup?"

"The parents, some Indian engineers and a firm of electricians I arranged from Marbella. The Spaniard's job was to install a meter, the three-phase distribution box, connect everything to the mains, and test the system so that the electricity company would activate the supply."

"What about Internet connection?"

"Fifteen years ago, inspector. Mobile telephone signals and the Internet were both weak and intermittent up here. They installed their own satellite system. I remember there was a huge disc on the roof of the data center.

"What caused the fire?"

"They'd built a backup power room," said Seb. "It contained six large diesel generators and a UPS device that evened out the fluctuations in current. Apparently, there was one of our infamous power surges, which overheated this device. It exploded. Somehow the fire suppression system failed and eventually, the fire spread into the computer room."

"Where were the Crowns?"

"We found what little remained of them on the generator room floor," said Seb. "It was assumed that they'd gone there to learn what the first explosion was about. The pathologist reported that he was unable to determine exactly what they died of. There was only ash and a few bones left."

"So, the coroner's verdict seemed reasonable," said Prado.

"As far as our, and the coroner's expertise in fires could diagnose, Yes, sir," said Seb. "But as you know, we don't have the forensic experience up here to really be sure."

"Did we take a DNA sample?"

"Both are in the file," said Seb.

"Then send me copies of everything please."

Gomez opened the front door with one of the larger keys and they went in.

Prado wandered around the farmhouse but saw nothing that interested him on either floor. Everything was clean, the kitchen fittings were luxurious, the windows, top of the range and there was a comprehensive heating and cooling system, but as

Gomez had said, everywhere lacked personal touches. The garage though, made him think. It was enormous, and an unusual shape, long and thin, more suited to housing a bus or truck, but there were no tracks on the concrete floor, and the wall-mounted shelves were bare but dusty.

Why would they build a garage for a truck that only came once to deliver the initial installation? Thought Prado. As for Crown's secret note, 'look in the darkness', look where, and for what? He could stay there all day and ponder on that one. He'd have to bring a search team up here and go over the place with a fine-tooth comb. He said his farewells, clambered into his car and headed off to Málaga.

17

"Not sure if I can face breakfast," said Amanda snuggling under the duvet cover of their bed in the Hotel Wellington. "I'm still full of steak. Could you bring me up some fruit please?"

"Shame, my love. Apparently, the buffet here is one of the best in Madrid," said Phillip.

"Then you go and enjoy it for both of us. I'm going back to sleep." With that, she turned over and snuggled under the duvet.

Yes, dear, thought Phillip as he slipped out of bed and headed for a shower. He smiled, amazed at how familiar they'd become in such a short time.

While walking along the long corridor to the elevator, he called Richard.

"You're up early," said Richard in his twangy Boston drawl. "A bit mean with the Arzuaga were they?"

"On the contrary, but it was just enough. Diego had other matters to attend to later."

"At that time of night?"

"Some female friends joined him for a nightcap."

Phillip took a seat on one of the sofas in the circular lobby waiting area outside the elevator. He admired the beautiful stained-glass window that overlooked the hotel terrace to the rear of the building.

"Some?" said Richard.

"There were two of them. They seemed more than familiar."

"Whatever?" said Richard. "After that final bull, he deserved to blow off some steam. More importantly, did they make an offer?"

"As we expected. They've guaranteed to replace any losses with stock in the Romero Company," said Phillip. "They've drawn up an agreement, which their lawyers will forward to ours."

"You happy with it?"

"Both Amanda and I are more than satisfied, but also extremely excited about the opportunity. It could raise our business to another level."

"Are you sure you want that? I thought you came to Spain for an easier life?"

"I did, but this is interesting stuff. It more than compensates for the extra work.

"Then it sounds good to me," said Richard. "Happy to agree, subject to any comments from the legal guys."

"Ok, good. I'm meeting Juan for breakfast, so will confirm that. Let's hope it's successful."

"If it doesn't, we're well-covered," said Richard. "So, relax and do your best with the film."

Juan was already queuing at the buffet as Phillip registered his room number with the congenial maitre d'. He ordered a coffee and walked over to join him at the incredible display of fruits, pastries, cooked meats, and cheeses. He opted to toast some crusty brown bread, drizzle some amazing quality olive oil from Jaen over it, then smeared some grated tomatoes on top before adding a couple of slices of cooked ham sliced from the leg. He joined Juan at a table by the window and took a sip of fresh orange juice.

"No Amanda?" said Juan, eyebrows raised.

"Overindulged last night. Me too, but I couldn't miss this breakfast."

"I know what you mean. I always go home three kilos heavier after staying here. Did you have time to speak to Richard?"

"I can confirm that subject to the legal stuff being OK, we're happy to work with you."

"Excellent, excellent," said Juan shaking hands, then reaching into his jacket pocket, extracting a pack of DVDs and handing them over. "These are the footage from the various cameras we had scattered around the arena last night. I've had a quick look, and they managed to capture all the key moments. I'm extremely keen to see what you can do with them."

"We're both looking forward to it," said Phillip. "No longer than two minutes?"

"Shorter if possible. People's attention spans seem to be nonexistent these days. Are you returning to Málaga today?"

"Yes, we're on the midday train. We'll look at these on the way. One question; assuming we can set the first film running in, say four weeks. That takes us up to mid-July, which leaves only six weeks to film and edit Fredo before La Goyesca in early September. Would it be possible to use the same crew who were filming last night to assist us as needed? They know what you want, I assume you trust them and more importantly, they have a drone camera and operator, something that we're not up to speed with yet?"

"Whatever you need Phillip, just ask. We can provide whatever resources you need to finish on time."

"Has Fredo prepared his script?"

"He's nearly finished. When we've agreed to it, I'll send it to you."

"Where should we film him?"

"At our ranch and the bullfighting museum in Ronda."

They finished their breakfast, chatted generally and left the breakfast room together, saying their farewells and exchanging contact details in the lobby.

Phillip smiled to himself in the empty elevator mirror as he headed back upstairs with a basket of fruit and a jug of coffee "This is going to be an exciting project," he said to himself. "I wonder where it will take us."

Amanda was sitting up in bed chatting with Ingrid on Skype when Phillip let himself back into their room. He poured her a coffee. She took it from him, sighing thankfully, and sipped it while finishing off her conversation. Phillip put the fruit basket on the bed by her side and started packing their things. He heard her say her goodbyes.

"Ingrid OK?" he said.

"She's nervous about this project but will go along with it because we all want to."

"That's quite normal with her. She's not such a risk-taker. Juan says Hi. He has given me the footage from last night and offered us any resources that we might need to finish our work as quickly as we can. How did he put it? I'd rather you concentrate on your creativity rather than doing all the physical work."

"Wow, that is fantastic news. Does that include the drone?"

"Yep, I also asked if it was possible to stick a camera on the bull's forehead to get a genuine bull's eye view."

"That would be amazing. What did he say?"

"He's going to talk to his cameramen. We need to leave for the station in about an hour."

"You know, I really like this bed," she said, patting the vacant space by her side. "I think we should buy one of these, don't you?"

"Then we better sample it one more time just to make sure," he said unbuttoning his shirt.

They only just made the train.

So concentrated were they in taking their seats and setting up Phillip's laptop to watch last night's DVD's of the bullfight. They failed to recognize the enamored young couple from the hotel lounge sitting three rows ahead of them.

18

The EasyJet Airbus A320 touched down at London Gatwick airport just before nine. Phillip and Prado had reserved the front seats so they could exit quickly. They were booked on the last return flight to Málaga later that night and were prepared for a long tiring day.

Forty minutes later, Phillip was driving the small rental car heading up the M23 Motorway in the direction of the busy M25, the outer London artery to join the M3, then M27 to Bournemouth.

It was raining and Phillip drove cautiously. It was his first trip back to the UK since he'd left for Spain some four years previously. It was Prado's first trip ever, consequently, for the first half an hour, he bombarded Phillip with questions about the UK. Why did they drive on the wrong side of the road? Why there was only one police force that didn't carry weapons? Why there were so many different nationalities, the roads so crowded, all the houses look the same, everything so green? Phillip did his best to answer the tirade, but eventually, Prado nodded off. It had been an early start.

It took Phillip a couple of hours to reach the George and Dragon pub car park some two miles from the Crown's house in the rolling countryside to the northeast of Bournemouth. They met up with the local detective who had arranged the visit and would accompany them. They got out briefly, shook hands and introduced each other.

He was Detective Sergeant Barker. A tall, thin man in his forties with a shaved head, wearing jeans and a leather jacket.

"Do you have anything on the Crowns?" said Phillip.

"Not even a parking ticket," said Barker. "And they keep a low profile in every respect. So much so, that the neighbors have never met them. They employ a few local people to drive them around, shop, maintain the garden and clean. We've spoken with them all, but they are tight-lipped and have nothing to say for or against their employers.

"Apparently, the Crowns travel a lot and are often away for months at a time. They always fly in and out of Southampton airport in a private charter that connects them to Amsterdam. From there, who knows where they go?"

After several more questions, it was obvious that there was no more information to be had about the reclusive twins, so they climbed back into their separate vehicles.

Barker led the way in his unmarked car down some narrow country lanes, bordered by high hedges, some completely covered with leafy bowers, to an isolated property hidden behind a high yew hedge. They stopped at tall white painted gates. Barker rang the security bell and they were admitted. After the impressive entranceway, they expected a much larger house, but it was a medium-sized thatched cottage with several outbuildings. The gardens and lawns were well maintained, but it was mainly trees and bushes. No wisteria, Virginia creepers, hanging baskets or pretty borders. By the time they had parked on the gravel driveway by the front door to the house, the twins were outside the door waiting to greet them under the porch.

Other than their different genders, they were identical. With their dark hair, mid-height, slender frames and thin faces, their resemblance to Malcolm was remarkable.

"Welcome to rainy England," said George.

Even his voice was like Malcolm's, thought Phillip as they showed their ID cards, then followed them through a large hall with a low beamed ceiling into a chintzy lounge and sat down in low soft sofas. A grandfather clock chimed twelve as they took their seats and looked curiously at each other.

"Tea?" said Georgina.

They all accepted, so she stepped outside, leaving them alone with George. He looked at each of them as if awaiting their questions.

"Thank you for seeing us at such short notice," said Barker. "But as I said on the phone my colleagues here from Spain need to ask you a few questions about your brother and parents."

"How can I help you?" said George.

"Yes, thank you again for seeing us," said Phillip. "As your lawyer in Marbella probably informed you, Inspector Prado recently returned from a visit to your property near Ronda. He's curious to learn about the data center and your parent's role there. For example, what kind of business or service was the data center providing and on behalf of whom?"

"I'll happily answer that," said George looking Prado straight in the eye. "Our expertise is in Information Technology. We have built a leading reputation for providing data centers for the travel industry throughout the world. Our parents started the business when we returned from Spain over thirty years ago now. Some fifteen years ago, they wanted to retire. At about the same time, a large Spanish hotel chain wanted to set up online booking, but on the condition that the data center was based in Spain, not in India where most of ours are today. We've always adored Ronda, and at the time there was a strong possibility that the Los Merinos project would go ahead. It seemed a no-brainer at the time to purchase the plot next door."

"Do you always pick isolated locations?" said Phillip.

"We used to when we had to rely on satellite technology. Nowadays, we go for the cheapest solution wherever fiber-optic is available. Which regretfully, isn't in the beautiful Ronda countryside."

"Can I assume that you were insured?" said Phillip.

"You may, and yes, we were fully reimbursed by the Spanish insurance company for our loss."

"Do you still provide the data center for the hotel group?"

"Yes, but now they are happy for it to be in India. They need more capacity and the price is substantially cheaper."

"Are there any cellars or other outbuildings on the

estate?"

"None."

"Any reason why the garage is so large?"

"None, but before it was a barn. We were obliged by the planners to retain the same footprint."

"Excuse me while I update the inspector," said Phillip turning to Prado and recapping the answers in Spanish.

Georgina came back carrying a tray laden with Chinese pattern tea service and a plate of chocolate digestives. She served everyone, passed around the biscuits, then sat down next to George.

"Now let's talk about the brother," said Prado before taking a nibble of a biscuit.

"If you prefer, inspector, we can speak in your language," said Georgina in perfect Spanish.

"Thank you, Señora Crown, that would be marvelous," said Prado. "I was wondering if you'd still remember after all these years."

"We use it often as we travel around the world," said George in Spanish. "Much of our business is in Spain, South America, and the Philippines. It's probably the only good thing that emanated from our education in Marbella."

"That's something at least," said Prado. "We read the school psychologist's report. She was worried about the cause of your unruly behavior, suspecting that you were being abused in some way. By your parents, perhaps?"

"That doesn't surprise me," said George. "We must have been more than a handful. However, we had a great relationship with our parents. Our problem was the other children. Without wishing to appear arrogant, all three of us were gifted, particularly Malcolm, we found the teachers bad and the pace terribly slow. The others in our class resented that and resorted to bullying. We never complained, but the three of us contrived to sort out the bullies who then went running to the teacher. We were never believed which just made us worse. We begged our parents to return to the UK and attend a school that would stretch us. Thankfully, they understood, and we came here."

"How old was Malcolm then?" said Phillip.

"Fourteen," said Georgina.

"Was that 1985?" said Phillip.

"Yes, we all moved back just after we were asked to leave the school," said George. "Mid-June, if I recall rightly."

"Yes, that's right," said Georgina.

"What went wrong with Malcolm?" said Prado.

"As he matured, his natural urges grew more confused and wilder," said Georgina. "No matter how hard we tried to help him, his behavior progressively went off the rails. Eventually, he fell in with the wrong crowd, and we severed all contact."

"When did you last see him?" said Phillip.

"At his last court case some five years ago now," said George. "We all went to support him, but when we actually heard the evidence against him, we realized how far he'd fallen. We cut him out of our lives there and then."

"How about your parents?"

"He appeared at the Cortijo about a year or so ago with an ugly giant of a man," said George. "It was just before the fire. They stayed for a few weeks while they sorted out some property. He said they were purchasing it for a new business venture that was most hush-hush.

"Malcolm had been recently released from prison in the UK and my parents were worried that he was breaking his terms of parole. However, he didn't seem concerned and they didn't press him on what he was up to. Where is he now?"

"He's in Alhaurin Prison awaiting trial for human trafficking and running a sex-slavery ring," said Prado.

"So that was the end of the hush-hush venture," said Georgina. "Then he certainly won't be coming out again?"

"It's worse than that," said Prado. "We suspect that he's terrified of a criminal organization, probably the people he's been working with, in the trafficking business. Nasty people, whoever they are, and he refuses to reveal anything about them. We are extremely concerned for his welfare."

"In prison?"

"It's likely that this organization has people everywhere," said Prado.

"I don't see how we could help," said George.

"We were hoping you might know some of your brother's contacts," said Prado.

"We have no idea. Sorry that we can't be of more help," said Georgina. "Will that be all?"

"Thank you for your time," said Prado standing and looking at them both carefully before asking. "Do you live alone here?"

The Crown's seemed unfazed by this personal question before George said. "We do, inspector, but we have help."

"So, no partners, husbands or wives?"

"No," said Georgina smiling. "With all the traveling we do, partners would be impossible."

"At least we have each other," said George looking

caringly at his sister.

They all stood, shook hands and the Crowns' escorted them to the front door. On the way out, Prado noticed a framed picture of snowy mountains hanging in the hallway. He stopped at the front door and turned back with a quizzical expression.

"One more question, if I may," he said. "Was anybody aware of your brother's whereabouts at the time of the fire?"

"I don't think the question was ever asked, inspector," said Georgina.

"And how would you describe the nature of the relationship between your parents and Malcolm?"

"Uncomfortable," said George. "They were glad to see the back of him, but sad that one of their flock had lost his way. They only ever wanted the best for all three of us and couldn't understand why two of us had succeeded and the other failed so miserably, especially considering his brilliant intellect."

"Thank you and adios," said Prado turning back and heading to the hire car.

They swept out of the gates, rejoined the A338 and headed into Bournemouth center. They parked the hire car at the central police station and joined Barker, who drove them to the bank, which was just off the Bath Road near the Pavilion Theater.

"Not quite the Costa del Sol," said Prado on seeing his first British beach. "And what is that thing sticking out into the water?"

"That's a pier," said Phillip.

"What's it for?"

"It's for fishing, taking a walk in the fresh sea air, playing slot machines, gorging on hot dogs and ice-cream, enjoying the views of the land and on some, there are theaters featuring smutty comedy plays, hence our saying seaside humor.."

"We should build some of those on the Costa del Sol," said Prado with an evil grin. "Along with all warm English beer and soggy fish and chips, it would be more like home from home for your countrymen."

Phillip glanced at Prado; eyebrows raised.

Barker parked up at the back of the bank and as instructed rang the door phone. A young blond girl let them in and escorted them through to the Manager's office.

Ben Newman, it said on a sign stuck on the full height glazing at the side of the door. They went inside, shook hands with a short, young officious man with dark hair and a dense covering of dandruff over his blue suit jacket. His oversized tie was askew between the collars of his white shirt, but he was well prepared with all the files on the Crown's personal and business accounts ready to hand.

"Have there been any transactions on any of the Crown's accounts during the last three years that might cause the bank any concerns?" said Phillip.

"None whatsoever," said Newman. "On the contrary, their accounts and tax affairs are dealt with punctually and efficiently. Our auditors are more than satisfied that the Crowns are excellent and trustworthy long-term clients with business interests spread all over the world."

"We would like to obtain copies of all their statements for the last three years," said Phillip.

"Of course," confirmed Newman. "Leave me your email address I'll send them to you."

Phillip handed over his card. Newman took it, glanced at it and tossed it on top of the Crown's files.

They stood, shook hands and left.

Barker dropped them back at the police station, they jumped in the hire car and headed back to Gatwick.

"Was that a waste of time?" said Phillip as they rejoined the M27.

"Yes and no," said Prado. "It confirmed that the Crowns are exactly what they appear to be. Successful, honest businesspeople. They maybe be a bit weird and I'm unclear about the actual nature of their relationship, but I can cross them off our list of suspects. The only rotten apple in the Crown barrel is Malcolm and we have him safely locked up.

19

"Thank you for sparing us some of your valuable time, Diego," said Bosque sitting in his usual place behind the table in the committee room of the Royal Taurino Society. "We won't keep you long."

Diego sat on the chair in front of them, relaxed in his usual white linen attire. He said nothing, but looked one-by-one at the line of seven old men on the other side of the table. Even if Zambrano had bothered to turn up, the Society no longer worried him. It had been a couple of days since he'd gotten his two pardons and his plans were taking shape as envisaged. He wondered what they were up to though. This polite request to appear before them was not their usual style.

"First we'd like to congratulate you on your magnificent performance," said Bosque. "Your two successive pardons will go down in the annals of bullfighting history as the finest achievement ever. However, even though it might not have been your intention, you have also achieved more for our marketing campaign in one night than we could in a month of Sundays. Would you have any objection to our agency using your images to promote our arguments to carry on killing bulls?"

"I have no objection," said Diego. "Under the terms of my license, the Society owns the rights to all images captured at events under its control. What will you use them for?"

"To justify why we should not take the blood out of bullfighting," said Bosque making a poor attempt to disguise a smug grin. "Your two pardons have reminded us of the most significant attractions of bullfighting. Death or the possibility of it. We believe that spectators prefer to be kept guessing about the outcome of a bullfight. Will the bull live or die, will the torero scrape through unscathed or will he be seriously injured, even killed? In the olden days, when we used to garrote people in public, there was never a millimeter of space to spare with a view of the executioner. In France, they used the guillotine. Thousands turned up to cheer as heads were severed from necks and women knitted while enjoying the gore. If they were sprayed with the victim's blood, all the better. In Great Britain, public hangings were more popular than Shakespeare's plays.

"Watching things die gives us humans a twisted sense of pleasure. It satisfies a base instinct and is the main thrust behind bullfighting's attraction, always has been, always will. Diego, they may adore your sublime Veronicas, and artistic nuances, but what they really came to see was you being killed, and if not you, then at least the bull. You see Diego, in short, if there is no killing, the pardon becomes worthless and bullfighting would die out rapidly, which is why we need you to support our campaign to keep blood in the ring."

Diego frowned. He wasn't surprised by their intransigence, but still felt disappointed that they hadn't moved a single millimeter in his direction. What else could he do? Was there some other way than to sit back, say nothing, support their cause and watch these old powerful men destroy his family's way of life. No, he thought. I, we, are doing the right thing, we must take the blood out of bullfighting.

"Meanwhile," said Bosque. "According to our records, a double pardon has never been achieved before. The Society wants to recognize your superb contribution to our national tradition by awarding you with our highest acclaim. The Medal of Honor."

With that Bosque opened a black leather box in front of him, extracted a gold disc, the center of which contained the green and purple livery of the Society in enamel. Threaded through the gold loop at the top was a green and purple ribbon. The committee stood and applauded almost enthusiastically, as Bosque walked around toward Diego. At that moment, the door opened and in came a photographer who snapped away as Bosque placed the medal over Diego's head. Adjusting the disc so that the enamel faced the table. He put his arm around Diego's shoulder, shook his other hand and smiled to the cameraman. Then gave Diego a wry grin and returned to his seat.

Diego waited until they had all settled. Then he waited again deliberately silent, fingering the medal with a pensive expression. He looked at each man. "Thank you, gentlemen. This is not what I was expecting. It's most gracious of you and I will treasure it always, no matter what transpires. As you know, my next fight will be in Ronda. I hope to see you all there."

He walked over toward Bosque, picked up the leather box, turned and walked out.

"Fuck," he shouted in the lift. He dug his phone out of his inner jacket pocket and called Juan. "Can you meet me at the Wellington in half an hour?"

"I'm just about to get in a cab to Atocha," said Juan.

"Then please catch a later train, we have a massive problem."

"Very well. I've checked us out of our rooms, so I'll wait in the lounge."

***

Juan was sitting in a corner of the lounge reading a newspaper when Diego rushed in and sat down in the armchair next to him. He threw the box containing the medal onto the coffee table.

"What's this?" said Juan opening the box. "Wow, it's the Society's..."

"Medal of Honor," said Diego.

"Why?"

"To thank me for my pardons."

"Well deserved then."

"But that's not the real reason. They're going to use medal ceremony photographs to promote pardons and how worthless they would be if there was no killing."

"What makes you think that?"

"You and I both know how fantastic it feels to have a bull pardoned in the ring."

"Right," said Juan wondering where Diego was heading.

"Paradise for the bull, the pinnacle of achievement for us and premium entertainment for the crowd, it's one of the rarest sights to treasure."

Juan nodded.

"But there's another way of looking at it," said Diego. "Let me ask you a question. Is watching a bull be pardoned, the principal reason people flock to bullfights?"

"It's one of them," said Juan. "Another is to see and be seen, but the main motivation is to watch a real live bloody death. Either the bull or the torero, they don't much care which."

"That's pretty much what Bosque said, but what shocked me most was that they intend to highlight this risk of death in their campaign using my bloody photograph. It just might work against us. Perhaps we need to rethink our plans."

Juan waved the approaching waiter away. "Diego, there's really no need to worry about this. It changes nothing. If they want to keep blood in the ring, bullfighting will continue to fade away. If the Society thinks that promoting the risk of death will attract youngsters to the ring, let them. We can do even better."

"Really, how?"

"In our new version, the bull's life is guaranteed, but because he's not lanced by the picador or stabbed by the banderilleros he's twice as dangerous. The risks of death for the torero and his team will be considerably higher than today. I suggest that our campaign emphasizes these increased risks."

"Wow. You're right. Gracias tio. Will you tell Phillip and Amanda?"

"Of course. Anything else?"

"That's it for now. I'm off to meet the Condesa."

"Don't forget to show her your medal," said Juan with a smile.

20

"Have you walked the Caminito del Rey," said Amanda raising her voice above the wind noise, her hair wrapped in a pink headscarf. They had the roof down in Phillip's Cabriolet and were driving up to Ronda yet again. This was the fifth time in the last few weeks since they'd started work with the Romero's.

They'd just passed the turnoff to the village of Ardales, the route up to the starting point of the popular suspended hiking path. The original Caminito used to be the most dangerous walk in the world along a deep gorge that cuts through hills linking two reservoirs. In the early twentieth century, a narrow path was suspended at the top of the gorge's vertical cliffs to provide access for engineers to check on the engineering works that controlled the water flow between the two reservoirs. It was opened by King Alfonso XIII in 1921. Over the years the path slowly crumbled causing the risk level for using it to progressively increase. Eventually, they had to close it, much to the disappointment of dangerous sports enthusiasts. An initiative by Málaga County Council prompted a new path to be constructed on top of the original. It opened to much acclaim in 2015 and is completely safe, but not recommended for the faint-hearted or sufferers of vertigo.

"The Caminito? No, my love and you?" said Phillip.

"Me neither."

"Then we should add it to our to-do list of videos."

"There are already several dramatic versions, one with a guy on a mountain bike. It would be difficult to better that," said Amanda.

"I'm sure we can think of something, especially after what we've learned over the last month about filming with drone cameras."

"We need to finish this project for the Romero family first. How much more is there to complete?"

"In terms of filming, there's only the interview with Fredo tomorrow, then La Goyesca on Saturday."

"Apart from the editing, and that will take us several weeks," said Amanda.

"At least. Did you look at the stats on the voting film?"

"Just before we left, they're incredible. We've never done anything that went viral so quickly. I hope Diego is satisfied."

"We'll find out tonight at the family dinner," said Phillip.

"I hope this wild goose chase at Cortijo Infierno with Prado doesn't take too long."

"They should be nearly finished by the time we arrive," said Phillip. "His forensics team has been tearing the place apart since the crack of dawn."

"What does he want from us exactly?"

"He thinks that Crown has hidden something up here and hopes that our English mother tongue perspective may spot something that he and his team have missed."

Amanda shook her head. "It's unlikely Crown stashed anything here. He would want to keep everything close, and not risk his parents finding it."

"We will see my love," said Phillip.

Amanda reached over and rubbed his thigh.

He glanced at her and smiled tenderly.

As the mountain road climbed nearer to Ronda, agriculture gradually changed from citrus fruits to cereal crops, olive trees, and grapes. Meandering ranks of towering wind turbines dotted the hilltops, rotating steadily. Occasionally, they passed ruined forts, some from Moorish times, standing forlornly on cliff tops. There were too many and isolated to bother with upgrading them to tourist attractions.

A Guardia Civil patrol vehicle was parked outside the entrance to Cortijo Infierno. They were expected, waved through the gate and onto the track leading up to the farm building.

A white saloon car and a National Police forensics van were parked in front of the house. An officer in a white suit was digging up the stones used to form the name of the farm. She looked up as they passed. It was Doctor Ana Galvez. She waved and smiled as they parked next to the van and clambered out. Prado came out the front door to greet them with a dour face.

"Pleased to see us?" said Amanda.

"Ecstatic," he said, frowning. "I'd be happier if we'd found something though."

"Anything of interest?" said Phillip.

"Not in, or around the house, the garage or the

estate, despite the latest scanning technology."

"What are you looking for?" said Amanda.

"No idea. Something containing papers, perhaps. I've been staring at the place for so long, I can't see the wood for the trees. Could you guys take one final look around," said Prado. "If you can't find anything then at least we can be convinced that 'look in the darkness' must mean somewhere else."

They set off into the hallway, heads turning in all directions trying to spot something out of the ordinary. All the light fittings had gone, leaving bare wires dangling. The downstairs ceiling was typical of old structures, exposed timber beams supporting timber planking. Cables were clipped to the wood in tidy pathways. Upstairs the ceilings followed the roofline, angled to a point. Dormer windows provided light. It was quickly obvious that there was nowhere to stash anything.

The garage was another matter. Compared with the whitewashed house, it was a relatively new brick building covered with typical Spanish roof tiles.

The forensic team and Prado stood by the door and watched them as Phillip and Amanda went inside and peered upward. There was no ceiling as such, just the inside of the roof lined with white plasterboard. However, the last meter or so was horizontal. In theory, there could be a void between that and the roof apex.

Phillip went outside to inspect the brickwork in the gable end opposite the door. Everyone trailed after him and looked up.

"Have you tested up there?" said Phillip. "Only the grouting just under the roof level seems cleaner than the surrounding area."

"I see what you mean," said Ana, asking a colleague to fetch an extendable stepladder.

Ana scrambled up the ladder to the area concerned with her scanner and held it against the wall. "There's something in there," she shouted.

Her assistant passed her up a small drill and a hammer. Ana removed the grouting from a few bricks, then hammered them through and peered in through the small hole with her torch. She withdrew her head from the hole, drilled out a few more bricks to enlarge the opening and asked for a rope with a lasso knotted at the end. It took her a few minutes to encircle the object, pull it to her and secure it.

"It's not that heavy," she shouted. "I'll lower it down."

Prado was beside himself with excitement as he watched a small boxlike shape lowered onto the floor. He went over to what was a thirty-centimeter cube of rusting black painted metal, with a door on one side. It was a small safe. He heaved it up and shook it. Whatever was inside made a rattling noise. He put it back down.

"A tin of some sort," said Ana jumping down from the ladder, squatting, and inspecting the solid lock in the safe door.

"It could also be booby-trapped," said Phillip.

"Unlikely, but best that we take it to the lab and ask a professional locksmith to open it," said Prado unable to hide his impatience.

***

Every year, during the last week of the Pedro Romero Festival, Pedro senior and his wife Marta now in their mid-eighties, invite the family for a formal dinner at their ranch. After filming Diego and his team practicing their maneuvers for the new style of bullfighting, Amanda and Phillip retired to a guest room on the top floor of the old house to get ready for the meal.

They stood in line at the entrance to the magnificent dining room studying the table plan mounted in a display cabinet hanging on the wall. Amanda looked stunning in a sleeveless lime-green silk dress, with bottle-green high-heeled shoes, and a matching purse. A wide bottle-green belt accentuated her shapely curves and a delicate silver necklace with a small emerald pendant and matching earrings complemented her hazel eyes. Phillip wore a dark blue suit and white open-necked shirt. They were in line behind Juan, his wife Maribel and Diego's mother, Maria all dressed in stylish outfits. The sisters were practically identical. Classic Spanish looks, high cheeks, delicate noses, full lips, olive skin, brown eyes and dark hair pinned back into a bun, with a red rose over their right ears.

Inside the dining room, the long table was laid for thirty-six people. It looked beautiful covered with crisp white tablecloths, fine china, silver cutlery, and crystal glasses. A large flower arrangement of roses set in Rosemary was in the center in front of where the hosts Pedro and Marta Romero would sit.

Eventually, it was Phillip and Amanda's turn. They shook hands and exchanged cheek kisses with the distinguished Matriarch and Patriarch, then walked along the table and found their seats at the far end of the table by the grand fireplace.

The two seats next to Phillip were empty. He reached over to look at the name cards.

Leon and Inma. They were late. Phillip wondered if there had been any developments with the contents of the strongbox they'd found earlier. Then Prado rushed in through the dining room door with a harassed looking Inma in a tight red dress that showed off her trim figure hanging onto his arm. They were the last to arrive, exchanged greetings with the already seated hosts and looked around for their places. Phillip waved and pointed to the vacant seats. They said Hola to everyone as they worked their way toward Phillip and took their places.

Prado introduced them.

"I love your dress," said Amanda to Inma in an attempt to calm her down, "And forgive me as you must have heard this a thousand times before, but you three sisters could be triplets."

"Thank you, and don't worry, I can never receive enough compliments. Makes up for the lack from his Majesty here," said Inma, looking grateful for Amanda breaking the ice. "Sorry, we're late. As usual," she nodded at Prado. "He was delayed coming back from Málaga. I thought I'd be used to it by now. Leon tells me that you two are making the films?"

"That's right," said Amanda.

"I saw the voting one yesterday. It was fantastic. Well done," said Inma, leaning forward and speaking quietly. "All the family are most impressed. They probably haven't said so, but I can assure you that they are. And to have been invited tonight to what is a purely family affair means that you've been more than accepted. Now they will listen to your advice so don't hold back."

"Thanks, Inma," said Amanda, reaching out and squeezing her hand.

The serving staff dressed in white Romero T-shirts and black pants arrived with the starter and commenced distributing the plates.

While he was waiting for the lobster cocktail, Phillip looked along the table and saw that Diego and his fiancée the Condesa, a beautiful, tall, slender girl in her early twenties with pixie cut black hair and engaging brown eyes, were sitting opposite Pedro and Marta. Fredo Ordoñez sat next to Marta, he was unaccompanied.

Prado cleared his throat.

Phillip looked at him.

"Guess what was in the safe?" Prado whispered across Inma now that she and Amanda had stopped talking.

"A treasure map?" said Phillip.

"No, a canister," said Prado frowning. "With an old roll of undeveloped film."

"And the pictures were?" said Phillip.

"And the pictures were not?" said Prado. "The film is stuck together. Ana is trying to find a specialist developer."

21

"Do you know who the guy in the portrait is?" said Phillip as he and Amanda lay entwined naked in bed the next morning in the guest room at Ganaderia Romero.

"I think it's Pedro Romero," said Amanda stretching and yawning. "But I'm not sure."

Phillip clambered out of the large bed and strode over to the picture at the end of the bed for a closer inspection. "There's no title, but it looks like Goya's signature," he said.

"Have a look on the back," said Amanda.

Phillip lifted the gilt frame off its hanger and peered at the back. "There's a label," he said. "It says, fine-art print of Pedro Romero, painted by Francisco Goya. Original completed in 1798, now housed in the Kimball Art Museum, Fort Worth, Texas.

"We could use the image as the introduction to the film, we're doing on the Romero dynasty," said Amanda.

"Good idea. Are you joining me for breakfast, or shall I bring you up some fruit?" said Phillip.

"I'll join you," said Amanda pushing back the duvet cover. "But only if you come back to bed first."

"Brazen hussy," said Phillip.

***

Most of the Romero family was seated at the breakfast table in the dining room when Phillip and Amanda entered holding hands. Amanda was dressed for her interview with Fredo in cream jodhpurs and brown boots with a red and black plaid short-sleeved shirt.

"Leon has left for Málaga, already," said Inma as they sat down next to her. Her magnificent hair was down, and she wore jeans and a Romero family T-shirt. "But he'll see you at La Goyesca tomorrow afternoon. We've been invited to join a dear friend in the Royal Box. He's the chief of Ronda local police and is this year's president. It will give you a chance to meet our sons."

Phillip went off to the buffet table, leaving the two women chatting. Diego joined him as he poured orange juices from the pitcher. He looked furious.

"What's happened to the voting video?" said Diego.

"Sorry?"

"It's been replaced by some sort of joke."

"But yesterday, it was fine, the votes supporting you were piling in."

"They were, but this morning, it's another story. I think we've been hacked. Look and fix it muy pronto, before it turns us into a laughingstock."

Phillip left his half-filled breakfast plate on the table,

ran up to their room and turned on his laptop. He called Richard while it booted up.

"Have you...?" said Phillip.

"Yes, we've been hacked, I'm working on it, but this is way too advanced for me. Any suggestions?"

"Give me five."

Phillip clicked on the Nuestra-España website and was horrified by what appeared. A cartoon featuring an extremely camp, male ballet dancer, dressed in a sky-blue suit of lights was dancing the tango with a bull dressed in a frilly pink tutu. Phillip was impressed; it was hilarious, but he could understand Diego's frustration.

"I have to take this down," he said out loud. "And now."

The bedroom door opened and in walked Amanda carrying a plate of croissants, ham, cheese, and a coffee.

"Diego told me," she said placing the plate next to his laptop. "Here, eat while you work. Will you be able to trace who did this?"

"Too soon to tell."

"I'll leave you in peace. I know you hate being disturbed when concentrating."

"Thanks, my love. It may take a while."

Phillip waited until the door closed, then turned his attention to the screen. He changed his password, replaced the current live site with his back up located on a different server. It was based in the UK and had impregnable security.

Immediately, the proper site appeared. The page that linked to Diego's website returned to its correct video, and the voting could continue as if nothing had happened. He checked how long the cartoon had been running. Fourteen minutes. It would have caused some amusement and turned off a few voters, but the yes voters were already making their presence felt. The meter ticked up to over thirty million supporting Diego's alternative, with some thirty-odd thousand against.

Now he had to track down the hackers.

He picked up the phone and called what used to be in his distant military past, a regularly used number.

"Four years with no card or message. Clearly you no longer love me," said a deep male voice.

"Dearest Theo," said Phillip to his former colleague in the British Intelligence Corps. "My life without your dulcet tones and acerbic wit has been incomplete but you are often in my thoughts."

"Yes, but only when your computer is giving you jip. Still in Spain?"

"Living a much quieter life, until this morning."

"The devil always finds temptations for idle hands, but I can't imagine you are just lying in the sun every day."

"Correct. I assume that you are still active?"

"I've quit GCHQ and turned private," said Theo. "Far more lucrative. How can I help?"

"Either someone gained access to my laptop or I've been hacked. I've rescued it quickly by switching my site onto the secure backup server, but now I'd like to clean up the original and trace the bastards who took me down. However, they may have installed some tracker malware on my systems."

"How about your phone?"

"Unsure."

"Is there a clean phone nearby?"

"Probably not."

"Then pop out and purchase a burner and call me

back with your system access details. I'll clean everything up, then find how they accessed your site."

"It'll be an hour or so."

"Fine."

"Later."

Phillip jotted down Theo's number on a post-it note and stuck it his wallet, picked up his car keys, and headed downstairs.

He popped into the breakfast room and spotted Diego looking at his phone. He seemed much happier.

"That was quick," he said, as Phillip approached.

"We are still vulnerable though. I need to pop into Ronda to buy a new phone just in case mine has been compromised. I recommend that you and Juan do the same."

"Really?" said Diego. "In that case, I'll come with you. I know a trustworthy shop."

"Family, right?"

"Second cousin."

"I'll tell Amanda and meet you outside."

Phillip whispered his plan into Amanda's ear. She was still chatting with Inma. She kissed his hand and waved him away.

He headed outside to his car and stared in horror at his precious cabriolet. All four tires had been cut.

He stood there scratching his head as Diego arrived wearing a Ronda Football Club baseball cap with his hair tucked up underneath and large sunglasses.

"What the?" said Diego. "We'll go in mine."

They ran to the massive garage. Diego unlocked it and slid back the huge doors. There was a choice of a yellow Ferrari, top-end Mercedes or a battered Landrover. They took the latter and moments later were chugging in the direction of Ronda.

"Is this the Society's way of saying, do what you're told?" said Phillip.

"Has to be," said Diego. "However, what I don't understand is, who disabled your car and how?"

"I don't think we should discuss it in the vehicle," said Phillip.

"You think...?"

"If they are going to these lengths to disrupt us, anything is possible."

"Then I'll stop at the first layby and we can discuss this."

Two kilometers later, Diego pulled off the road into a picnic area. They clambered out and walked away from the vehicle."

"At night," said Diego. "We have two ferocious Doberman dogs that patrol our grounds. Anybody that smells familiar, they leave alone, but any stranger would have been pinned down. The noise would have woken us all up."

"Are you suggesting that there is a mole in your house?"

"I can't think of another explanation. The dogs were fine this morning, so it had to be someone staying in the house and known to them."

"Someone working for the Society?"

"Charged with slowing us down and keeping them informed of our plans. Tell me, where was your laptop last night during dinner?"

"I left it in our room, but it was off and is password protected."

"Perhaps, someone has your password?"

"But how?"

"When was the last time you used public Wi-Fi?"

"That was weeks ago, on the train back from

Madrid after meeting you and Juan. I also used your house system on several occasions."

"Maybe, they had someone on the train?"

"To be fair, I didn't think about it, but you could be right. Any ideas on who the mole could be?"

"I've been racking my brains since we left. My first conclusion was that it must be you or Amanda, except why would you cut your own tires?"

"I can assure that it's neither of us," yelled Phillip, waving his arms in anger. "We both support your project wholeheartedly. Why would we shoot ourselves in the foot?"

"Sorry, but I had to test your loyalty. Then there is only one other possibility."

"Who?"

"Fredo."

"I thought he was your whistle-blower."

"So did I."

"Are you going to confront him?"

"I think not. We'll use him to feed false information back to the society."

"Be careful where you discuss your plans. There could be listening devices everywhere."

Diego nodded. They climbed back aboard and continued to Ronda, remaining silent as the elderly diesel engine labored up the hills to Ronda.

They parked near the bus station, left their old phones in the glove compartment and walked to the phone shop on Calle Infantes.

Diego insisted on paying.

Five minutes later, Phillip called Theo.

"Who is that?" said Theo.

"I have my new phone," said Phillip. "I'm texting you my IP addresses and login details for both the old one and the server that has been hacked. Also, could you look at my laptop? It may have been compromised."

"Is it switched on?"

"No, but I'll arrange for it when we're done."

"I'm on it," said Theo. "I'll call you back when I have something. Until then, don't use any of your devices."

"One more thing; what's the best listening device scanner nowadays. I've been out of the loop."

"The joys of living in Spain," said Theo. "Tell you what. Text me your address, and I'll send one over by courier along with my invoice. Should be there in forty-eight hours."

"Thanks, Theo," said Phillip tapping out his villa location.

"Welcome back to your old world. I've missed you."

"Thanks. I'd rather not have to bother you but needs must. Ciao."

Phillip called Amanda who was in their room getting ready for their session with Fredo. She turned his machine on.

Diego took Phillip to a discreet café further along the street. "Not family," he said as they took a seat at a terrace table. "The mechanics are on their way to the ranch with four new tires for your car. Should be ready by the time we get back."

"Thanks."

"Only fair. I said that you shouldn't be out of pocket because of working with us. I've also ordered surveillance systems for the ranch. If the society wants to play nasty, we need to protect ourselves. I'm defending my home, but what can you do to fend off any more hackers?"

Phillip delayed his response until the waiter had taken their order for coffee and molletes and was out of earshot.

"I've taken care of it with a former military colleague."

"You were in the army?"

"British Intelligence Corps."

"Then we're in safe hands. How long?"

"A couple of hours, and we'll know more about who attacked us, where they are, and with a few options of retribution, should you want to take them down."

Diego extracted his new phone and checked the voting statistics.

"Looks like it's really going global," he said. "The pro voter numbers are still increasing. Now, all we need is Fredo's interview and the La Goyesca documentary to complete your project for us."

"You still want Fredo speaking on your behalf?"

"Probably not, but he's expecting to be filmed this morning. Best if we don't disappoint him. He'll think we don't suspect him, but we don't have to broadcast his film. What concerns me more though is, why is he helping the society? He's family and we should be his priority."

"Perhaps the society has a hold over him?"

"Such as what?"

"Could be any of the human frailties?"

"But he's such a sweet guy?"

"Do we really know everything about each other?"

Diego stared at Phillip with a quizzical expression.

"I guess not. Enough of this. What did you think of the Society's campaign?"

"Professionally made," said Phillip. "Its patriotic theme will no doubt stir the hearts of many Spaniards and will probably result in a temporary increase in bullfight attendees. It's bound to reinvigorate interest among those lapsed spectators. But, once the good feeling has died down, the audiences will sink to their usual numbers because it contains nothing that appeals to potential new attendees, especially the younger generation."

"I agree," said Diego before munching his mollete. "They've wasted all that money on advertising that won't work. What are your thoughts about how we can get our message over to the youngsters?"

"We need to capitalize on your growing celebrity status," said Phillip. "It shouldn't just be factual about the new style of fighting, but more about why you and your supporters seek to modernize bullfighting for the benefit of future generations. The Society used your two pardons to illustrate the importance of killing the bull. We should use them to make a hero of you for saving the bulls' lives as part of your strategy to change bullfighting and protect animals from such barbarity. A brief history of your family's involvement in changing bullfighting over the centuries will more than qualify you to change it yet again. One more thing. Fredo told me last night that you are going for a third pardon at La Goyesca? Is that right?"

"I've been telling everyone," said Diego. "That I intend to go for a third pardon. However, between, you, me and Juan only; that won't be happening. We have another plan in mind that will be revealed on the day. After my first bull, I'll need a cable-free microphone to speak to the crowd. Can you have one available near the bullfighter's gate?"

"No problem," said Phillip.

They finished their coffee, returned to the Landrover and headed back to the ranch in silence.

***

Phillip's car was being worked on as they pulled up in front of the ranch. Fredo was waiting at the main door chatting with Amanda. He looked up as Phillip and Diego walked toward the house and smiled warmly at them both. Diego ignored Fredo and went indoors.

Amanda handed Phillip their increasingly large camera bag.

Phillip fitted them both with throat mikes and they walked to the stables located near the bullring. Fredo and Amanda mounted a pair of beautiful gray Arab horses and headed off across the rich green meadows of the Romero ranch chatting as they went. Fredo's leg didn't seem to impede his riding skills.

Phillip checked that the recorder was grabbing their conversation and drove around them on a golf cart filming from various angles and occasionally flew the drone camera over them to provide aerial views of their interview. It was the first time he managed to use it without crashing into a tree or lamppost.

***

Diego kissed his fiancée goodbye and waved as she drove away in her Mercedes back home to Salamanca. She would not be attending La Goyesca.

He went for a run around the estate, conscious of the fear gathering momentum for tomorrow's fight. He knew from experience that until he sat in the chapel at the Ronda bullring, and could complete his mental preparations, there was nothing he could do to assuage or escape the sense of foreboding gnawing away at his guts.

He was drying himself after a shower when his old mobile phone parked on top of the laundry basket rang. Assuming it might be his fiancée missing him already, he didn't bother to check the caller ID, picked it up and said, "Hola."

He was surprised when a gruff man's voice said in English, "Is that Diego Romero?"

"Who is calling?" said Diego in the same language.

"I want to make you an offer that you cannot resist," said the man.

"Goodbye," said Diego and went to press end call.

"Then you'll be saying goodbye to half a million Euros," said the voice.

"Is this a joke?" said Diego.

"We have never been more serious in our life," said the man.

"Who are we?"

"I represent a discrete group that wagers on the outcome of bullfights."

"And you want to bribe me to do something?"

"Yes, we do, but you'll find that our requirements are pretty much the same as the Royal Society, so it's hardly onerous."

"And your requirements are?"

"We need you to win a pardon for your first bull."

"That's impossible, nobody can guarantee a pardon, and there are too many variables, including me being on the receiving end of serious injury."

"No, you don't understand Diego, this is an offer that you may not fudge or decline. If you win a pardon, you will be paid, but if you lose, then the outcome will be extremely unfavorable. I suggest that you do some research into a colleague of yours. He was one of the few foreigners on the bullfighting circuit, a Scotsman named Donald MacKinnon. I'll be waiting for your call."

"Fuck off," shouted Diego and swiped end call. He then went to settings and blocked the number.

"Shit," he shouted out loud. "How did they trace my number? With all that's going on, the last thing I need is some damn foreign crook muscling in on our plans."

***

Amanda was impressed with Fredo's articulate and personable manner. He explained the history of Toro de Lidia and went on to describe the effects of centuries of selective breeding. Occasionally, they would stop to film individual bulls, cows, and calves. Fredo knew many of their names and pedigree, having been involved in their nurturing from birth.

Some two hours later they returned to the main house. Fredo limped off to the dining room. Phillip and Amanda packed their luggage and equipment into Phillip's trunk. Then headed off in the freshly shod cabriolet to the Parador Hotel in Ronda to meet their camera team and prepare for tomorrow's La Goyesca.

Halfway there, his new phone rang.

It was Theo.

"Let me park up," he said.

Phillip stopped the car at the next layby and climbed out.

"OK, shoot."

"I've cleaned your server and old phone. There was Malware on both, but until you've checked for listening devices, I wouldn't say anything compromising in the car or at home."

"What about my laptop?"

"It's not been hacked, but according to the log, someone accessed it last night, and loaded the cartoon and some malware. I've cleaned it all out so you can use it again now."

"Terrific, did you find any trace of hackers?"

"They certainly know how to cover their tracks. The malware was being monitored via a massive data management center located in Mumbai, India. However, I haven't been able to penetrate beyond their servers to an actual computer, so it's a dead end."

"Have you learned anything about the data center?"

"It's operated by a local company that is owned by an offshore company working out of Turks and Caicos Islands. However, other than local nominee directors and shareholders, I have no names worth anything."

"What's the name of the offshore company?"

"CVS Holdings Ltd."

22

"Have you voted?" said Sebastian.

"Not since the council elections," said Tobalo, to his lifelong friend and brother-in-law.

Seb and Tobalo were the two local police officers that had accompanied Prado to Cortijo Infierno. They were well built, good-looking men in their early forties, clean-shaven with trim black-hair, and brown eyes. They'd stopped off at their regular café for breakfast which was in the back streets near Plaza del Socorro, Ronda's quaint, central square.

However, today they were not dressed in their customary local police uniforms, but were wearing cherry-red tight-fitting pants, royal-blue bolero jackets, white linen shirts with lace frills, and black leather ornate boots.

This was the final and most exciting of three days of bullfighting at Ronda's annual Pedro Romero Festival and known as Corrida de Toros La Goyesca, Ronda. Seb and Tobalo were sub-contracted as ushers for the Royal Box at the bullring.

It was their second day on the job. On Friday they'd had some time between duties to watch the Novillos, young bullfighters. Today was the main day for the bullfighting stars. Sunday, the closing day of the Festival, would be for fighting bulls in the old style on horseback.

"I didn't mean the political elections," said Seb digging his phone out of an inner jacket pocket. He swiped the screen a couple of times and presented it to Tobalo. "I'm referring to this."

Tobalo placed his glass of café con leche on the aluminum table, took the phone and watched.

The silent film started with a picture of cattle grazing peacefully in a rich green meadow. After a couple of seconds, a text question appeared over the beautiful scenery. 'What is your preference for bullfighting?' The image switched to that of a dead bull being dragged unceremoniously out of a sandy arena by a team of mules. The word 'Option One?' Appeared over the animal's bloody torso. Followed by, OR...?

The film morphed to a close-up of Diego Romero's face, then slowly zoomed out to reveal him standing before a fierce black bull in a small arena surrounded by timber posts and beams. It had no darts in its back, or blood dripping down its shoulder. Diego shook his muleta. The bull charged, Diego twirled his cape and together they whirled around each other, the bull's horns narrowly missing Diego's chest. Then fast forward until the bull was too exhausted to move. Diego turned his back on the bull waved his arms in the air, then took a harness from an assistant. The camera zoomed in on the bull. He was appraising Diego. Was he about to charge?

The camera zoomed back out.

Just as he had when the two bulls were pardoned in Madrid back in June, Diego walked toward the bull, holding the harness. He stretched his hand under the bull's chin and stroked him, before slipping the harness over its head. They then walked side by side around the arena to the open arena gate where Diego released him into rich green pastures.

'Option Two?' Appeared as the bull trotted off contentedly. More text followed. 'To vote now, click below.'

"I'd heard about this," said Tobalo. "But how does Diego propose to change bullfighting to get to this. I understand the ending, best of friends, let's go walkies with the bull bit, but what happens during the remainder of the fight to replace the current life or death drama? Is he proposing that all fights become like what they do in the province of Aragon, the recortes?"

"Isn't that where the bullfighter dodges around the bull without a cape or sword?" said Seb.

"Yes, there's no killing. It's more like an acrobatic display, but it shows little respect for the bull. I couldn't support that."

"Perhaps you'd prefer what the Basques do?"

"A few lads teasing a cow. Where's the courage and grace in that?"

"You're right. I can't believe that Diego would support anything clown-like, disrespectful or barbaric. It rules out running with the bulls, as in Pamplona, and I can't imagine Diego sanctioning bull wrestling, as in Portugal. And as for Toro de La Vega?"

"What's that one?" said Tobalo.

"In Tordesillas, they run a bull through an open area

and over a bridge across the River Duero. The crowd, on foot or horse, attempt to kill the bull using spears and lances before it crosses to the other side. Supposedly, it's considered a traditional spectacle by the government of Castilla y León."

"Now that is barbaric."

"As is coating a bull's horns with tar, setting them alight and letting it run so drunken idiots can dodge and weave around it. Apparently, one bull was so terrified it killed itself against a post. My point being that Diego is right to address change. Us Spaniards cannot continue with these outdated customs and ourselves be respected by other cultures who left these barbaric entertainments alone centuries ago."

"You're being irritating again. Perhaps, after I've seen what Diego intends, I'll be more supportive. I suppose you voted for option two?"

"That's my secret, but over fifty-six million have voted for change."

"How many voted for option one?"

"Look for yourself, the numbers are under the voting buttons," said Seb.

Tobalo scrolled down and saw that only thirty-seven thousand had voted to keep killing bulls.

"Are you going to vote," said Seb.

"Of course," said Tobalo.

"Then you'll need to use your own phone. It won't let you vote twice with the same device."

Tobalo extracted his phone from inside his jacket, swiped to the YouTube video and voiced his opinion. The thirty-seven thousand went up by one as he watched.

He finished his coffee and looked at Seb with raised eyebrows.

"You ready?" said Seb.

Tobalo sighed, frowned and nodded.

They finished their coffee, left some coins on the table, put on their Cordoba hats, and exchanged some brief farewell banter with the other regulars before heading out the café entrance.

"I bet you voted for option one," said Seb as they walked side-by-side along the narrow street in the direction of the bullring.

"That's the beauty of democracy, the freedom of choice and anonymous participation, but to you, I'll admit that I voted to keep bullfighting as it is. It's been our national tradition for centuries. I see no reason to change it just to assuage distant politicians in Brussels, a bunch of animal lovers who can't understand the pleasure of a tasty steak, or ignorant youngsters who have no idea of the role bullfighting has played in Spanish history."

"Fair enough. At least you're being consistent. You hate change of any sort."

"I like my life as it is, why should others keep trying to change it?"

"What do you think of your smartphone?"

"I don't know how we existed before them."

"That's because it keeps changing. Every year, they bring out something new."

"Yes, but change is what's expected of technology. Bullfighting is a well-established cultural thing like classical music. They don't change Isaac Albeniz's scores to suit a more modern taste. They remain the same, and so should bullfighting."

"You are grumpy today, but listen, my friend, people aren't going to bullfights anymore. Look at Ronda, the finest bullring in Spain used only twice per year. If bullfighting doesn't change, it will fade away. In ten years, there will be no more Goyesca, and then we will both lose our prestigious part-time jobs. If we want to continue earning a bit extra, we need to get behind Diego. Yes, I know we aren't aware of the details of his alternative, but he's a caring man and everything he does reeks of duende - style. Whatever it is, it must be good and will be different from those other examples we were chatting about earlier. As you saw from the voting statistics, most people take the view that killing noble beasts for fun is barbaric. In addition, as you so rightly pointed out, this is a democracy, the majority rule. So, make the most of today's death in the afternoon. It won't be around much longer."

"You're probably right," said Tobalo. "There you go with your irritating ways again. However, irrespective of what you say, I'm making a bet with everything I possess that Diego will make it three pardons in a row today."

"Such a large wager is a hell of a risk, dear friend," said Seb. "Ronda spectators rarely demand a pardon for any bull, for three in a row, you can forget it."

"I'm aware of that," said Tobalo. "Most of the pundits are saying the same thing, yet the Royal Taurino Society is confident that Diego will make it."

"Have you seen the Society's ads?" said Seb.

"I have. Blood stirring, I thought. Makes you proud to be Spanish."

"I'm not so sure, they remind me of the former glories of our national soccer team. To me, that is the old Spain. Now we're a modern egalitarian democracy with more female ministers in the new Socialist government than men. They won't support killing animals for fun and have already stopped all taxpayers' money going to support bullfighting. Next, they'll be taking on the old buggers at the Society to modernize or face extinction. You should be betting on that, not wasting your money on a third pardon."

"Of course, you're right... again... but...."

"Then why be so foolhardy?"

"If by some miracle the bull is pardoned, I could win thousands. Where I bet online the odds are fantastic," said Tobalo, eyes shining."

"Always dreaming of the big win. You're the same with El Gordo lottery at Christmas, and how much do you waste on La Primitiva every week, when are you going to learn?"

"You will see my friend. This time the money is coming my way. I feel it in my bones."

"Does my sister know about your wager?" said Seb.

"No, but this is too good an opportunity to miss," whined Tobalo. "If the bull survives, I could pay off the mortgage."

"Yes, but if you lose, you'll have to increase it. My sister will kill you."

"Yes, but think how happy she'll be if I win."

"Knowing my sister's opinion on taking risks with family money, pigs might fly, cuñado."

"I'm thinking positively, brother-in-law, not about the elevation of bacon prices."

"Then I wish you well, as always," said Seb shaking his head sadly. Tobalo maybe his bestie, but when it came to finance; his light did not shine so brightly on the money tree.

The noise of the crowd increased the nearer they approached the bullring.

Intelligible conversation became impossible as they joined the throngs all heading the same way to watch the procession.

They worked their way through to their favorite location by the bronze statue of Antonio Ordoñez at the front of the Plaza de Toros. 'El Maestro,' as he was christened by his army of fans, had managed the first La Goyesca event originated from the brilliant idea of his father Cayetano Ordoñez in 1954. The concept was to combine the bicentennial anniversary of Pedro Romero's birth with the Art of Francisco Goya and his connections with Ronda and bullfighting.

Many of the spectators were wearing a variety of festival clothing. Some were in Cordoba hats, black pants, white shirts and red bandannas around their necks. A few were dressed as Bandoleros, celebrating the area's long bandit history, others wore elegant clothing reflecting the rich, bold colors of Francisco Goya's paintings.

Any moment now, the procession carrying the bullfighters to the arena would pass in front of Seb and Tobalo. The noise was deafening as everyone shouted at each other sharing their excitement at seeing Diego, his rumored new ideas and the possible outcome of his performance.

Mobile phones were raised aloft everywhere, recording the event, albeit as yet nothing was happening. Selfies with a passing police officer seemed to be the favorite activity. Several camera drones hovered over the street until one smashed into an overhead cable and fell out of the sky, causing much amusement when it landed on a mounted police officer's horse's head. For a moment the crowd stilled, anxious that the animal might react violently, or bolt, but it swished its tail, twitched an ear, snorted and carried on calmly. The officer though was furious, he turned the horse and set off to confront the inept drone pilots while muttering about air traffic control not being part of his job description.

The boisterous, tightly packed, but mainly good-natured crowd jostled the two men back and forth, as they waited for the approaching procession edging slowly toward them. They had stood in this same location for years and should logically have been accustomed to the excitement that buzzed among the crowds. However, La Goyesca was special and this year it could go down in history.

Seb and Tobalo perspired in the late afternoon heat. Their broad-brimmed gray Cordoba hats provided some shadow against the relentless Andalusian sun. They peered up Calle Jerez and could see the mounted police riding slowly past the sixteenth-century Mudejar style church, Iglesia de Nuestra Señora de la Merced Ronda some 400 meters away. Both sides of the street were jammed solid with eager spectators.

Local police struggled to contain the amiable masses on the pavements and bar-fronts in order to maintain enough space for the procession to squeeze through. The onlookers talked animatedly among themselves while enjoying a modest glass of vino fino, dry sherry, or the local deadlier potion, vino de terreno, a strong, sweet raisin wine, the traditional beverages of choice for such refined social celebrations. On the balconies above, elegantly dressed families appreciated the unimpeded bird's-eye views of the proceedings below. A couple of kids were trying to catch the passing camera drones with a fishing net.

There wasn't a bed available anywhere in and around the city and every entrance-ticket into the arena had been sold out for weeks. Touts mingled among the crowds. They had nothing for sale but were bidding five times face value for any tickets.

Nobody was selling, this was a one-off event with the potential to become quixotic in the world of bullfighting. Attendance would be passed down through family histories. It might be a worthless asset for inheritance purposes, but of incredible value for prestige and was sure to remain the focus of heated discussion for centuries in the colorful city squares and vibrant cafés.

Most people in the crowd were straining on tiptoe for a glance of Diego Romero as his carriage went by, however, some were not so enthusiastic.

Next to the brothers-in-law, being closely monitored by local police, were a mix of some thirty animal rights lovers and vegans chanting their demands. They appeared to be led by a tall, sour-faced, long red-haired man wearing huge sunglasses. He prowled among them limping quite badly, supporting his right side on an ebony walking stick. Occasionally, he waved it threateningly at his fellow protesters if their enthusiasm for the task dared to falter. At one point, he stood right next to Tobalo for a second or two, then led his disparate group off to reassemble opposite the main entrance to the bullring to the rear of the stadium.

"Stop murdering bulls," shouted one man in Spanish as they barged their way through the crowd to their new position.

"Animals have rights," whined another.

"Humans don't need to eat meat," cried a woman's shrill voice.

The spectators ignored them, resolved not to let such rude behavior and ignorance spoil their favorite day of the year, especially on this occasion when bullfighting history was likely to be rewritten and render some of their complaints unfounded.

Seb looked at Tobalo, now they could hear the music approaching. Usually, Tobalo would be excited by this glamorous display, but today his expression was glum. He is clearly preoccupied with something, thought Seb, stretching out his arm and hugging his brother in law's shoulder.

"Whatever it is, don't let it bug you," said Seb.

"Easier said than done," said Tobalo.

The procession was headed by the mounted brass band of the Real Maestranza De Caballería De Ronda in their smart blue cavalry uniforms, ostrich feathers fluttering from their helmets as they played a slow trotting march. The trumpet blasts echoed between the whitewashed adobe buildings while the metronomic thud of the bass drum was intoxicating. The pulsating rhythm penetrated deeply into the hearts and souls of the spectators, fueling their anticipation of what was yet to come.

A loud cheer rippled towards the two men as the band approached, "Viva El Bailerin," someone shouted.

"Viva," was the deafening response.

Following the band was a sleek, highly polished black open-top carriage bearing the cavalry's coat of arms on each door. It was drawn by five, matching, finely muscled gray Arab horses; three leading a pair. Their long manes fluttering as they trotted slowly along, horseshoes clicking metallically on the tarmac. Their glistening coats groomed to perfection, the brasses on their immaculate leather tackle sparkling in the sun; they were magnificent. Their movements precise and elegant, as if they had been trained at the

Royal Andalusian Horse School in Jerez de la Frontera, just over a hundred kilometers to the west.

El Bailerin sat in the forward-looking bench seat dressed in his trademark sky-blue suit of lights. To his left was his picador. Opposite were two of his three banderilleros. His other assistants were waiting in the arena, not enough space for them.

Following Diego's carriage were the other two teams in equally splendid regalia. In the second carriage was torero, Macca Cienfuegos. In the third sat torero Sammi Bettencourt. After the toreros came two more carriages with the beautifully dressed Damas de Ronda, the La Goyesca welcoming committee representing the womanhood of the city.

The final notes of the band faded as they came to a halt outside the Parador Hotel. The carriages headed to the main entrance at the rear of the bullring. One by one, they reversed up to the doorway, their passengers climbed out and walked into the marshaling area to prepare for their parade around the sandy arena to show themselves to the crowd.

That was the last Seb and Tobalo would see of the procession. As the final carriage passed, they went to the staff entrance and took their places at the door of the Royal box. This was their thirteenth year as the president's ushers. The routine never changed.

They paused for a moment by the museum door to watch Diego climb down from his carriage and head off to the arena chapel on his own.

Seb thought that he looked calm and relaxed as his solitary figure walked through the museum in the direction of the chapel.

23

"Everyone ready?" said Phillip into his headset microphone.

He was standing between the inner and outer ring of the bullring near the bullfighter's gate waiting for Diego's team to enter the arena while directing the actions of the five members of his camera crew. Three were spread around the arena using normal TV quality devices; another was flying a drone camera with a powerful zoom lens, the last was Amanda. She was stationed by the stables. One by one, the team acknowledged that they were indeed ready.

"Do we have a method to fix the button-camera to the bull?" he said.

"We've cobbled together what we hope will work," said Amanda. "We've hidden the camera workings inside the owner's rosette which will be fixed as high up the neck as possible with the usual mini-harpoon just as the bull is about to enter the ring. Simultaneously, the other stable - hand will smack the lens button onto the bull's forehead. I've turned the device on, Bluetooth is working, and I have a clear image on my monitor. However, as the planet is a tad short of adhesive for sticking stuff to bull's hair, we're worried that it might wear loose as the bull heats up or shakes his head. I hope that I can grab enough footage before that happens. How's the drone?"

"It's hovering above the bull's entrance gate at about twenty meters," said Phillip. "We'll zoom in on the bull and fly along with it as soon as the gate opens. Between that and the button-camera, we should be covered."

So much for an easier life in Spain, thought Phillip. I've never worked this hard, but at least, it's enormously satisfying.

***

Seb ushered the president and his two advisers to their seats in the Royal Box while Tobalo minded the door. The president was also their boss, the chief of local police accompanied by invited guests, old friend, and colleague Detective Inspector Prado, his wife, and two strapping sons. The crowd applauded politely as they made themselves comfortable. Four couples from the Royal Taurino Society plus Pablo Bosque took the remaining seats. Zambrano, Lorenzo, and Agustin had sent apologies; other business had beckoned.

Don Bosque was last to take his seat and was traveling solo. It was well known that the Duquesa detested bullfighting. He might be all-powerful in board and committee rooms, but with his wife, that was another matter, especially when it came to blood sports. Occasionally, and more often than he would admit, he wondered why he continued this escalating battle to protect Spain's shrinking tradition. For seventy-eight years old, his burning flame was starting to flicker, and his doctor had warned him that he ought to begin taking things easy. His heart wasn't what it used to be. The appeal of a quieter and more harmonious life was increasing with every passing year. However, not until he'd won this battle.

He shook hands with everyone and took his seat next to the president.

The committee members exchanged positive nods and glances with each other.

***

Diego's mouth was bone-dry, sweat streamed down his back, his thighs twitched, and his mind was a turbulent storm of flashing thoughts. None of them making any sense. "Why me?" he whispered to the small white statue of Christ on the cross standing in the wall niche a couple of meters in front of him.

As was customary before any fight, he was sitting on a pew in front of the altar in the bullring chapel, leaning forward; chin resting on his right hand.

The tiny chapel in Ronda bullring had no windows, but good ventilation and moody lighting. A small rectangular table, covered with an altar cloth, stood in front of the statue, a poorly polished brass cross and two fake white candles that flickered, providing someone had remembered to renew the batteries. Facing the altar was a single, well-used, wooden pew, large enough to accommodate four people. In the corner next to the door, was a rudimentary confession cubicle built out of buttermilk painted plasterboard, its entrance closed by a purple curtain. Diego wasn't praying or begging forgiveness for his undoubted multitude of sins. In fact, he was struggling not to think at all. The idea was to rid the clutter from his mind, so he could focus on the job soon to be in hand.

For this, he needed no distractions and the statue.

Diego would shortly join his cuadrilla in the arena to fight his first four-legged monster of the day. He'd seen his adversary earlier and it was a mean-looking beast, lethally sharp horns, a fearsome temper with an incredible turn of speed. Yet, his forthcoming contest against the bull was not the main item on his thought agenda. It was the telephone call from the gambling syndicate who was the cause of his mental turmoil.

Diego hadn't doubted for one moment that what the man had said was sincere. He'd checked out Donald MacKinnon which had certainly added a fresh dimension to the challenges before him. The Royal Society was no longer the only group trying to deter him from changing bullfighting.

He stood, contemplations over, his mind now ready for the dangerous challenge ahead. He was about to head toward the exit when the door opened and in stepped Fredo who closed the door behind him. They hugged.

"Sorry to barge in on you," said Fredo. "But I have to talk to you urgently."

"What do you mean?" said Diego, not wanting to be distracted from his freshly prepared mindset.

The door opened. Diego's team was outside.

"Come, we have to go now," said the picador.

"We'll talk about this later," whispered Diego as he headed past Fredo tapping him gently on the back.

Diego dismissed the Society, the gambling syndicate

and whatever Fredo's problem might be from his mind, and with a determined expression strode out to join the parade. He had a bull to fight.

24

Behind the gate where the bull enters the arena, is a narrow area where the animal is held until the president signals the go-ahead. The space is secured by two swing doors that close the gap between the inner and outer rings. The inner door opened, and the bull moved nervously forward into the space looking curiously about him, sniffing and snorting.

Amanda stood by one of the swing doors only centimeters from the bull. It was her first time up close with a fully grown Toro de Lidia and she was amazed at how massive and well-muscled it was; and those horns were terrifying. One stable hand jammed the tiny harpoon holding the owner's rosette high on its neck, the other smacked the button camera onto the bull's forehead.

The bull didn't even notice. The hands turned to Amanda with quizzical expressions. She checked the monitor. The picture was perfect, but for now, it showed the top of the arena gate.

The trumpet sounded, the gate opened, and the bull trotted into the center of the arena.

"Bull camera working," she said over the headset while watching the small monitor showing the bull's eye view of the arena. Ahead of the bull were four distinct shapes of which only one was moving. Amanda gasped as the bull charged. The image frightened her as it accelerated incredibly quickly straight at Diego, the image moving up and down slightly with each footfall of the bull. As Diego executed his Veronica, the bull's view was blinded for a second as the cape passed over his eyes. The bull stopped, spun around and attacked the shape again. She heard the crowd gasp as the bull turned and twisted relentlessly.

The camera caught Diego's expression in mid-Veronica; a look of intense concentration watching every centimeter of the bull's movements as they turned together. What a great picture, she thought.

After a while, she noticed that Diego's elegant passes with the cape were in perfect harmony with the bull's speed and head movements. Instead of appearing to be a lumbering beast, chasing a man with spindly legs and a gaudy rag, the two of them moved like well-rehearsed dance partners.

"Viva El Bailerin," yelled someone.

The responding, "Viva," was deafening.

After several minutes of nonstop charging around, Amanda noticed that the bull had started showing signs of weariness. Twisting such a weight in tight, narrow circles must be energy-sapping, she thought. She lifted her head from the fascinating action on her screen to see what was happening in the ring and spied that the bull had stopped in the center of the ring, panting heavily, head turning left and right. To her, it appeared as if he was appraising the situation. She watched as the bullfighter's gate opened and two picadors cantered in, riding blindfolded and protected horses. They were carrying long lances in their right hands and reins in their left.

She heard murmuring from the audience who seemed puzzled and mumbled questions to each other. She heard a woman nearby ask why the horsemen were carrying lances. Apparently, in the morning's newspaper, there was an article saying that today, Diego would be demonstrating his new style of bloodless bullfighting and now he wasn't.

Amanda marveled at the horses galloping around the ring. They stopped in front of the Royal Box, bowed their heads and turned to confront the bull now standing in the center of the arena unsure of himself.

The two picadors then gave a superb demonstration of horsemanship. Goading the bull to charge, then deftly avoiding him at the last moment with elegant sidesteps that forced the bull to stumble as he desperately tried to change tack and keep up with them. At the last minute, the bull was trapped between them. The riders bore down on his morillo with their lances. Then galloped off in opposite directions to thunderous applause and out of the arena.

The bull's blood began to flow.

Amanda shuddered, the injuries sickened her, and she worried about the poor bull being in pain.

The bull returned to the center of the ring. Panting heavily and looking frustrated.

Diego stepped back to the bullfighter's gate with a bow and flourish of the cape. The audience cheered. The trumpet sounded and the three banderilleros stepped forward each carrying their pair of darts. One at a time they flirted with death as they ran at the bull, dodged and leaped away at the final second with graceful athletic movements. It was an incredible spectacle that would form part of their new style of fighting. One that they had been rehearsing with live animals at the ranch all summer. One-by-one, they placed their darts precisely on target into the bulls' massive shoulders, bowed to the audience and withdrew. Their act drew a standing ovation.

"I didn't realize there was so much blood," Amanda said to the stable hand as the bull's back and shoulders slowly stained red. "Are those wounds painful?"

"Hardly," said the stable hand. "His hide is so thick the darts will feel like a pinprick."

"But surely the loss of blood tires him," she said.

"The blood will congeal," said the stable hand. "While it looks bad, the loss represents a small percentage of his total. The main objective of the lances and darts is to weaken his shoulders so that he hangs his head lower. Then it's safer for the torero to deliver the killer sword thrust over his horns."

***

Diego studied his men's performance carefully while standing by the bullfighter's gate. Their rehearsals had paid off. Using two horses instead of the usual one had added a new dimension to their show. In the new style, they would do more of this and the horses would not be blindfolded or covered in their protection. Furthermore, precisely calculated, deliberate near misses would increase thrills levels. It meant that everyone would have to increase their fitness levels as without bloodletting and muscle weakening it would take double the effort to tire the bull to a level where he could walk up to it and stroke it under the chin.

Today, however, although they were fighting under Royal Society rules, and would have to kill the bull, Diego had resolved to show a hint of their new way of fighting. So far, the crowd seemed pleased.

Let's hope it continues, thought Diego.

***

Up in the Royal Box, Diego's plan wasn't going unnoticed.

"Clever bastard," said Bosque.

"Don't worry, it's all for show," said Escobedo. "Just a hint of his blood free solution, but his fighting is still more than good enough to warrant a pardon."

"And totally within our rules," said Bosque. "Are our supporters ready?"

"Payment has been promised, providing there is a pardon. They have practiced their indultos, and will wave two handkerchiefs each," said Escobedo. "Should be a cinch."

"Amazing achievement though," said Bosque. "Three pardons in a row."

"You can't help but admire the man," said Escobedo.

***

Juan was watching from within his enclosed TV commentary booth opposite the Royal Box. So far, so good, he thought to himself.

"An amazing display," he said into the microphone. "Unprecedented athleticism and incredible bravery against a strong and intelligent bull with just a few hints on how Diego intends to change bullfighting. Now he's about to commence the final stage, the question on everyone's lips must be will he, or won't he, go for a third pardon?"

***

The trumpet sounded. Diego exchanged his capote for the red muleta and stick. The bull, though panting, seemed to have developed a second wind and was far from exhausted.

Diego's men pulled back to the perimeter. He handed his hat to his assistant, stepped toward the bull, draped the cape over the extension stick and held it in front of him.

"Toro," he called and shook the cape firmly.

The bull charged straight at Diego, but the intelligent animal had learned from his previous efforts. Instead of following the cape as Diego positioned it above his left eye, he swung his head to the right, going for Diego's ribs.

The crowd gasped. Diego stood his ground and curved his body gracefully without any hint of panic. The point of the horn missed his chest by a fraction of a millimeter. Diego span around to face the next attack. This time he was ready for the bull's new tactics and was far enough away to avoid the horn, but still close enough to draw a gasp from the crowd. This relentless attack by the bull continued for eight minutes, each time the bull lunging, and turning to lunge again and again. Diego repulsed each charge with flawless footwork and superlative Veronicas. The crowd was on its feet, many biting their fingernails as slowly and inevitably the bull began to grow weary. Eventually, Diego saw the bull's head start to droop and he paused between each charge, then finally stood still, panting. Diego stepped right up close, shaking his cape, but the bull had had enough. It was time.

Diego turned his back on the bull, bowed to the crowd and exchanged his stick for the sword. He looked up at the president and saw the white handkerchief waved to confirm the go-ahead to kill the bull. He took his stance, a couple of meters in front of the bull's head. Held the cape in his left hand and aimed the sword over the horns at the tiny killing zone between the bull's shoulder blades. He waited. The crowd fell silent.

But not for long.

A few calls of indulto echoed around the ring. Then handkerchiefs appeared by the hundred and the shouts of indulto gathered momentum.

The president waited.

The president's hand hovered over the orange handkerchief. His assistants leaned over and said something in his ear.

To Prado, it looked like they had mouthed; wait.

"Wave it, man," shouted Bosque at the president who turned to him with a confused expression.

In the sunny seats, the audience stood as one, pointed their thumbs down, and began booing. They rapidly outnumbered the indultos.

Seconds later, the President lifted his white handkerchief. It fluttered in the mild breeze.

The committee members all stood, waving and cursing at the president who appeared even more confused. His assistants made to console him and by the pats on the president's shoulder, Prado suspected that they were confirming that he'd made the right decision.

Down below, ignoring the chaos in the stands, Diego lowered the cape to the floor and shook it. The bull's eyes followed it and his head dropped. Diego leaped forward; his chest perilously close to the bull's right horn. The sword hit its small target precisely and the blade disappeared down into the bull's torso up to the hilt. The bull shook his head, staggered and dropped to the floor mortally wounded. Within seconds, it was dead. Most of the crowd applauded and cheered frantically, knowing that they had just seen the master at his best. The remainder slumped back in their seats, commiserating their lost earnings.

The president waved his blue handkerchief. Then added two white and a yellow.

The blue confirmed that bull's corpse would be dragged once around the arena for a lap of honor respecting his bravery and determination. Two white signified two ears would be awarded to Diego for such a fine performance. The yellow confirmed that Diego had made a perfect clean kill with one thrust of the sword.

The mule team entered. One assistant cut off the ears and brought them over to Diego, who showed them to the crowd to rapturous applause. Another tied a sturdy rope around the bull's front legs and torso. They towed him once around the ring and out through the stable gate.

Diego walked to Phillip, reached over the perimeter wall and accepted a cable-free microphone.

He turned it on and tested it over the arena

loudspeakers.

"Toreador," he sang from the musical Carmen in a passable tenor voice.

The crowd laughed and quietened.

***

Bosque was on his feet rushing over to the president.

"You must stop this," he said. "That man must not be allowed to speak."

"I'm sorry Don Bosque," said the President now on surer ground. "But under your own rules, a torero can thank the audience for their applause. If you look carefully, it's in the small print on the program."

Bosque returned to his seat, blue veins bulging from his nose.

"Wait until we hear what he says," said Escobedo.

***

"Señor President, honorable members of the Royal Taurino Society, Ladies and Gentlemen," said Diego. "Thank you for your recognition of what was today probably one of my hardest ever contests with a bull. It may not have been what you were expecting, and for this, I make no apology. Only to say that this contest has been arranged by the Society. It is therefore right that the bulls are fought according to their rules and regulations. You have all seen their ads promoting our national tradition and I'm sure that some of you feel proud and happy that there will be no changes under their leadership. They have made their position quite clear. Bullfighting should continue as it has for decades.

"I regret that they have been unable to accept our ideas for a more modern and caring approach. One that recognizes that bullfighting, as it stands, is a dying art. The staggering reduction in audience numbers, of which I am sure you are all aware, proves my case. Sadly, the Society's well-meaning campaign will not bring back large numbers of spectators because it addresses only those who are already avid fans. It totally ignores the youth of this country and their wishes for the future. In ten years, bullfighting will be as dead as the corpse they towed out a few moments ago.

"As the Society is not prepared to save our art, the Romero and Ordoñez families, whom you have admired in this ring and all over Spain for centuries have to come together to offer you an alternative. I give you my family and fellow supporters."

The bullfighters' gate opened and in walked twenty-three toreros dressed in their suits of light. They lined up in front of the Royal Box, bowed, turned and repeated this to the audience.

The audience stood as one and cheered louder than they had all afternoon.

Diego waited until the noise faded before continuing.

"No doubt you recognize all the familiar faces here. They need no introduction except to say that we represent twenty-four of the top forty bullfighters. Together, at the end of today's program, we are going to resign in mass from the contracts tying us to the Society and their outdated rules." Diego paused.

"We will form our own league of bullfighters and subscribe to new methods and rules that do not involve disrespect, pain, bloodletting or killing of the Toro de Lidia. Shortly, we will be broadcasting online, a documentary demonstrating what kind of entertainment you can expect to see at our contests. And no, they will not include the life and death possibilities that attract many of you to today's events. They will still offer gripping high-quality drama that exposes bullfighters to even more danger than we currently face, but more importantly, they will be much more artistic and graceful while showing respect for all the animals that we work with. Our goal is to extend the life of Spain's long relationship with man versus bull but leaving the barbaric methods of yesterday behind. We do this for our children, our grandchildren and for the good name of our country.

"We all love our toro, now it's time to stop killing him for sport, fun, art or tradition. We're about two thousand years too late but let us finally catch up with the Romans and condemn blood sports to the past. Thank you and I look forward to seeing you again for our first live entertainment here in Ronda bullring in a couple of weeks' time. It will also be broadcast on free to air TV and online. Commentary of course by my uncle, Juan Romero. I'll be back to kill my last bull ever in about forty minutes. Thank you."

25

As Diego and the members of his new league departed the arena, Inma and their sons Felix and Carlos walked down from the Royal Box to use restrooms and order a beer, closely followed by the president and his advisers.

Prado stayed behind, he wanted to keep an eye on the committee members. He'd seen their angry reaction to Diego's speech and was listening intently to their chatter. They'd huddled around Bosque in the front row. Some members expressed concern about being overheard, Bosque had taken one look at Prado who was fiddling with his mobile and plugging in his headphones. They had no idea who he was and dismissed him as unimportant.

"If I was a younger man, I'd go down and shoot the bastard," said one.

"I know how you feel," said Bosque. "However, Diego is just one member of this new group. Much as we'd like to, we can't eliminate them all. What we must do is prevent them legally from setting up in competition against us. Surely, between us, we know enough of Spain's finest lawyers to bury them in litigation. They'll be too busy defending themselves in court to actually run an event."

"Actually," said Escobedo. "There's not much in our small print to stop them. We've never discussed this possibility and our contractual wordings include nothing that we can use to even take them to court. Gentlemen, we've been lax in our responsibilities. We should have seen this coming. This young man has wiped the floor with us, and now it's too late to do anything about it."

"What do you suggest?" said Bosque tight-lipped.

"As I said before, we need to keep our enemies close," said Escobedo. "I propose that we try to make an agreement with Diego."

"Preposterous," said Pizarro, his usual apoplexy rising to the surface.

"No listen," said Escobedo. "Let us negotiate to participate in Diego's league. With the well-established and respected Society on board, working as we have always done, in a supervisory capacity, making sure of fair play and treatment of the animals and workers. It will add credibility to their offering."

"They'd insist on sharing power," said Pizarro, banging his walking stick on the seat below.

"That's reasonable," said Bosque, visualizing a tranquil retirement with the Duquesa. "It would also deter others from setting up their own league. Because once one group has split off, what is to prevent another then another? We'd be in danger of ending up like the boxing world. Six different associations, all spinoffs from the other because the greedy board members couldn't strike an agreement."

"What shall we do then?" said another.

"I propose that we vote on the matter," said Bosque.

"Seconded," said Escobedo.

"Who is for the motion to discuss a joint venture with Diego?" said Bosque. Four hands shot up. "Those against?" No hands, they'd abstained. "Then the majority has it," said Bosque relieved. "I'll go see Diego and his family at their ranch, see what we can cook up? Meanwhile, the next fight starts shortly, and I need the restroom."

Bosque grabbed hold of the low wall at the front of the box and heaved himself up. He negotiated his way carefully past the other seated members to the steps and headed down to the exit.

As he stepped into the main circular passageway leading to the restrooms, a massive pain hit him in his left arm and chest.

26

Amanda and Phillip squeezed into Juan's tiny commentary booth and leaned against the wall.

"What is the audience saying?" said Juan.

"It's mixed," said Amanda. "I was at the bulls' entrance. The people around me were probably more in favor than against but wanting more detail on what comprises the new event."

"It was the same near me," said Phillip. "Pity that we couldn't use today to demonstrate the whole thing, not just bits of it."

"I agree," said Juan. "But our lawyers insisted that while we operate under contract to the Society, we must abide by their rules. As it is, they'll be spitting blood after Diego's speech. Sorry, but I've got to squeeze this in before Macca starts with the second ball."

Amanda and Phillip listened in as Juan spoke into the microphone.

"There's a real buzz here this evening in the Ronda

bullring where Diego Romero failed to achieve his third pardon in a row. However, after an incredible display against an exceptional bull, he was awarded maximum honors. Let's have a look at the audience in this magnificent bullring as they prepare themselves for the second contest of the evening with torero Macca Cienfuegos.

"The stadium was built by the Real Maestranza de Caballería de Ronda, The Royal Cavalry. The designer Martín de Aldehuela was also the architect for the Puente Nuevo, New Bridge here in Ronda which crosses the Tajo de Ronda gorge joining the old and new parts of town. The construction of the arena took some six years and it was finally inaugurated in 1785 with a bullfight starring famous toreros including my ancestor Pedro Romero and Pepe-Hillo. It is the second oldest bullring in Spain after Sevilla, but it was the first to hold an event.

"The design concept was to portray a building of substance, in effect, a monument to bullfighting. As you can see, there are two floors, each with five rows of seats. The double gallery of arcades built in stone, with no exposed seating creates a solid, egalitarian ambiance. One hundred and thirty-six Tuscan columns form sixty-eight arches supporting a gabled roof of Arab tiles that can accommodate 6,000 spectators. At sixty-six meters diameter, the arena is considered the largest in the world. It's a spacious and elegant place for slaughtering noble beasts, and today there is not a spare seat in the house. Here's Macca now, let's wish him luck."

***

Inma and the boys returned to their places. Prado squeezed her hand as she sat next to him.

"Sorry, it took us so long, but someone had passed out in the main passageway by the east gate," she said. "The stewards directed us back here via the next entrance along. Did the old guys finish their chat?"

"Yes. I'll tell you about it later," said Prado. "Now I need the restroom. I'll be right back. Macca is about to start."

"Won't be long," he said to Seb on the way out. "Where's Tobalo?"

"He's had a bit of a shock, inspector," said Seb looking worried. "I told him to go buy himself a large Scotch."

Prado squeezed against the flow of the returning crowd in the direction of the restroom. While standing at the urinal he pondered on the committee members' conversations. It was clear that Diego was a thorn in their side but was impressed by their democratic agreement to go talk with him. A sensible solution. He concluded. They can work together to ease out bullfighting with blood, and phase in Diego's new politically correct methods. Everybody wins. On the way back, one of the stewards recognized him and beckoned him to come over.

"We have a problem," he said. "An elderly man has had a heart attack."

"Then call an ambulance," said Prado.

"We have, but it's Pablo Bosque."

Prado stopped dead in his tracks.

"Show me," he said.

The steward pressed his way through the crowded circular corridor shouting, "Medical emergency, excuse us please." The crowd moved aside, allowing the two men to rush forward. Prado saw Bosque's legs twitching but the rest of him was hidden by a green-uniformed medic on his knees, bending over Bosque's bare chest triggering a portable defibrillator. After several attempts, the medic tested for a pulse and shook his head.

"He's gone," said the medic.

The surrounding crowd hushed respectively, and stewards urged them to return to their seats.

"Someone found this near the body," said a steward to Prado showing him a mobile phone with a smashed screen.

"Thanks," said Prado, and slipped it into his pocket. "Any signs of injury?"

"No, it seems like a straightforward heart attack," said the medic.

"Nevertheless, I'd like the pathologist to check him over," said Prado. "Please deliver him to the police morgue. Should there be nothing incriminating, we'll release the body to his family immediately. I'll inform his fellow committee members and next of kin. Meanwhile, the fight is to continue."

Prado returned to his seat. Tobalo was still absent, he noted. In the arena below, Macca was about to kill his bull.

Prado stopped by Quintanilla, stooped, presented his ID, and then whispered in his ear. "I'm sorry to inform you that Señor Bosque has had a serious heart attack in the passage outside. Regretfully, he died. They'll be taking his body to the police morgue shortly. Do you have a number for his next of kin?"

Quintanilla turned pale.

"What is it?" said the woman sitting next to him.

Quintanilla indicated Prado, who repeated his

message. By now, the other members of the committee were showing an interest in Prado. Quintanilla's wife passed the message along. A heated, but whispered discussion ensued. Eventually, they all stood up, gathered their belongings and left.

Escobedo's wife slipped Prado a scrap of paper as she passed him on the way out. Prado glanced at it, it contained the name Duquesa de Aragon and a number.

Prado went up to Inma.

"What's wrong," she said. "And why have the Society members all gone?"

"The man that you saw passed out was Pablo Bosque, the chairman of the Society. Sadly, he died."

"Oh, no," said Inma putting her hand to her mouth. "What a terrible place to go?"

"Rather fitting, I thought," said Prado. "That the head of the Royal Taurino Society would pass at the bullring during one of the most significant fights of the modern era."

"I suppose you're right. You'll need to inform Diego?" she said. "His fiancée is the Duquesa's niece. "If you go now, you'll catch him before he goes into the chapel."

27

"Thanks for coming guys," said Diego to the group of bullfighters standing outside the main entrance, "Our next meeting will be at our first event. See you all in two weeks."

They raised their arms and cheered, then climbed into their respective chauffeur driven cars, and departed.

Diego went to prepare himself for his second bull. He used the rest room, then went through the solid chapel door and closed it behind him.

The confession booth curtain was closed.

He walked to the pew in front of the altar, sat down, leaned forward, rested his chin on his right hand and closed his eyes to compose himself.

Seconds later he opened them again, focused on the statue of Christ and tried to cleanse his mind of all the recent clutter.

It proved impossible.

The threat from the man at the gambling syndicate

nagged away at him. Would there be any consequences for not obeying their instructions? He wondered.

After a minute or two spent wrestling with the possibilities, he cleared his thoughts of everything and concentrated on the next bull, hoping that it would be easier than the last.

A faint noise distracted him momentarily. He turned his head towards the confession cubicle but saw nothing. He returned to his contemplations, head bowed, eyes focused on the statue.

Finally, he felt at peace.

The mental clutter began to dissipate.

He was concentrating so hard on sustaining this mindset, he failed to hear the swish of a curtain, a light footstep, followed by a scrape of metal.

He felt a thump in the center of his back. An irritation swelled his chest as if someone was scratching his heart from the inside. A vision of his beloved fiancée appeared before him and then; an inner peace settled over him.

28

Prado slipped out of the now practically empty Royal Box on his way to inform Diego about Bosque. The president was waving his white handkerchief for the next bull to enter the ring. Torero Sammi and his team were in position and ready. The trumpet sounded.

It took Prado several minutes to cover the several hundred meters along the circular stone corridor and down a flight of stairs, to the chapel entrance down on the ground floor. By then he could hear the crowd cheering the first moves of the third bull.

The chapel was located just off the main passage and only a few meters from the bullfighter's entrance into the bullring itself. The passage was deserted, but the noise of the crowd made it impossible to hear. He knocked gently on the white painted double door of the chapel and put his ear to the timber to listen for a reply but heard nothing. After a brief pause, he pulled open the door, but there was nobody there.

The purple curtain to the confession booth was

open but other than a pile of prayer books, a black robe hanging on a hook, and boxes of candles stacked on the floor, it was empty.

He shut the door behind him and went off to continue his search in the bullring café next to the main entrance. It contained a self-service counter and vending machines. Full height glazing provided views over a small terrace laid out with black metal tables and chairs, and the entrance into the arena and bullfighting museum. A hot food counter was at the far end behind which stood a couple of uniformed male chefs who looked at him expectedly.

"Any sign of Diego?" he said.

They shook their heads. "Try the guys on the terrace," said one. "They are his team."

"Thanks," said Prado going back outside.

He approached the six men dressed in their suits of light sitting around one table drinking bottles of mineral water

"Where's Diego?" he said, showing them his ID card.

"He's saying goodbye to all the toreros," said a picador. "They're outside the main gate. Then he'll go straight to the chapel."

Prado nodded and headed back into the café, through the exit into the enclosed ticket office and out to the main gate.

"Hola Raffa," he said to the steward manning the turnstile. He was a burly retired local policeman who Prado knew from old. "Have you seen Diego?"

"Yes Leon, he's gone to the chapel," said Raffa.

"How long ago?" said Prado.

"About five minutes," said Raffa.

"How come I or his men did not see him?" said

Prado. "Shouldn't we have crossed on his way there?"

"There's a short cut through this door in the outer bullring wall behind me that goes directly to the chapel and restrooms," said Raffa. "He went that way."

"Show me," said Prado.

Raffa pulled open the door and sure enough, there was the chapel door opposite and some five meters to the right, the restrooms.

Two bandoleros, one with a walking stick, were about to exit.

Prado invited them through first and then entered.

He didn't bother to knock on the chapel door this time. He opened it and went straight in. In the gloom, he could see Diego sitting upright, head bowed.

"Sorry to disturb you, Diego," said Prado. "But I have some alarming news that requires your urgent attention."

Prado waited near the door giving Diego time to finish whatever communication he may be processing. After a minute of no reply or movement, Prado cleared his throat, but there was no response.

His patience expired.

He moved forward, hand reaching out to touch Diego's shoulder, and froze.

He spotted an object sticking out of Diego's back. Prado touched his neck.

He was still warm, but there was no pulse.

29

Prado closed Diego's glassy eyes, dug out his phone and called his chief.

"I thought you were taking a few days off," said el jefe.

"Me too, but Diego Romero has been murdered in the chapel at the bullring," said Prado. "Stabbed in the back. No sign of a culprit."

"You'll be wanting the forensics A-team, then?" said the chief.

"Ana Galvez, and if possible, our top pathologist. By helicopter immediately would be even better."

"Give me a few minutes."

Prado ended the call and drew the now-closed curtain of the confession box. The black robe was no longer hanging on its hook,

but was lying on the floor in a heap.

The chief called back a few minutes later. "Helicopter ordered," he said. "The team are on their way and should arrive within the next half an hour.

You'll have to clear a landing space as near as possible to the scene and call that location through to Ana. She'll direct the pilot."

"Thanks, boss," said Prado.

"No problem, but I'm mildly concerned you investigating this case. The victim is a close relative and that could cloud your judgment."

"There's no one else up here capable, sir."

"I'm aware of that, which is why I've decided to let you run with it, but keep me informed, please. Every detail and your thoughts on the case. If I see you breaking the usual protocol, I'll pull you out immediately. Understand, inspector?"

"Yes, sir."

Prado shook his head. Of course, he understood that it should be another officer leading the case, but he was on the scene, knew the town, the people and the key players in bullfighting. No one was better qualified to lead this case than him. He brushed it from his mind, took a few photos of the scene with his phone and returned it to his jacket pocket.

He rubbed his earlobe while surveying Diego and the immediate vicinity. His mind was in a whirl, and emotions torn between duty and sadness. He'd known this young man since he was a baby, even bounced him on his knee at the occasional family event. Later, he'd admired him for his skills in the ring, and respected him as a kind and loving person. Let's find the bastard that did this, he resolved, cleared emotions out of the way and applied his head to the task.

There are no pockets on a torero's suit and there was no sign of a phone or any other items. The only potential pieces of evidence were the robe, the murder weapon and that someone had closed the confession booth curtain between his first and second visits.

Prado glanced at his watch. The timing must have been tight. He thought. It was only eleven minutes since Prado left the apparently empty chapel then returned. Eleven nerve-racking minutes hiding in the booth with the curtain closed waiting for Diego to arrive. Hoping he didn't check the booth before taking his seat. Then he had to creep out, kill Diego, and check the passageway, then leave.

"Whoever it was must have nerves of steel," muttered Prado.

Prado went around to examine Diego's back. He concluded that there was only a small spread of blood in the sky-blue suit around the entry wound and no other holes. What does that imply? He asked himself. A single blow and not a frenzied attack? The shape of the murder weapon handle reminds me of a bullfighter's sword. It must be long enough to have penetrated the heart, which explains the lack of blood. Diego must have died instantly. It's a similar killing stroke to that a bullfighter makes on the bull, I'm unsure if that was intended as an appropriate form of justice or not, he thought, but whoever did this has anatomical knowledge, and to have hit the target at the first attempt implies a person well-practiced in the art. Not necessarily strong, but an expert. Could be any gender, but with the skills of a torero or a surgeon? It also suggests that the killer may not have any, or at least a miniscule amount of blood, to clean off their person. Perhaps they went straight from here to the nearest restroom to check but leaving the chapel would risk exposure. Perhaps there was an accomplice minding the door? However, I didn't see anyone outside when I arrived, but there again, I wasn't paying attention, being too preoccupied with what I would say to Diego about Bosque.

Prado looked at the time. It was only sixteen minutes since he was first in the chapel.

It didn't give the killer much opportunity to escape, perhaps they were still in the arena? If not, what with all the crowds they couldn't have gone far. He dug out his phone again and called the local Guardia Civil captain.

"How can I help you, inspector?" said the captain.

"Someone has killed Diego Romero up here at the bullring," said Prado.

"That is a huge loss for bullfighting," said the captain.

"And his family," said Prado.

"Isn't your wife related?"

"She's his aunt," said Prado, grateful for the captain's kind words. "Listen, it's only been minutes since he was found, and the killer can't have gone far with all these crowds and lack of parking. Could you put up some roadblocks on the three main roads out of Ronda, and photograph the registration plate of every vehicle leaving town?"

"It will be difficult, inspector and will cause big problems when the crowds vacate the bullring, but I'll give the orders straight away, and call you if we find anything out of sorts."

"Thanks, captain. Much appreciated."

That was the city contained, thought Prado, now for the arena.

Prado left the chapel, closed the door behind him and ran to the café.

Diego's team was just finishing their drinks.

"Sorry to butt in gentlemen," said Prado. "But I

have some terrible news. Diego has been murdered in the chapel, and I need someone trustworthy to guard the door until forensics arrive. I also need to clear space outside for a helipad for my team. I don't have time to explain more now, but I will need to talk to you all later. Who will guard the chapel?"

"I will," said the picador, a tall, gritty man with medium length dark hair, brown eyes, and a few days stubble. He wiped the tears from his eyes with his sleeve, clearly distressed.

"What is your name?" said Prado.

"Emilio Cambron."

"Thank you, Emilio, I appreciate that it's a shock, but it's quite OK to be upset. Who will help me with the helipad?"

"Where do you want us," said the most senior of the three banderilleros.

They all followed Prado as he jogged through the yard to the exit barrier.

"Is this the only open entrance to the bullring?" he said to Raffa.

"Until the last bull is killed, all the other gates are closed," said Raffa. "This is the only way in and out, other than the staff entrance. Why what's the problem?"

"I'll tell you why later. Is someone manning the staff entrance?"

"No, access is by fingerprint scan in both directions."

"Can the staff entrance be locked?"

"Yes, I can radio my colleague in the office, he can do it from the control panel."

"Please do so, and do not let anyone in or out of here until further notice," said Prado as they ran out to liaise with the local police supervising the outer areas of the bullring.

He sought out the most experienced man and was relieved to find Pepe, a former colleague from his Legion days, talking with two officers outside the east gate.

Pepe stiffened to attention as Prado approached.

"Stand easy, Pepe. Listen, Diego Romero has been murdered in the chapel. Forensics will be leaving Málaga shortly in their scene of crime helicopter. I need a place for them to land on the bullring concourse. Can you arrange it, please? These three are members of Diego's team and will help. I must run. Any questions?"

"No worry, sir," said Pepe. "Leave it with us."

Prado headed back to the main entrance dug his phone out of his jacket and called Phillip.

"Where are you?" he said, when Phillip responded.

"In the hotel room looking at the footage we've taken so far, why?"

"Someone has killed Diego; I need images of the crowd to look at later. Can you request your drone cameraman to do that please?"

"Straight away, anything else we can do to help?"

"Not at the moment, talk later."

Prado went back to Raffa at the bullfighter's entrance where a small crowd was gathering bombarding Raffa with questions.

"Sorry, but you'll have to leave this area," shouted Prado. "There'll be a helicopter landing here shortly."

Pepe came over from standing by the statue of a running bull outside the main entrance and escorted the curious onlookers away.

"Thanks, Pepe," said Prado.

"We've sorted a landing spot, sir," said Pepe. "It's between the bull's statue and the rear entrance to the hotel Parador but the pilot will have to drop straight down. There are power and communications cables all over the place."

"OK, I'll inform the pilot when they're on their approach, thanks."

Prado turned to Raffa.

"Do you have any security cameras covering this or any other gate?" he said.

"The only camera is at the ticket office," said Raffa.

"Have you let anyone in, or out of here in the last half an hour?"

"Several; let me think a minute," said Raffa his mind churning as he recapped the visitors. He held up his hand and tapped each finger as he explained his mental list.

"As I recall," said Raffa. "Diego and the toreros came out first and said their farewells. Diego went back in on his own, then there was...."

"Did they have tickets, passes or some kind of authority for you to grant them access?" said Prado taking a notebook and pen out of his inner jacket pocket and jotting down Raffa's list.

"The toreros had guest passes that they all handed back to me as they left."

"Does that mean everyone who enters this building is identified by a ticket or pass?"

"Everyone except those in the Royal Box such as yourself Leon. Furthermore, in order to buy a ticket, the purchaser must register their National ID, any foreigners their passports."

"What about when they leave?"

"We don't check them leaving, only if they intend

to return. Then they have to inquire at the security office for a passout stamp."

"Are you sure that all the toreros left?"

"Positive. I counted twenty-three in, and the same out."

"And you recognized every one of them?"

"Of course, they've all fought here over the years."

"So, you're sure that none of them could have switched suits and remained behind?"

"Absolutely."

"Good, continue with the list," said Prado.

"Fredo Ordoñez left about fifteen minutes ago. He didn't look at all well and ignored me when I offered assistance. He hasn't been back. A couple of stewards popped out for a smoke. A priest arrived a few minutes before Diego went back in."

"What was the priest wearing?"

"The usual black robe."

"Did you recognize him?"

"No, but he had a pass. He explained that he was standing in for Father Ignacio Martin who was off sick. Then there were two bandoleros. They didn't have a pass, but one needed a pee desperately and I felt sorry for him, so admitted them through the short-cut."

"Was there anything special about them that earned such kindness?"

"The one that wanted the restroom was disabled. He used a walking stick and occasionally, his friend had to help him over the tricky cobble-stones."

"How long were they inside?"

"No more than ten minutes."

"Can you describe them?"

"Difficult, they wore baggy clothes, sunglasses and bandanas partly covered their heads although the disabled one had some strands of red hair sticking out from under the bandana."

"Were they Spanish?"

"The disabled one didn't say anything, but the guy that spoke was definitely, but not a local accent, more Madrid."

"Anything else distinguishing about them?"

"Both about my size, the guy with red hair looked about mid-forties. The other much younger; twenties or so, I would guess."

"OK, thanks. From now on people may leave but make a note of their name and ID number. Forensics will be arriving within half an hour or so. You will be relieved then."

Prado headed for the arena manager's office in the administrative block to the rear of the café. On the way, he phoned the Duquesa's number. Her voicemail answered.

"I need to speak to you, it's urgent," he said and hung up the phone.

She called him right back.

"Sorry, Inspector Prado, but I never answer unknown numbers," she said in beautiful Spanish. "How can I help you?

"I'm sorry to disturb you Ma'am, but I'm the holder of some bad news and wanted to inform you as quickly as possible before the TV news picked it up."

"Is it my husband?"

"Yes, ma'am. He's had a major heart attack here in Ronda Bullring, sadly, he didn't survive."

The line went dead.

Prado considered calling again but thought it politic to leave her alone with her grief. He texted a message offering his services at any time.

He arrived at the manager's tiny office at the back of the café to find complete chaos. Several journalists were demanding to know what was happening with the ambulance crew. They were also complaining about the entrance to the chapel being blocked by a picador as they were keen to interview Diego about his speech. Just to add to the bedlam, a couple of stewards were demanding permission to open the gate nearest the ambulance to transport Bosque's heavy corpse, the shortest possible distance.

The manager was a man of similar age and height to Prado, but a lot thinner. He had well-defined crow's feet, cropped hair, and a Roman nose. He was harassed and refusing to open an exit gate. Prado barged his way through to stand by the manager. He held up his ID and waited for silence.

"My name is Detective Inspector Prado of the National Police," he said. "I regret to inform you that the bullring is now a serious crime scene, and I need the calm cooperation of everyone. First, we need to extract the body of a heart attack victim as soon as possible before our helicopter arrives. Stewards, please open the east gate immediately, and then close it as soon as the stretcher has gone through."

Prado waited while the stewards departed, then said.

"Would everybody else, except the manager, leave now. Either return to your seats or leave the stadium."

"What is going on, inspector?" said a journalist holding up a camera and taking photos of Prado.

"Why aren't we allowed in the chapel?" said another.

"Leave now," shouted Prado. "And if I see one single image of me in any of your publications, you will personally be arrested. Am I clear?"

The journalists left, saying nothing.

Finally, Prado was alone with the manager.

There was a plastic sign on his desk. Mateo Chacon, it said.

"Señor Chacon," said Prado as he took a seat opposite. "This is not your day; we also have a murdered torero in the chapel."

"Is it Diego?" said Chacon.

"I'm afraid so," said Prado. "He's been stabbed. Have you seen anything suspicious in the last half an hour?"

"No, I've been busy in here. How can I help?" said Chacon.

"I need a list of all staff, visitors, guests, and the audience," said Prado. "Is that possible without too much work?"

"Yes, I can collate the data into an Excel file and email it to you," said Chacon. "By Monday morning?"

"That's fine," said Prado. "Do you have any procedure in place for eventualities of this nature? Only, I don't want to alarm or disappoint the crowd, and I'm conscious that Diego was due on next."

"We have an emergency evacuation plan," said Chacon. "But the only similarity to this I can think of is when a torero is killed. He's carted off to the morgue and the next on the list finishes off his bull then carries on as usual with theirs."

"Mmm...," pondered Prado. "In that case, can we announce that due to unforeseen circumstances, Diego's bull will now be fought by Macca? The crowd should still receive full value for their tickets and at the end, we can announce Diego's death. By then forensics should have arrived and have taken any samples they may need before the crowds trample over everything."

"No problem, inspector. When Sammi has finished with his current bull, we'll make the announcement. Normally, I would inform the president, but now, won't have time. Could you tell him?"

"Yes, I have to inform my wife in the Royal Box. She'll be wondering what I'm up to."

"Anything else?"

"Yes, I require the restrooms nearest the chapel sealed off, but with subtlety. Can you arrange something?"

"Locked doors with an out of order sign should do the job."

"Tell me about your regular priest."

"Father Ignacio usually attends. Some of the toreros like to confess prior to their fight. Others are worried that they may be seriously injured or killed and prefer a priest is on hand to deliver the last rights."

"I understand that Father Ignacio was off sick."

"I wasn't aware of that. Then who came instead?"

"You tell me."

Chacon tapped his desktop computer and read whatever page he'd found.

"It was a last-minute replacement. One of the Franciscan monks from the local monastery stood in for him, a Father Jacobo. He called the office some twenty minutes before Diego's first bull, and we emailed him a pass."

"To what address?"

"Fatherjacobo@gmail.com."

"Does the monastery not have its own website or email server?"

"Not that I know of. Father Ignacio also uses Gmail."

"Do you have a photo or any ID?"

"No, just his name. As I said, it was a last-minute thing. Normally, we wouldn't be so obliging, but he was a priest after all, and we had to have one here."

"Do you have the monastery number?"

"Not even sure if they have a phone. I have Father Ignacio's if that will help."

Prado stabbed the father's email addresses and numbers into his phone.

"Thank you, Señor Chacon," said Prado. "Please keep me posted with any abnormalities. Especially, among the staff."

They exchanged visitor cards and Prado headed back up to the Royal Box. He went via the chapel where the picador was pacing up and down outside the door struggling with his emotions. He stopped pacing when he saw Prado, his eyes moistening.

Prado gripped his shoulder and tapped it a couple of times.

"Any idea who did it, inspector?" said the picador.

"Not yet, Emilio, but don't worry. We'll find them. You were obviously close to Diego. Can you think of any enemies that might have wanted him dead?"

"Bullfighters have many adversaries especially among animal lovers, but they want to stop him killing bulls not see him dead. It could have been those bastards at the society, but recently some new rumors have started doing the rounds."

"Such as?" said Prado

"Apparently, a bookie has been offering large sums for bullfighters to throw fights or get themselves deliberately injured in specific body parts at an agreed time."

"Did any of you know bullfighters that might be doing that?"

"No, it was only a rumor."

"There's often no smoke without fire," said Prado. "But thank you, I'll keep the society and bent bookies in mind."

"Will it be long before I can be relieved? It's just that our team has a lot of talking to do about our future. Without Diego, I don't see how we can continue with this new version of bullfighting."

"I understand, but knowing the Romero family as I do, they'll be even more determined to make it work now. Diego wasn't working alone, and each family member won't want to see his death go in vain. We'll relieve you in about twenty minutes, OK?"

"I'll be fine. No one will enter this chapel. Believe me."

"That I do."

"Thank you, Emilio."

Emilio puffed out his chest, set his jaw into a grimace and went about the business of guarding the body of his boss.

Prado jogged back to the Royal Box on the upper floor. A pale Tobalo had replaced Seb on the door. "You OK?" said Prado as Tobalo let him in.

"Thanks for asking, inspector, I've had a few personal problems but I'm recovering," said Tobalo nervously.

The Royal box was practically empty. Inma and the boys stood as Prado climbed up the steps towards them.

"Are you OK?" said Inma. "You've been ages."

"Sorry my love and darling boys but there's a lot more going on than the demise of Pablo Bosque." He put his arm around Inma and hugged her tight. "It's

Diego," he said. "He's been murdered in the chapel."

Inma looked up at him failing to comprehend the meaning of his words. She shook her head and said, "Diego what?"

"Diego has been killed my love. I am so sorry."

Inma burst into tears. Prado patted her back. Their boys stood and joined them, each struggling to control their emotions. Diego was a favorite cousin with whom they had spent many happy childhood hours.

"Sorry, everyone, but as the most senior officer on the scene, I've had to take charge. I can't stay long."

"I must tell Diego's mother," said Inma recovering quickly. She sat back down and extracted her phone from her purse.

"Darling, can I leave you to inform all the family and Diego's fiancée," said Prado.

She nodded vigorously and said, "Go; get the bastard," said Inma waving him away urgently.

Prado moved the few rows down and stood behind the president who was busy awarding a blue handkerchief to Sammi's first bull. Prado bent down and whispered the situation in his ear. The president gasped but nodded and continued his hankie waving with renewed vigor.

Prado's phone buzzed. It was a text message from Ana Galvez, the helicopter was approaching Ronda. Prado called her with the landing directions. As he walked towards the exit, he called Pepe to warn him of its imminent arrival.

On his way back past the chapel, Prado heard the manager's announcement over the PA system about Diego's unavoidable withdrawal from the contest. Prado heard the crowd's reaction. It was a mixture of anger and confusion.

30

The downdraft from the police helicopter stirred up a whirlpool of dust and scraps of paper, as it hovered over the bullring concourse. What with overhead cables, valuable statues, dense crowds, and trees, the pilot had a tricky job to find a clear landing place. Delicately, he lowered the noisy machine into what seemed an impossible space. As soon as he touched the ground, the side door opened and out jumped Ana and Daniel Hidalgo, the provincial pathologist, bags in hand, already dressed in white protective suits.

Prado led them to the murder scene, pointed out the restrooms that needed their attention and opened the chapel door. They donned their head and shoe covers then went in. Prado released the picador from his guard duties and followed.

While Ana scanned the chapel interior and confession box, Daniel, a short, slender man with dark hair, brown eyes and a pencil mustache, examined Diego's body. Prado waited by the door. Despite the inherent urgency he wanted to inject into their slow and painfully detailed work, he knew from experience, it was best to leave them to it. They were thorough professionals. If there were anything to be found, they would discover it eventually.

Ana bagged a few samples and recorded several prints then examined the discarded robe in the confession box. She confirmed that there were some bloodstains on the outside around waist height.

Prado accompanied her to the male restroom and watched as she scanned the sinks, the urinals then the cubicles for bloodstains. She shook her head and they moved into the ladies. There was nothing there either.

"I suggest that the killer wiped their hands on the robe then threw it on the floor," she said. "Other than several prints and a few hairs, I've not found anything useful."

Prado extracted Bosque's phone from his jacket pocket and passed it to Ana. "This belongs to the Chairman of the Taurino Society, the heart attack victim. He was using it when he collapsed. As he's a potential enemy of Diego, test it, and if possible, let me know his recent calls and texts. Then analyze his contacts for anything out of the ordinary and crosscheck with our databases."

Ana took the phone, bagged it, and then added it to her backpack. They both returned to the chapel to find the local police morgue crew ready to take the body.

"I've done all I can here," said Daniel. "Time of death within the last two hours. The post-mortem may reveal more but I doubt it. He died instantly from a single thrust into the heart with what I am sure will turn out to be a bullfighter's sword when I've pulled it out. This was not a lucky blow. The killer knew exactly what they were doing."

"You think it could be another bullfighter, or a surgeon?" said Prado.

"Yes, but also consider veterinary, butcher or military," said Daniel. "And no student either. Someone most proficient at what they do. Is there a relative around that can confirm ID?"

"His father's deceased and his mother's at home. I'll bring his uncle to the local morgue. While you're there, can you take a quick look at Pablo Bosque? He had a heart attack shortly before the murder. I don't suspect any foul play, but just make sure. I'd like to release the body to the family as soon as possible."

"I will inspect his body thoroughly, inspector," said Daniel. "There is no such thing as a quick look in this profession."

The bearers lifted Diego from the pew, laid him on the stretcher face down, zipped him into a body bag and carried him off to the mortuary van. Daniel followed them carrying the discarded robe now sealed in a clear plastic bag and labeled.

Ana had gone back to the helicopter to use the onboard equipment to analyze the prints and compare them with the police database.

***

The crowd's initial enthusiasm had mellowed, thought Prado as a steward led the way up the steps into the banks of concrete seats. Anyway, they're certainly quieter and are chatting among themselves rather than watching the next fight. Perhaps, it was the manager's announcement that Diego would no longer be participating that afternoon, and they're speculating as to why. He made up his mind there and then to tell them personally before they left the arena.

Prado was surprised to see that the priest seated at the end of the front row was a slender young man in his mid-twenties, with an unruly mop of black hair wearing blue jeans, a loose white linen shirt, and expensive-looking sunglasses. Unlike his neighbors who were busy chatting among themselves, he was keenly watching the action. Prado crouched next to him in the stairway and spoke quietly into his ear.

"Sorry to disturb you, Father," he said showing his ID. "There's been an incident in the chapel that I need to discuss with you privately. Would you mind accompanying me there?"

"Certainly inspector," said the priest, a concerned expression darkening his mood.

They chatted as they walked up the terrace steps, through the entrance and into the circular corridor that provided access to all the ground floor seating areas.

"Is there anything wrong with Father Ignacio?" said Prado.

"Regretfully, a dose of food poisoning," said the Father. "Some dodgy mussels for lunch on his way to the visit the good sisters at the convent; so, the mother superior informed me."

"Hence your last-minute replacement. Have you been in Ronda long?" said Prado.

"I arrived at the monastery from Toledo only a couple of weeks ago," said Jacobo. "May I ask as to what sort of incident you want to discuss. Might it be something connected with Diego? It's just that the crowd were speculating about him. What with the ambulance sirens, then the manager's announcement, followed by the helicopter noise?"

"How long have you been in your seat?"

"Regretfully, I just missed Diego's epic performance."

"Have you left for any reason?"

"No. I wouldn't miss a minute."

"You enjoy bullfighting?"

"I love it, my father was an avid attendee at Pamplona bullring. He always took me with him, and I ran with the bulls as a teenager. However, that was before my calling."

"Thank you, father, but what I really need to talk to you about concerns Diego," Prado checked to ensure that nobody was near enough to hear before saying quietly, "He's been murdered in the chapel."

The father crossed himself.

They arrived at the chapel where a local officer was now guarding the door. He nodded to the inspector and opened it for them. They walked in.

"Does everything seem as it should be?" said Prado.

The priest looked around. "When I left, the curtain to the confessional box was open like now but the robe that I hung on the hook has gone."

"I can confirm that there was a robe there," said Prado. "Was it yours?"

"Yes, I hung it up before leaving for my seat. It's too hot to wear outside."

"We found it in a heap on the floor. We think that the murderer used it to wipe their hands. There were a few blood stains."

"Will you need some samples from me for elimination purposes?"

"We will indeed. Do you mind if we go and see our forensics officer by the helicopter now?" said Prado escorting the father back outside in the direction of the concourse.

"I have some photos of the robe," said Prado swiping his phone screen and showing them to the father as they walked. "Can you confirm that it resembles yours?" The father regarded the images closely and nodded. "We are keeping the robe in the lab for more tests. You'll get it back in due course."

At the helicopter, Prado introduced the priest to Ana and watched as she collected her samples from him.

"When you've finished with the Father," he said. "He's free to go."

His phone rang. It was the captain of the Guardia Civil.

"My roadblock team has just delivered a man to the barracks," said the captain. "They stopped him while driving a shabby white Range Rover on the road to Jerez. We suspect that he's Diego's killer."

"Why?" said Prado.

"He was desperate to get away from us," said the captain. "And he's in hell of a state, but more importantly for you has a bloodstain on his shirt, his right sleeve, and traces of dried blood on his hands."

"Name?" said Prado.

"He won't tell us," said the captain. "Insists on talking only to you."

"Have you checked his documents?"

"He's not carrying any, and the vehicle is registered to a company."

"Can you bring him to the bullring?"

"We could. However, given that it will be emptying out soon, it will be quicker for all if you could walk to the barracks."

"I can't leave the crime scene just yet; can you hold

him for a while?"

"No problem."

"What charges are you using?"

"Take your pick. He damn near killed one of my officers at the roadblock. We had to shred his tires to stop him. Add to that speeding, dangerous driving, no vehicle safety certificate or insurance and while he passed the breathalyzer test, we think he might be on something."

"Then hold him pending my arrival, but don't leave him on his own, he sounds deranged and could be suicidal. I'll need the results of some tests before I see him. Remove his shirt, take his prints and a scraping of the blood on his hand. Have an officer deliver them by motorbike to the forensics helicopter on the bullring concourse as soon as you can please."

Prado swiped end call turned back to Ana and said, "A suspect has been arrested at a Guardia Civil roadblock and is being held in their cells. Before I interview him, I need his prints checked and some blood samples found on his hands and clothing analyzed. They will be delivered to you directly. I'll be in the arena if you need me."

He had an announcement to make to the crowd.

Prado was well accustomed to informing distraught relatives about the unexpected death of a loved one, but he'd never had to tell six thousand fans about the loss of their favorite celebrity. Rather than use the public address microphone hiding away in Chacron's cubbyhole of an office, he wanted to address the crowd personally. The manager escorted him to the bullfighter's gate, where Sammi was waving a pair of bull's ears to the crowd. They were cheering, but only out of politeness. With all the distractions, the crowd had understandably lost their initial verve and enthusiasm for this year's La Goyesca.

Chacron handed him the same cable-free microphone that Diego had used earlier. Prado waited until the mule team had dragged out the sixth bull and as most of the audience stood to collect their belongings, he spoke.

"Ladies and Gentlemen," he said. "My name is Detective Inspector Prado of the National Police. I'm sorry to interfere with your valuable time, but before you go home, I need to advise you of some alarming developments at the arena this afternoon. After that, I need you to help me."

Prado paused for them to turn and face him. He glared at the people nearest to him, and gradually an expectant silence settled over the arena.

"I regret to inform you that two of bullfighting's outstanding personalities have died here this afternoon. The first was Don Pablo Bosque, Chairman of the Royal Taurino Society. He suffered a fatal heart attack.

"The second was Diego Romero. He was found murdered in the bullring chapel shortly before his second appearance."

Prado waited until the crowd's astonished reaction calmed down.

"Now, how can you help?" Prado said. "If you visited the restrooms, walked around the arena, or passed by the chapel, you could have seen something, or someone, that might give us a clue to finding Diego's killer. If anyone does have such information, no matter how insignificant it may seem, there will be several officers standing by each gateway as you leave.

Please tell them what you saw and leave your contact details. Thank you."

Prado returned the microphone to Chacron and instructed.

"Please keep the stadium open until I return and provide drinks to my officers."

Chacron nodded and walked off in the direction of his office.

Prado walked along the inner ring toward the gate that led up to the commentary box. He politely forced his way against the stream of spectators and went up to see Juan. He wondered how he was feeling.

He found Juan with his head in his hands, weeping quietly. His headset discarded on the table in front of him. Prado put his arm around his dear friend's shoulder and hugged him. Juan looked up, tears rolling down his cheeks. Prado had never seen his usually tough friend so upset about anything.

"I suppose you need me to identify him?" said Juan.

"Sorry, but there isn't anyone else," said Prado passing Juan a handkerchief. "But only when you're ready."

Juan wiped his eyes and stood up. "Any ideas on who killed him?"

"Several," said Prado. "However, the Guardia have arrested a suspect trying to smash through their roadblock. He has blood on his shirt and is acting in a disturbed manner. I'm on my way to interview him at the barracks now. Care to walk with me?"

"Then let's get it over with," said Juan collecting himself.

They joined in the mass exodus edging their way through the main exit out onto the concourse. It was usually a fifteen-minute walk from the bullring to the

Guardia Civil barracks on Avenida Málaga. This evening, the streets were hot and with all the perspiring bodies in such proximity, the humidity was uncomfortable. They took off their jackets and draped them over their shoulders. Prado couldn't help but listen in to conversations as he walked among them. The majority were asking the same questions as he was to himself. Who would want to kill Diego Romero and why?

"This might seem a little insensitive right now," said Prado. "But Diego's team are already talking about the future. They'll be looking to you to take over and launch the new version."

"I'm aware of that," said Juan. "I'm thinking about calling a meeting with everyone."

"Did Diego have any particular requests?"

"All bullfighter's leave descriptions for their disposal, Leon. When can you release the body?"

"Probably tomorrow, maybe sooner, it depends on what the pathologist has to say," he said.

Some twenty minutes later, Prado and Juan arrived at the Guardia Civil. The captain, a rough-looking stocky man in a smartly pressed uniform came to the reception to meet them.

"Cristobal Mendez," he said shaking hands. He escorted them to the police morgue next door.

Daniel had been supervising the local pathologist in his laboratory. They'd finished their work and were cleaning their equipment when Prado and Juan arrived.

"Ah, Prado," said Daniel. "We've had a look at Don Bosque and can confirm that he died of natural causes, a severe heart attack. Ana has checked his phone and there's nothing on it that causes concern. The family undertakers are collecting his remains in the morning.

Is this Diego's relative?"

"Juan Romero, his uncle," said Prado.

"I'm so sorry for your loss," said Daniel. "Step this way, please."

"Have you finished with Diego?" said Prado.

"Yes, I still need to type up my report, but it was just as I explained at the chapel. A bullfighter's sword straight into the heart. He would have died instantly."

"After we've seen the body, could I take a look at the sword?" said Juan. "I may recognize it?"

"Certainly," said the pathologist stopping by a stack of fridges. He opened the middle one, slid it out and slipped back a white cloth to reveal Diego's face. He looked peaceful but pale. Juan looked at Diego for a second, nodded at the pathologist then bent over and kissed his nephew's forehead. Prado did the same. The pathologist replaced the cloth and slid the drawer back into the rack, closing the door with a solid clunk. He walked over to a side table, slipped on a pair of white gloves and picked up a short sword. He held it up for Juan and Prado to inspect.

"Can you hold it upright and show me the top of the blade under the hilt," said Juan.

The pathologist followed his instructions. Juan peered closely at three initials stamped into the shiny metal. 'S.M.B'.

"Do they mean anything to you?" said the pathologist.

"Samuel Martinez Bettencourt," said Juan. "It's one of Sammi's swords, but it couldn't have been Sammi that killed Diego. He abhors being left alone on fight days. His team would have been with him every second. This is probably one of his reserve swords, bullfighters carry at least three."

"Where are spare swords kept during a fight?" said Prado.

"The sword assistant would carry one and hold one spare by the ring edge, any others would be in their changing rooms at the bullring," said Juan.

"Is it possible to access these changing rooms without being seen?" said Prado.

Juan thought for a moment. "Unlikely, the entrance is through a locked door next to the café. Only bullfighting team members have keys."

Prado dug his phone out of his jacket pocket, called Ana and said, "Can you talk with Sammi and have him check the whereabouts of his swords, then check the changing and restrooms for prints and samples."

Ana confirmed.

He then called Chacron.

"Can you escort my forensics officer to the bullfighter's changing rooms, please? She needs to know who has access to them and to check for prints etc."

"Of course, inspector."

"Are we done, inspector?" said the pathologist.

"For now, yes. When can you release Diego?" said Prado.

"His body holds no more clues for us I'm afraid. You may take him as soon as you wish."

Prado raised his eyebrows at Juan.

"I'll have to consult the family first," said Juan digging his phone out of his pocket and flicking through his contacts. "I'll let you know in the morning."

"Inma would have informed the family by now," said Prado.

"What would I do without you dear friend?" said

Juan as they returned to the Guardia reception.

"You'd cope, just as we all have to in tragic circumstances."

They hugged and said their farewells. Juan walked out the front door, phone to his ear.

The Guardia captain escorted Prado to the cells. Down in the basement, they entered a dimly lit passageway with three cells on each side. A warder was standing by the first cell door. He inserted a key, opened it, checked the prisoner and stood back.

The captain indicated that Prado should go first. Prado strode into the tiny, hot and humid room. The cell stank of urine, unwashed bodies, and a hint of vomit. A cockroach scuttled under the lower bunk bed. There was a full bucket in the corner, a small skylight was jammed shut, and the solitary ceiling light flickered on and off.

Sitting in the shadows of the lower bunk sobbing and looking extremely vulnerable and sorry for himself was a bare-chested Fredo wearing jeans, belt, and slip-on shoes. He looked up as they entered. His tear-stained eyes said it all. Prado's instinct was to take him in his arms and hug him.

The pathetic look on Fredo's face turned into one of relief as he recognized his brother-in-law.

The captain touched Prado's arm and passed him a slip of paper.

"From Doctor, Galvez," he said.

Prado glanced at the message. 'Blood on Fredo's shirt and hands matches Diego's. Fredo's prints on handle of murder weapon. Blood on priest's robe was Diego's."

"Fredo," said Prado. "As we're related, we will

interview you formally under caution. Captain, could you have Fredo cleaned up, find him a shirt to wear then bring him up to an interview room?"

"Sure," said the captain.

***

The brightly lit interview room was on the first floor. It was sparsely furnished with a wood laminate table, four blue plastic chairs and a stained framed photo of the King on one wall, a large rectangular mirror on the opposite. The glow of streetlights and fading twilight outside could be seen through a barred frosted window.

Prado and the captain sat down. A pen, notepad and an antiquated MP3 recording device were on the table. Fredo was brought in by his warder in handcuffs now wearing a white round-necked Ronda soccer team shirt. He sat down opposite them; the warder stood behind him.

The captain turned on the recorder, then announced the date, time and those present. He then deferred to Prado.

"Fredo," said Prado. "Tell me in your own words what happened in the bullring chapel this afternoon."

Fredo looked at Prado, his right eye twitching. He shook his head. "I didn't kill him, Leon."

"You'll have a hard job convincing me Fredo. A court would have no problem convicting you on the evidence currently against you," said Prado.

"I realize that, but when I entered the chapel, Diego was already dead."

"What made you draw that conclusion?"

"At first, I thought he was praying, but as I drew

closer, I saw a sword handle sticking out from the top of his back. I checked his pulse and realized he was dead. For the following few seconds, I'm not sure what happened to my head. It was like a brainstorm. Thinking about it now, it must have been a mixture of shock, sadness, anger, and terror. When I recovered, I found that I'd stupidly attempted to pull the sword out but couldn't move it, and then I heard voices outside. I looked at the blood on my hands and wondered what it would look like if someone came in. It was then that I twigged that the situation could look bad for me, so I waited by the door until it was quiet. I then headed home to give me time to think it through."

"Before you left. Did you notice the curtain on the confession box?"

"It was open. There was a black robe on the floor"

"Did you wipe your hands on anything?"

"There wasn't much blood, I cleaned what little there was from my hand onto my shirt and pants and then inside my pocket."

"Why were you in the chapel?" said Prado.

"I had no choice."

"Why?"

"Because I'm in a terrible mess."

"What sort of mess?"

"I'm an addicted gambler and owe vast sums of money to my bookie."

"How much exactly?"

"Over two million."

"That's far worse than a terrible mess," said Prado standing and raising his fist to strike Fredo. "It's a fucking disgrace. What the hell were you thinking?"

The captain restrained Prado with a hand on his shoulder and indicated that he should resume his seat.

Prado turned off the recorder and slumped back in his chair. "Have you considered the shame your actions will do to the family?" he said. "Or the damage it could do to Diego's campaign against the Society, let alone how Diego's fiancée might be feeling?"

"Of course, but I couldn't help it. It's er… like a sickness."

"That's pathetic."

"I know. Will sorry help?"

"I doubt it. OK, so you're in a mess and you go to the chapel," Prado was calmer now. "Were you going to ask Diego to pay your debts?"

"I considered it but chickened out. Actually, I went to the chapel twice."

"When was the first time?"

"Just before Diego's first bull. I went to warn him."

"Despite the fact that he hates being disturbed before a fight?"

"As I said, I was desperate, and wasn't concerned about his feelings."

"What were you going to say to him?"

"That the Society would not be happy if he killed the bull."

"And how did Diego react?"

"I arrived too late to tell him. He was just leaving for the ring."

"Tell me what the Society asked you to do."

"They didn't ask. It was made quite clear, that unless I did as I was told, I would be banned from my job as their adviser, wouldn't be allowed to practice my profession with Toro de Lidia bulls, and, they would expose my gambling and financial mess to the media."

"Powerful motivations for murder Fredo."

Fredo put his head in his hands and wept.

"Fredo," said Prado. "Did you kill Diego?"

"No," said Fredo raising his head, his eyes bloodshot. "However, I admit that I went to the chapel the second time to kill him."

"Kill a member of your own family, but why?"

"If Diego did kill the first bull, the society ordered me to execute him."

"Who in the committee instructed you?"

"Zambrano."

"When?"

"Last week, I went up to Madrid to collect a silenced pistol and final instructions from him."

"Where did you meet?"

"In the Society's offices."

"Was anyone else there? Bosque for example?"

"No, just Zambrano."

"Clearly you didn't shoot him, but where did you get the sword?"

"I told you. I didn't have a fucking sword. He was already dead."

"What did you do with the pistol?"

"I dumped it in a trash can by the restrooms at the car park before I headed home."

"Which parking?"

"The lot behind the church on Avenida Poeta Rilke."

"You realize, we will check that?"

"Leon, I'm not lying to you," said Fredo.

"You better not be. Tell me about the bookies and how you got into this mess?"

"I was bored. I live on my own with just the housekeeper for companionship. I have no girlfriend, hobby, or interests other than my work, so I started betting on bullfights and found I was good at it. After a while, I grew frustrated with the limited options and small stakes. I wanted larger risks and bigger rewards. I asked around and someone told me about Dabblers."

"What are Dabblers?"

"It's on the dark web, a site that specializes in bullfight betting."

"Who introduced you to them?"

"Zambrano."

"Didn't you think that might not be a coincidence?"

"No. I was too obsessed to think beyond my immediate lust for higher risks and rewards."

"So, you signed up with Dabblers?"

"Yes. At first, I played the standard stuff on their members' website, but the limit was five thousand per bet. I was doing well and wanted to up the stakes but wasn't sure how. Then at the end of my first membership year, a man called Patrick contacted me and said that, as I was such a good customer, he could offer me a more personal service for larger stake betting. We met, and he explained that in addition to their website, they provided tailor-made betting. I could negotiate a credit limit and bet as much as I wanted on any category. I preferred betting on bullfighters' likelihood of injury because I know bulls so well and can tell if a torero is likely to survive unscathed or not. Sadly, I've lost my touch. I've been losing for months now and have stupidly accumulated this huge debt. Today though, I've really gone way over the top and completely blown all my wealth, and all because of Diego. He had let it be known among his immediate circle that he was going for a third and fourth pardon, I'd bet the remainder of my credit limit on him doing just that. If he succeeded, I'd balance my account and more but as you saw, he killed the bull.

Why did he change his mind?"

"No idea, but don't try blaming your own mistakes on what Diego said, or didn't say. This is all down to your own failings Fredo. Where do you go to place your bets?"

"I do it on my phone."

"Do you know where your payments go?"

"All the financial transactions are offshore in Gibraltar. I transfer money to them, and any winnings are paid to me there."

"Where is the Dabbler's account located?"

"I don't know where. I just have an IBAN number and BIC code, but I guess my bank could find out from those."

"What happens when your account is empty?"

"I meet Patrick's representative outside my bank in Sevilla or Ronda and pay cash."

"Is this always the same person?"

"Apart from the twice I met Patrick, yes."

"What did Patrick look like?"

"Sort of Viking type. Long red hair, big sunglasses, your height, well built. Not a man you'd argue with, but I did feel some empathy with him."

"Why?"

"He has a bad leg like me and uses a walking stick."

"And the other guy?"

"He's a Spaniard, ex-military I would say. Good looking, dark hair. Actually, I have them both on film."

"Where?"

"It's at the ranch on my pen drive, along with other stuff."

"What other stuff?"

"I can't recall everything, but there are recordings of conversations with Patrick about credit limits and arranging payments."

"Why did you record the meetings?"

"Er… not sure. I guess I knew I was getting in deep and wanted back up if the shit hit the fan."

"OK, makes sense I guess," said Prado. "How do you contact Patrick?"

"We communicate using WhatsApp in English."

"He's English?"

"I am no expert, but I'd say Scottish or Irish. Not sure though."

"Where did you meet him?"

"As I just said, I've only met him twice, both times outside my bank in Ronda."

The captain looked at Prado and rose from his seat. "Can I have a quick word," he said glancing at Fredo. "In private."

"OK," said Prado.

Prado stood and the two men walked to the corner of the room.

"May I suggest," said the captain, his voice was hushed, little more than a whisper. "That we adjourn this interview for now. I'm concerned that Señor Ordoñez is answering incriminating questions without the presence of a solicitor. Furthermore, you two are closely related, which could be deemed a conflict of interest. For the purposes of further interviews with this suspect, I recommend a solicitor and an independent officer."

Prado looked long and hard at the captain but to no effect. He didn't flinch.

Prado sighed. "I am well within my rights, captain. I am leading this case and Fredo is our only suspect currently. We don't know for sure if he is the killer or it's somebody else still out there. We have to eliminate him or charge him urgently."

"Yes, I agree but don't push it too far. You don't want a judge to throw out any potential evidence."

"OK… OK," said Prado. "One more thing and we'll stop."

The captain nodded. Prado walked back to the table but remained standing. "You should know Fredo that Pablo Bosque died of a heart attack at the arena this afternoon. It was around the same time as you were planning to shoot Diego."

"Really?" said Fredo. "What a shame. I liked Bosque. He was desperately worried by Diego's plans. I was working with him to help disrupt them and keep him informed of what Diego and Juan were up to. However, I find it incredible that Bosque personally had anything to do with Diego's death."

"I can't see Zambrano instructing you on behalf of the society on his own bat. Bosque and the other committee members must have known about it."

"You're right," said Fredo. "In that case, Zambrano must have been working on his own account."

"Have you considered that Zambrano might have been working on behalf of this Patrick?"

"No. When Zambrano gave me the gun, I was in the Society's office. Why wouldn't I assume that it was a genuine instruction from them?"

"Perhaps that was just a ruse by Zambrano to mislead you into thinking the society wanted him dead, not Patrick?"

Fredo looked horrified as his mind grappled with this new possibility. He shook his head as the realization hit him hard.

"Do you concede that Zambrano may have misled you?" said Prado.

Fredo slumped down into the chair and nodded.

"Fair enough Fredo. I must go now. I'll do all I can to help you, as I'm sure will the rest of the family, but the truth must come out and you will have to pay whatever price is necessary for your crimes and disloyalty."

Fredo buried his head in his arms and shuddered.

"It will kill my mother," mumbled Fredo.

"You should have thought of the consequences before committing your stupid and inconsiderate squandering. Captain, please return Fredo to his cell while I call the family law firm. I will also need to find a replacement for myself."

***

Prado waited outside the main entrance of the Guardia Civil for a motorcycle officer to take him through the crowds to search for Fredo's gun at the car park. He called his boss.

"I hear you've arrested Fredo," said el jefe.

"Word travels fast. I need to step away from interviewing him further though. Conflict of interest and all that. I'd prefer not to leave him to someone from Ronda though. Can you spare an officer from the serious crime squad to come up here with me tomorrow, and take over the questioning?"

"Good idea. Come down in the morning and I'll sort something for you."

"Thanks."

A huge Guardia Civil motorcycle pulled up by Prado as he waited outside the entrance. The driver passed him a helmet which he strapped on and clambered awkwardly aboard.

The driver set off slowly and wound their way through the crowds who were still filling the sidewalks and the roads, although not as busy as earlier.

The driver stopped the bike outside the car park entrance barrier and they both climbed off. The driver heaved the bike onto its stand and together they went into the car park. The office was empty and locked, so they walked to the restrooms and searched the trash can.

All they found was half a dozen empty beer cans.

No pistol.

"Let's split up and check the other bins," said Prado.

They found nothing.

Had Fredo been lying? Wondered Prado. Or had someone seen him dump the weapon and taken it after Fredo had driven off?

"Thanks for your help," said Prado. "Can you drop me off at the bullring concourse please?"

31

"Captain, I'm back at the bullring," said Prado. "What I really wanted to say, was a big thank you for your time and patience with me and Fredo. I've spoken to my boss, and I'll be bringing up my replacement from Málaga to continue with Fredo tomorrow afternoon."

"Just doing my job, inspector," said Captain Mendez. "Did you find the weapon?"

"No."

"So Fredo was lying?"

"Possibly, or someone removed it after Fredo had gone."

"Any cameras at the car park?" said the captain.

"Yes, but only to record registration numbers."

"Would it be helpful if I send a man to the car park tomorrow to collect a list of yesterday's numbers?"

"Thank you. Meanwhile, charge Fredo with Diego's murder and hold him there until I see you tomorrow."

Prado walked to the helicopter, where Ana and Daniel were stowing their equipment.

"Ah, inspector," said Ana. "We're ready to take off."

"Did you find anything in the changing rooms?" said Prado stifling a yawn.

"Diego's backpack, phone, and laptop. The devices are both password-protected, so I'll take them to the lab technicians. In Sammi's room, we found red hairs like those in the chapel and fibers from clothing that were inconsistent with anyone on his team. Also, Sammi confirmed that his spare sword was missing. We showed him a photo of the murder weapon, and he confirmed that it was his."

"Anything helpful come in from the crowd?"

"Several hundred statements, opinions and offers of assistance from a few amateur detectives, but nothing of value, except about the two bandoleros. Some saw the one without the walking stick standing outside the chapel door, others recall them in the café, or coming in through the main entrance. A few spotted them leaving the main entrance. The timings fit with the statement from the main gate security officer."

"Mmm…," said Prado. "Were the changing rooms locked?"

"No, but the outer door that provides access to them is always locked. Each team is issued with a key."

"Did anyone see these bandoleros go through the door?"

"No, but one person was positive he spotted them hovering nearby," said Ana.

"So, it's possible they had a key?"

"Yes."

"The bandoleros sound suspicious," said Prado. "However, their involvement complicates things. We've just charged Fredo with Diego's murder. The evidence against him is overwhelming, plus he had motive and opportunity."

"Perhaps Fredo was working with the bandits," said Ana. "They stole the sword, while he did the rest."

"Possibly. Anything else?"

"I think that's it for now," said Ana.

"Amanda and Phillip have video footage of the crowds," said Prado. "I'll go and see their footage now. I'll just see you off first, and please let me know the results of your tests, no matter what time."

Ana and the team climbed aboard and strapped themselves in. The pilot took off vertically. When he was high enough to avoid the cables, he banked the machine southeast toward Málaga. Its flashing lights rapidly disappeared into the star-studded sky.

Prado had a final walk around the bullring.

The bullfighting teams had returned to their hotels. A few cleaners were brushing the concrete seats, piling the trash into plastic bags and stacking them by the exit. Several local officers were guarding the now locked gates. Prado dismissed them all and went to the manager's tiny office.

"Ah, inspector. Are we all done?" said Chacron.

"For tonight yes," said Prado. "We may have to come back tomorrow. Will you be here?"

"Yes, I'm here every day during La Goyesca. I would imagine that in addition to the crowds coming for the final fight, there are bound to be thousands of the curious and morbid wanting to see the chapel. Do you still need it?"

"No, we're finished. I'd appreciate those lists as soon as you can though, and thanks for your cooperation this afternoon."

"My pleasure. It was tragic but interesting. I look

forward to learning more about Diego's plans. Any idea who will take over from him?"

"Not sure yet. We have to bury him first."

***

Prado found Phillip and Amanda on the enormous roof terrace outside their room on the top floor of the Parador. They were sitting at a table scrutinizing Phillip's laptop closely, which glowed cozily in the darkness. A bottle of red wine, several glasses, and plates of Serrano ham, Manchego cheese, and crusty bread stood untouched at the end of the table. Prado poured a glass for everyone and helped himself to some food. He was starving.

"Anything interesting?" said Prado with his mouth full.

"Remember those topless demonstrators in Madrid?" said Amanda taking a sip of wine.

"I heard about them," said Prado.

"We discovered where they went after their protest was over," said Phillip.

"Where?" said Prado.

"The Las Ventas bullring," they both said together. Amanda giggled.

"See there," said Phillip indicating that Prado should look at the screen. "They were in the cheap sunny seats, accompanied by about a hundred or so of their fellows. There were also another hundred or so scattered around the stadium. The girls from Pamplona were sitting opposite us."

"And your point is?" said Prado after swallowing another slice of ham.

"It was them that started shouting indulto," said

Amanda. "Look how they're egging their neighbors on to stand up and join them waving handkerchiefs like crazy."

"Are you suggesting that they were paid to go to the arena and encourage both pardons?" said Prado.

"Why else would they go to a bullfight?" said Amanda. "They abhor them."

"You think Diego or someone close to him paid for two hundred people to attend the bullfight?" said Prado.

"Yes," said Phillip.

"Do you realize how much that would cost?" said Prado.

"Plus, food, accommodation, and travel costs, we reckon some fifty to sixty thousand Euros."

"That's a lot of money even to Diego," said Prado.

"But there's a lot at stake," said Phillip. "Sixty, even seventy thousand is not much for someone of Diego's substance to make sure he won his pardons and could safeguard his future career."

"OK," said Prado. "But what has this to do with his death?"

"We were taking a look at the Ronda crowds, as you requested," said Amanda. "Here is some footage from the drone camera that we were messing about with before the fight started."

"Take a close look at the animal protesters," said Phillip. "Amanda didn't recognize any of them, so we sent their pictures to the girls in Pamplona, and guess what?"

"Go on," said Prado intrigued by their discoveries.

"They didn't recognize any of them either," said Amanda. "They also confirmed that they had been paid to attend the Madrid bullring on the assurances that it was part of a plan to stop killing bulls."

"Did they say who paid them?" said Prado.

"No, only that as they arrived at the bullring, they had to find a man wearing a red Cordoba hat with rosemary stuck in it and tell him the password, Ronda. Then they were given an envelope containing an entrance ticket, a white handkerchief, two hundred and fifty Euros in cash and instructions to stand, shout indulto and wave the hankies like crazy at the end of Diego's fights."

"Mmm…," said Prado. "Any thoughts on today's protesters?"

"We've found several issues worthy of consideration," said Phillip clicking another file.

"At the beginning of the procession, the protesters were located at the front of the bullring. Other than the odd shout and waving a few placards, they barely seem enthusiastic about being there."

"You think they are fake protesters?" said Prado.

"Possibly," said Amanda. "Look at the big guy with the walking stick and red hair. He bullies them to shout, then goes to stand by those two uniformed men by the statue."

"They're the ushers to the Royal Box," said Prado. "But their main work is for the local police."

"Really?" said Amanda. "We can't see exactly, but it looks like one of the ushers is passing the red-haired protester something. Their arms touch for a moment while the protester studiously turns the other way and the usher starts a new conversation with his colleague."

"That's Tobalo," said Prado. "He went missing after Diego killed his first bull. His colleague Seb said that he'd had a bit of a shock, we'll need to talk to him. Now, what happened to the red-haired protester?"

"When the procession had ended, and everyone was heading into the arena," said Phillip pausing to take a gulp of wine. "He moved the group around to opposite the main entrance. You can see them here." Phillip pointed to the screen. "They seem to be in a huddle as if hiding what the people in their midst are up to. When we resumed filming the concourse after Diego's fight, they'd disappeared."

"Excellent work," said Prado.

"Do you think the protesters had anything to do with Diego's death?" said Amanda.

"I saw two bandoleros coming out from the area near the chapel immediately before I discovered Diego's body. One of them had red hair and used a walking stick like the chief protester. They may have had something to do with it. However, we have irrefutable that someone else killed him."

"Can you tell us who?" said Phillip.

"Fredo."

"Fredo," said Amanda. "Murdered Diego; you're joking?"

"Unfortunately, not. Shortly after Diego's death, Fredo was stopped at a roadblock speeding out of town, they found Diego's blood on his shirt and his prints on the murder weapon. I've just spent the last hour questioning him."

"I knew Fredo was up to something, but I didn't think it would come to that," said Phillip.

"What," said Prado.

"Diego was convinced that Fredo was spying on him and us on behalf of the society. They'd hacked my server, and we strongly suspect that it was Fredo who cut the tires on my car yesterday morning."

"Why would Fredo do that?"

"To disrupt our filming and slow Diego's project down," said Phillip. "Why would Fredo agree to help the society against his family?"

"He had massive online gambling debts," said Prado. "Which made him vulnerable to blackmail. He was given a pistol by a committee member of the society, with instructions to kill Diego if he didn't win a pardon. However, I'm still unclear whether this committee member was acting on behalf of the society or Fredo's bookies."

"Who are the bookies?" said Amanda.

"Dabblers. It's an illegal site specializing in bullfight gambling. See what you can find out about it."

"I find it difficult to believe that Fredo would kill his own nephew," said Amanda. "He's such a sweetie."

"Desperate men go to extraordinary lengths," said Prado. "However, I happen to agree with you, but based on the evidence against him, we had no choice."

"Diego was stabbed," said Phillip. "Not shot, so maybe Fredo isn't the killer?"

"That's what I'm hoping," said Prado. "But who else and why?"

"There could be another motive?" said Phillip.

"Such as?" said Prado.

"Currently, bookies make massive profits under the traditional bullfighting regime. People bet against the torero being injured, even killed. Under Diego's new system, much of that betting revenue could disappear. Surely, it's a powerful motive to stop Diego from going ahead. Perhaps, the bookie was trying to force Diego to throw a fight. He refused to and was killed."

"Maybe," said Prado. "However, it still leaves us with the question about Fredo. Did he kill Diego, or not?"

32

Prado let himself in the front door just after midnight, took his shoes off and left them tidily on the hallway floor next to several pairs of Inma's. He spent most of his time here now, with only a couple of nights a week in his Málaga apartment. Teleworking was suiting him, and Inma treasured his shorter working hours. Today's lateness was a rare exception.

He crept upstairs to the master bedroom. Inma was sitting up in bed with the bedside lamp on, wearing a revealing cream nightshirt, phone to ear and chatting with her sister. On seeing him, she smiled, cut the call short, and patted his side of the bed.

"I've loads to tell you," she said. "Be as quick as you can in the bathroom."

She started to chatter as he cleaned his teeth and slipped into his sleeping shorts. He put his phone on charge and clambered into bed, yawning, half-listening to her ramble on about her long conversations with the Duquesa, Condesa, Diego's mother, grandmother, and

Juan. He fell asleep halfway through. An hour later, his ringing phone dragged him back to consciousness.

"This better be good," he whispered.

"It bloody had," said Inma. "I thought we'd left all this behind."

"Me too," he said turning on the lamp and answering the unknown number from Madrid.

"DI Prado," he said.

"This is DI Campos calling from Madrid Central. Sorry to disturb you at this time of night, but I've just heard about Diego's death and have some information from a cold case that will interest you."

Prado swung his legs out of bed and sat up, now wide-awake again. "Tell me," he said.

"Have you heard of Donald MacKinnon?" said Campos.

"No," said Prado.

"He was a torero, one of the few foreigners on our circuit, from Scotland. Four years ago, he was murdered in the chapel at Las Ventas bullring."

"How?" said Prado.

"He was stabbed in the back with his own sword in what sounds like an identical method to Diego. Blood was found on the confessional cubicle curtain which we presumed to be the killer wiping his hands. We have no witnesses, but several long red hairs were found on the floor by the victim. We've made no progress, and the case is still open, it's been assigned to me, but frankly, I've put it on the back burner until now. Would you like me to send you a link to the file?"

"Yes please, and a few of the hair samples, by courier. Have you any thoughts as to why he was killed?"

"No, but the man left his wife in serious debt."

"Did she have any ideas about how he accrued the debt?"

"I don't know. She disappeared before we could talk to her. Our last trace of her is on a flight to Mexico. It's possible from there she went by train back to her homeland in Bolivia. I have no idea where she is now.

"Thank you, inspector, I look forward to reading the file. May I contact you with any questions?"

"Of course, any time."

Prado ended the call and stood up. Inma had fallen asleep. He went down to the kitchen, poured himself a glass of milk and carried it through to the study. He turned on his work laptop and logged onto the national police server. The link to the file on Mackinnon was in his inbox. He read it through, but it told him nothing additional to what Campos had said on the phone, except a photo, and an original home address in Bearsden, Glasgow. He noted that no inquiries had been made about MacKinnon's life prior to moving to Spain. Perhaps Phillip could gather some background material. He searched Donald MacKinnon and found his page on the torero's website. It wasn't flattering.

Prado switched the laptop off, stood and stared out of the window overlooking the garden. He concluded that the two murders were practically identical especially with the red hairs and sword stroke. Did this mean the same killer, the same motive? However, four years between murders was a long time. Probably too long to imply this involves a serial killer. They were also quick professional executions, not the typical complex games played by the mentally disturbed. Was Fredo involved with both crimes? Were the two deaths linked by gambling? With that question burning in his mind, he went back to bed.

33

Prado joined Phillip and Amanda for breakfast in the Parador. The view of the gorge and new bridge was spectacular, as they munched their own versions of a healthy start to the day, Prado appraised them of last night's call from Madrid and asked Phillip to do a background search on Donald MacKinnon.

"Perhaps there'll be a few articles in the Scottish papers," said Phillip. "Should I start with him or the gambling site?"

"Prado shrugged, and with a twinkle in his eye said, "Don't you do multitasking?"

"The impossible we do at once, miracles take a little longer," said Phillip. "Seriously though, any preference?"

"Mmm…," mumbled Prado chewing his olive-oil smeared roll. "Then start with the Scotsman."

"Any pointers as to why he became a bullfighter?" said Amanda. "It's not exactly an obvious career path for a Glaswegian."

"There's nothing on file. All we have is an old address in Glasgow and that his wife was a mysterious girl from Bolivia who likely skedaddled back home shortly after his death. Dear Donald, left her with a massive debt pile. Can you find out to whom he owed money, and why?"

"You want me to fly to Glasgow?"

"See what you can find online first. If there's anything promising, then you should go."

"I've been thinking about this red-haired animal protester outside the bullring," said Amanda. "It's not a common Spanish feature. Could he also be a foreigner?"

"He might be the Irishman Patrick, that Fredo mentioned," said Prado.

"Wouldn't there be a number on Fredo's phone records, perhaps we could trace Patrick that way?"

"As yet we don't have Fredo's phone," said Prado. "He didn't have it on him, it wasn't in his car and to be honest, what with the shock of discovering my own brother-in-law was the prime suspect in a murder case, I forgot to inquire. Now I've had to withdraw from interviewing Fredo; conflict of interest and all that. However, I'm still leading the case and a replacement has been found to interview Fredo. I'm off to Málaga shortly to collect him and the family solicitor."

"Before you go, we need some advice," said Phillip. "Juan is probably in shock and we're not sure if we should bother him at this time. We're wondering if Diego's death changes their plans to launch the new version of bullfighting or not. Obviously, we're spending their money staying in this hotel and need to know if we should carry on with the filmmaking or move out. Have you had any discussions with Juan along those lines? Would it be all right if we called him?"

"I spoke to him last night," said Prado. "He was deeply upset but pulled himself together when he realized that he had a funeral to arrange. After that, I'm sure he'll take over from Diego and carry on. They've gone too far to stop now."

"That's what I assumed," said Amanda. "In that case, we'll stay here for another few days. Any idea when the funeral might be?"

"As you know, we don't hang about burying people in Spain. Last night, Inma was mumbling something about the day after tomorrow, to give time for the long-distance travelers to make it, but I'll confirm the exact time later."

"Have they considered filming the event?" said Phillip. "We'd be happy to do it and sharing the family's grief for Diego should attract masses of new followers to the blood-free version of bullfighting."

"Good thinking. I'll text Inma. She'll know who to talk to." Prado picked up his phone from the table, tapped in the message and sent it off. He took a sip of his coffee and his phone buzzed. He looked at the text from Inma and placed it back on the table.

"Ok, Inma will keep you posted on the funeral arrangements and any filming requirements. I'm off to Málaga. Later."

Prado stood, put his blue suit jacket back on along with his Panama hat and headed out of the restaurant.

34

Prado pulled the unmarked police VW into the café on the Málaga Road just before Ronda and stopped by the main entrance. He and his two passengers clambered out and headed inside for a quick lunch. Cesar Forero, the family solicitor, an overweight, dark-haired man with blue eyes and a full beard, walked next to him. Detective Sergeant Alberto Santamaria, a huge but timid man with fair curly hair in his early thirties, trailed along behind feeling somewhat overawed to be working with the respected Prado.

One of the waiters was taking down a Serrano ham hanging on a stainless-steel rail above the bar. They stood by the bar and watched fascinated, as he set it up in its cradle and attacked it with a long sharp knife. He removed the outer skin before carving wafer-thin, bite-size slices of the succulent tasty meat and placed them on a serving plate with a pair of tongs.

"Ration of ham and some warm crusty bread?" said Prado.

"Two rations would be better, along with some cured Manchego," said Cesar.

"Whatever," said Alberto.

Prado ordered up and they sat at the only available table in the center of the Comedor surrounded by noisy truck drivers enjoying their menu of the day.

It was just after two when they arrived at the Guardia Civil barracks in Ronda and parked in the white-walled yard at the front packed with liveried Guardia vehicles. The rectangular-shaped barracks were located just outside the center of Ronda in a relatively modern white and ochre painted two-floored building with a terracotta roof. The windows were fitted with white roller blinds and decorative wrought iron grills secured the ground floor. A Spanish flag hung limply on a pole near the street and over the front door was a painted scroll bearing the words, 'Todo por la Patria, Everything for the Homeland.

Prado led the others through the front door where Captain Mendez was waiting with Fredo's warden. Prado made the introductions.

"How is the prisoner today?" said Prado.

"He seemed OK last time I looked," said the warden. "A bit depressed perhaps and our Michelin Star menu doesn't seem to inspire him to eat anything. He has had some juice though."

"Then bring him up to the interview room, please. I'll watch from the observation room."

The captain led everyone along the corridor to the interview room. The warden went to collect Fredo.

Two minutes later the warden came rushing into the interview room extremely agitated and breathing heavily. Prado watched him through the mirror as he gasped. "The prisoner has killed himself."

Prado flung open the door and charged down to the cells. The others were close behind him but he, was the first to see his brother-in-law hanging from the top bunk post, a leather belt around his neck, face a dark bluish color, body unmoving.

Prado picked up Fredo's hand gently and grabbed his wrist.

There was a faint pulse.

"He's still with us," said Prado lifting Fredo up to relieve the pressure on his neck. "Captain call an ambulance now. Santamaria help me get him down."

They lifted Fredo off the bedpost and laid him out on the floor.

Prado gave him mouth to mouth resuscitation and occasionally pumped his chest. He kept that going for several minutes stopping occasionally to check the pulse, but there was no improvement. He watched anxiously as Fredo's facial color turn paler and the pulse weakened. Then he saw it.

Written on the wall in a brown liquid were some letters and numbers. Drops of the liquid had dripped down the wall misshaping the letters. How Gruesome. Thought Prado, then spotted Fredo's untouched lunch plate on the floor. There were finger marks in the thick, greasy gravy.

"Santamaria," said Prado quietly, still pumping Fredo's chest with two hands. "Take a photograph of the writing on the wall and email it to me."

Then the ambulance crew arrived.

Prado went with it. Sitting in the back holding Fredo's hand as the medics worked on him, but they kept shaking their head then tried something else.

It took eleven minutes to reach the hospital on the edge of town. However, all their determined efforts were in vain. Fredo was declared officially dead by the Ronda hospital doctor at two twenty-five in the afternoon.

***

After the doctor had finished explaining the cause of death and morgue arrangements, Prado went out into the hospital car park where he walked around and fought back the tears. Half his brain was flashing over Fredo's struggles and his joy when appointed to the Royal Taurino Society as their advisor. The rest of him wrestled with his treatment of Fredo during their interview. Had I been excessively brutal with him? Was that because he was family? Did I overcompensate to put any potential fears at rest among my colleagues that I was treating him favorably? Perhaps if I'd taken a softer line, Fredo would not have killed himself and could eventually have returned to the bosom of the family.

"Fuck it," he said aloud, startling a passing nurse who glared at him. However, it helped settle him.

Prado still wasn't sure if Fredo had killed Diego, but despite the strong evidence, he preferred to give him the benefit of the doubt. As his emotions calmed, he realized that with Fredo dead there was no further need for any involvement in the case by his DI colleague. He wiped his eyes on the back of his hand, took his phone out of his trouser pocket and called el jefe.

"I'm sorry for your loss," said el jefe after Prado's update. "A sad day to lose another family member so quickly after Diego. I assume you're thinking that Fredo's death eliminates your conflict of interest and you want to resume the investigation on your own?"

"Right, sir," said Prado.

"You do realize that technically, I should take you off the case altogether. Our regulations clearly state that officers should not investigate crimes involving family members."

"I understand, but with my knowledge of the case so far, the area and people involved, it seems logical that I continue."

"Just this once I agree. However, we have another case that needs your attention. There's been another inter-gang shooting in Marbella between Albanians and Scandinavians."

"Can't we just let them finish each other off, sir?"

"We could but I'm concerned about collateral damage. Innocent Spaniards could be caught in the crossfire."

"How long can you give me?"

"Two more days."

"I'll keep you posted, sir."

Prado swiped end call

"Bastard," he muttered and checked his emails.

Santamaria had sent the image of the writing on Fredo's cell wall.

It read.

Shares, pen drive, safe.
Patrick, 519920333
Sorry. Love you.

Prado teared up and called Patrick's number. The number had been disconnected. He called Inma.

"This is a pleasant surprise," she said. "When are you coming home?"

"Not yet, there's no time but listen you need to sit down my love. Sadly, I have some more bad news."

"Fredo?"

"Yes, he hung himself in his cell."

Inma went quiet. Prado could hear her sniffing.

"Where are you?" she said.

"At the hospital. Does Fredo have a safe?"

"Yes," she said. "It's in his bedroom at the farm behind a portrait of our father."

"Then I need to go to the farm immediately. He left a message on the cell wall pointing me to something in his safe. Do you know the safe code?"

"No, but by the time you arrive, I'll have found it. When can I instruct the undertaker to collect Fredo's body?"

"It will be released tomorrow morning. Are you up to letting everyone know?"

"It won't be easy," she said. "But yes."

"Is there someone who can let me into the farm?"

"Yes, the housekeeper is there."

"Could you call her and tell her that some local cops will be arriving shortly to keep an eye on the place."

"Why?"

"Fredo was involved with some nasty people. We're concerned that they will also want whatever is in the safe."

"What had Fredo been up to?"

"Gambling. He was in serious debt to his bookies."

"Oh no. Bloody fool. How much does he owe?"

"A couple of million at least. I'm hoping the safe contains a copy of his contract so I can find out where the bookies are based. I suspect that they had some involvement with Diego's murder."

"So Fredo didn't murder Diego?"

"Possibly, but it depends on what we find in his safe."

"Are you taking the solicitor with you?"

"Yes, and Phillip."

Prado called Santamaria.

"Bring Cesar from the Guardia Civil, Phillip from the Parador and the car to the hospital, we have to drive to Sevilla urgently," he said then called his contact in the Sevilla police to arrange a patrol car to meet him at Fredo's farm.

***

Prado was a competent driver but threw all caution to the wind. It was a difficult road. Initially through tight mountain passes and hairpin bends, but down on the plain it straightened out and he could put his foot down. The hundred and fifty-odd kilometers to the Ordoñez ranch took just over an hour and a half. Prado screeched to a halt at the entrance, picked up the entry phone and the housekeeper buzzed them in.

They drove up a long concrete track lined with oak trees with white fencing on each side. Cattle were grazing as far as the eye could see. After five minutes, they arrived at an enormous two-floored, white painted house with a terracotta roof, fronted by a large fountain in the center of a garden laid out with square flowerbeds encased in low hedges. Various outbuildings and stables adjoined the house. An archway in one outbuilding led through to a courtyard. A brand-new tractor was driving out through the arch towing a trailer full of hay. It sped off along the drive and turned off in the direction of the grazing animals. A local police car was parked by the garden. Two officers climbed out as the dust settled over Prado's car.

Prado jumped out and went over to the policemen.

"Any suspicious vehicles come up the drive?" said Prado.

"Nothing, inspector," said one of the officers.

"OK, thanks, you can go now."

Santamaria, Phillip and Cesar Forero, clambered out looking pale, but relieved to be in one piece as the Sevilla police car drove off. Cicadas chirped loudly, birds tweeted and there was a distinctive agricultural smell in the air.

The housekeeper opened the front door. Bianca, a petite, middle-aged, well-rounded woman with short, tidy, dark hair wearing a green apron over a cream blouse waved them inside and led them up to Fredo's bedroom on at the top of the stairs overlooking the front garden. The picture had been swung back on its hinges revealing a small wall safe. Prado dug his phone out of his inner jacket pocket, checked his messages and saw that Inma had delivered the entry code. Prado turned the dial back and forth, turned a handle and the door opened. Inside, was a laptop on top of a pile of papers, along with its cables and a pen drive. Prado removed the machine and gave everything to Phillip.

"Your department," he said showing him the message from Inma. "The password is the same as the safe."

Phillip carried the computer over to a desk in the corner, plugged it in, sat down and opened the lid. Prado lifted out the pile of papers and flicked through them. Some were sealed envelopes. "Anything you recognize?" he said.

"Yes, as expected, there's his will," said Cesar. "Plus, tax returns, property deeds, car papers, and various business letters, but the envelopes are new."

Prado picked up a letter opener from the desk, slit

open the envelopes one-by-one and handed them over to Cesar. Cesar peeked inside each one. "This one is unusual," he said after several minutes. "Copies of blank stock transfer sheets but signed by Fredo. Each one has a note stuck to it with a scribbled number. Probably a quantity of shares. Then there's a note on the front of the envelope. It says, copies of what was delivered by hand to Patrick's representative, on twentieth August, at eleven in the morning outside my bank in Ronda. Purpose to provide security to cover the debt with Dabblers of two point two million Euros."

"That's a fuck of a lot of money," said Prado. "

"Large enough to have complete control over a man," said Cesar.

"Is there any way you can stop the share transfers?" said Phillip.

"Yes, Fredo was breaking the major shareholder agreement to disclose and agree on all transfers prior to implementation. As Company Administrator, I can call an extraordinary board meeting followed by a letter to the share registrar freezing all transfers until the board is satisfied that there is no longer a risk of criminal manipulation of its assets."

"Can you do that by phone?" said Prado.

"I can do it on Skype now."

"Then do it," said Prado.

Cesar stood, picked up his phone and went out into the hallway. Prado went over to Phillip who was scrolling down Fredo's search history.

"Found anything?" said Prado.

"Other than a massive overdraft and large cash withdrawals, the rest seems tediously ordinary."

"Any links to the Dabblers website?"

"No. Perhaps he did all the gambling from his phone?"

"He said so, but there's no sign of it. He didn't have it with him when he was arrested, and it wasn't in his car. So, either he left it at home or dumped it in Ronda. I'll ask Bianca." Prado went off to talk to the housekeeper but quickly returned shaking his head. "Apparently, he took it with him but without the charger."

Phillip inserted the pen drive. It was also password protected and the access code was different from that of the safe. It would have to wait until he could use his more sophisticated computer at home in Nerja. They cleared the safe of all its contents and left.

35

Prado dropped Phillip back at the Parador. He and Amanda wouldn't arrive back in Nerja until late that evening. They grabbed some sandwiches from the hotel bar and some mineral water and had supper while they drove.

Just under three hours later, they arrived at Phillip's villa. Amanda went to deal with their several days of laundry, while he went straight into his study, paused to appreciate his collection of old Apple computers then sat down at his workstation. He turned on his desktop, googled 'Dabblers' and found zero results.

Must be dark web, he thought, clicking on the Green Onion TOR logo. After several minutes of searching unsuccessfully, he concluded that it must have been taken down.

He plugged in the pen drive, loaded it into his special password cracking software and went to pour a glass of Verdejo for them both.

He gave her a hug and returned to the study sipping

his wine. The computer screen presented him with the list of folders on the pen drive. There was one near the top titled Dabblers. He clicked on it. It was immediately obvious that Fredo might have been an idiot with his gambling, but he'd produced a detailed report of what he'd learned about his bookies.

There was a screenshot of the Dabblers website's front page consisting of a fancy collage of bullfighting photos and a strapline inviting punters to join for Instant access to the best odds.

Fredo had created a spreadsheet of all his wagers, winnings and receipts and losses. Phillip opened the file. Three years ago, when Fredo first started with Dabblers he won consistently. Phillip quickly calculated some six hundred thousand Euros that Dabblers had credited to an account in Gibraltar in Fredo's name. The bank name and log in details were at the top of the spreadsheet. Phillip clicked through to the banks' website and logged in. The account balance was just over a thousand Euros. All the transfers were there along with the Dabblers account details, which proved to be another bank in Gibraltar.

There was a further spreadsheet named Dabbler's cash payments. After each entry, was a link to a video. Phillip clicked on the first and a man's face appeared with red-hair and wearing large sunglasses. Phillip recognized him as the leader of the animal protesters, the man with a walking stick.

By the angle of the image, Phillip guessed that Fredo was wearing a buttonhole camera. In the background was Fredo's bank in Ronda.

"Is it all here?" said the man in English with a broad southern Irish accent.

"As always."

"To be sure Fredo, you're such a good customer that I've decided to increase your credit limit."

"To how much?"

"How much would you like?"

"The maximum I could afford is two million. What collateral would you accept?"

"I would need something to cover the full amount, what can you provide?"

"Shares in the family company?"

"Yes, but I'd need you to sign a credit agreement and some blank stock transfer forms, which I would return when the debt is repaid. However, I do have another solution that would avoid any collateral being necessary."

"Such as?"

"Speak to your nephew. Tell Diego that he must secure the third pardon with his first bull at La Goyesca."

"What will he get in return?"

"You won't need to pay collateral and he will be paid half a million."

"I can't see him agreeing to that, half a million is nothing to him."

"The money is not the point Fredo. He will comply with the offer or end up like Donald MacKinnon. You remember him, don't you Fredo?"

"Sorry Patrick, but I refuse to be involved, you'll need to find another way to communicate with him."

"Then give me his number," said Patrick, his expression mean and ugly.

Fredo dug out his phone and gave it to him.

"That's great now Fredo, now I'll just be wanting those shares."

"Sorry?"

"I want your shares as collateral to cover your new credit limit. Call me when they are ready."

Patrick turned and walked away, eventually disappearing among the crowds of tourists leaning heavily on his walking stick.

"Amanda," said Phillip. "Come and see this."

36

Prado parked under the Málaga Comisaría, grabbed something to eat in Cortijo de Pepe and went to meet Ana Galvez and el jefe at the forensics lab located on the ground floor. They sat around Ana's wooden desk in the corner overlooking workbenches, fridges and a variety of machines.

"Given the strong evidence against Fredo," said el jefe. "Are we all agreed that Fredo was Diego's killer and we can cease investigating further.

"I don't agree," said Ana. "We also have a person, according to the security gate guard, whose red hair was found in the chapel and in the changing rooms from where Sammi's sword was stolen."

"I'm with Ana," said Prado. "It's not yet cut and dried against Fredo."

"You would say that," said el jefe.

Prado's phone rang.

He put Phillip on speakerphone.

"I've uploaded some new material from Fredo's pen

drive to the police server," said Phillip. "Could you log in and click on the video titled Patrick and Fredo."

"So, this Patrick, could be our killer?" said el jefe as the video finished. "He has red hair and his limp certainly looks genuine; he almost winces every time he puts his right foot down."

"He's a strong contender and I agree about the limp," said Ana. "However, not all of him is so bona fide. The red hair actually belongs to a woman."

"Really," said Prado. "It didn't look like a wig."

"Who can tell nowadays?" said el jefe.

"Do the hairs in the chapel match those in the changing room?" said el jefe.

"Yes. They also match the samples from Madrid," said Ana.

"Meaning that the same perpetrator killed MacKinnon and Diego?" said el jefe.

"Can we find out where Fredo was during the Mackinnon case?"

"Four years ago, he was still in Mexico," said Prado He didn't return until three years ago."

"So, we have a man called Patrick who walks with a limp and wears a lady's wig," said el jefe. "Not sure how we can put out an all-points bulletin to our colleagues with that, and the media would have a field day. What else do we have that puts Patrick at the Ronda crime scene?"

"The two bandoleros admitted into the bullring for a pee wore beige clothing," said Prado. "And according to the security guard, the limping man had red hair sticking out from under his bandana."

"That's convincing," said el jefe. "Anything on Diego's phone?"

"His log listed a call from the same WhatsApp

number written by Fredo on his cell wall," said Ana.

"When was the call?" said Prado.

"Thursday afternoon before La Goyesca," said Ana.

"Anything on Diego's laptop?" said Prado.

"Only lots of notes about new bullfighting plans," said Ana.

"What about Fredo's phone?" said Prado.

"The phone company can't trace the actual phone, but has sent us a list of activities," said Ana. "A call was made minutes before Diego's death to a mobile number in Barcelona. The device is registered to a Wind Turbine Manufacturer owned by Joshua Zambrano."

"Possibly, a last-minute call to confirm that Fredo should go ahead with Diego's execution," said Prado.

"It must have been," said Ana. "I wonder if Zambrano will confirm that."

"As soon as we've finished here, I'll arrange for an arrest warrant for Zambrano," said Prado. "We'll go talk to him tomorrow."

"There are some more items on Fredo's pen drive," said Phillip. "But before I get on to them, I've found a few snippets in a local Glasgow newspaper archive about our Scottish bullfighter," said Phillip. "They did a feature on his first fight and sent a journalist to Madrid to interview him and take photos. When asked why he had chosen this unusual career path Mackinnon confirmed that he loved taking risks. I emailed the journalist, who is now an online blogger, and requested any additional background information that might have a bearing on his murder. Apparently, our Donald loved to gamble. He'd won a small fortune on the horses at Ayr races and used the money to buy his lifetime's dream, which was to become a bullfighter."

"Where his luck ran out," said Prado. "And he ended up owing large sums to the bookies, didn't pay and was killed."

"And the bookies must surely have been Patrick and Dabblers," said el jefe. "The similarity in MacKinnon's and Diego's deaths must link Patrick to both murders. It can't be a coincidence."

"There is another aspect to think about," said Phillip. "Patrick would need his stable of bent bullfighters more afraid of him than the bull. If they didn't throw a fight or contrive an injury at an agreed time in a specific part of their body. They would end up as dead as Mackinnon. What I mean is, that perhaps both deaths were a warning to other bullfighters to comply with his demands?"

"But that could mean that the whole industry may be riddled with bullfighters taking backhanders from Patrick," said el jefe.

"Other bookies too perhaps, but it is understandable," said Prado. "It's only the premier league, where fighters are well paid. The lower divisions earn a pittance, especially now that most of the TV companies have withdrawn coverage and the fighters no longer receive a percentage of the TV rights."

"Are you saying that Diego was on the take?" said Ana.

"No, but if he had refused Patrick's demands," said Prado. "Death could have been his reward."

"It's certainly a powerful motive," said el jefe. "Patrick stood to lose huge revenues if Diego was successful in setting up his new league. His death would mean that business could continue as usual?"

"I agree," said Phillip. "But only for ten years or so

before bullfighting dies out altogether."

"That's still long enough to fleece a lot of punters," said Prado. "So, it just leaves us with the question who killed Diego? Fredo or Patrick?"

"As yet we don't have anything to disprove it was Fredo," said Ana. "But we do have a lot that says it could have been Patrick. All we have to do now is find him."

"Anything else on Fredo's pen drive that could help us with that?" said Prado.

"There is," said Phillip. "Which I'll get to in a minute. First some bad news. The Dabblers website has been taken down but Fredo's pen drive has revealed their bank account details."

"Don't tell me, Gibraltar."

"Afraid so, but it's a different bank to Fredo's," said Phillip.

"Would the Gibraltar courts allow us access to the Dabbler's account?" said Prado.

"Allow me to deal with that," said el jefe. "Email me the account details please, Phillip."

"On their way," said Phillip.

"What else do you have?" said Prado.

"There's another film of Fredo making payments to a different man outside his bank in Ronda," said Phillip. "I think this man is representing Patrick and you'll never guess who he is?"

"Surprise me," said Prado.

"It's the usher at the Royal Box," said Phillip.

"Sebastian?"

"No, the other one, Tobalo."

"Really, I've known the man for years," said Prado. "However, I recall he was away from his post at the time of the murder, and it was him that Amanda suspected was giving the red-haired protester something just before La Goyesca started."

"A key to the bullfighters changing rooms perhaps?" said Phillip.

"Could be or the other way around?" said Prado.

"You mean, the protester was giving Tobalo the key?" said el jefe.

"Yes," said Prado.

"Which would put Tobalo in the frame for the murder," said Ana.

"This is getting messy," said Phillip. "And sorry, but there's one more thing that could complicate matters further. Fredo filmed two more incidents that might have a bearing on the case. He was in the Society's offices on both occasions. The first shows him talking to an elderly man who says that the committee wanted Diego dead unless he delivered at least one pardon at La Goyesca."

"And the second incident?"

"About a week ago, according to the camera's date," said Phillip. "The same man is giving Fredo a small package wrapped in a black felt bag and says, 'only if Diego doesn't deliver a pardon.' When the man has gone, Fredo films himself opening the package to reveal a pistol and silencer."

"Any idea who the elderly man is?" said el jefe.

"I've checked the Society website. It was Joshua Zambrano."

37

DI Campos: a tall rangy man around forty, with an unruly mop of dark hair wearing a beige waterproof jacket and black pants rang the bell of an elegant apartment block in the centrally located exclusive Chamberí district of Madrid. It was just before seven in the morning and had just stopped drizzling. The street was quiet, birds were chirping their morning chorus, and the occasional taxi splashed by on the damp tarmac. "How may I help you?" said a man with heavily accented but good Spanish.

Campos presented his ID to the video lens. "It's DI Campos of the National Police, I'd prefer not to announce my business with Señor Zambrano over the door phone. Please admit us so we can talk with him."

"Very well," said the voice and the door buzzed open. Campos and his youthful male assistant took the elevator to the top floor. As the doors slid open, a gray-suited butler met them. "Come this way please," he said and led them down a short marble-tiled corridor to a double width timber door. He pushed one side open, stood back and waved them in.

Zambrano was sitting in a comfortable armchair in the spacious hallway reading a document. He was a mid-height slender man with small, elegant hands, smartly dressed in a dark navy blue suit, his silver hair and mustache neatly trimmed. "I trust this isn't going to take long, Inspector Campos, my chauffeur is arriving shortly. I have a meeting in Segovia."

"Regretfully, sir, I'm afraid that won't be possible," said Campos reaching into his inner jacket pocket and extracting a folded paper. I have a warrant here for your arrest."

Zambrano didn't bat an eyelid and inquired, "On what charges?"

"Conspiracy to murder Diego Romero," announced Campos.

"Ah, I see, may I call my solicitor?"

"Of course. You'll be taken to Madrid Central Comisaría. Your legal advisers can meet with you there."

Zambrano picked up his phone from the hall table, spoke quickly and ended the call. "I'm all yours," said Zambrano standing. "Do we need handcuffs?"

"That won't be necessary, sir. A police car is waiting in the street for us."

"Nowak, please accompany me in the elevator," said Zambrano to his butler. "I need to cancel various arrangements. Would you mind, inspector?"

"Not at all, sir."

***

Prado was on the early AVE to Madrid with Phillip when his phone rang. He looked at the number with some surprise and yet pleasure. It was the Duquesa de Aragon.

"How may I assist Ma'am?" he said.

"Thank you, inspector, but I think I may be the one to help you. I've been going through my husband's personal effects and found a laptop computer in the safe with a post-it note stuck to the lid. On it, is written a scribbled message that says, in the event of my death, give to the National Police, and that's you, right?"

"Indeed Ma'am, although I do have the odd colleague or two. How may I collect it from you?"

"I'm in Salamanca visiting my niece for some mutual consoling before she catches the noon train to Ronda for tomorrow's funeral. Sadly, we've run out of tissues, so I thought I'd attend to a few outstanding matters such as this. If you could give me an address, I'll have my driver deliver it to you muy pronto, where are you?"

"On the train to Madrid, should be at the central police station on Calle Legonitas in a couple of hours."

"He's leaving in my Bentley shortly. If he's ticketed for speeding, perhaps you could kindly deal with it?"

"Of course, ma'am, thank you."

"He should also be there in a couple of hours. I hope it's of some use."

"Will you want it back?"

"Not at all, one knows nothing of such devices. Give it to a worthy cause."

"Certainly ma'am. Should the contents reveal anything untoward, should I keep you informed?"

"Most sensible."

"Adios ma'am."

"Royalty?" said Phillip.

"With a wicked sense of humor. It was Bosque's wife. She's sending us a laptop found in Bosque's safe, it was marked for police attention. Her driver is due to deliver it at about the same time as we arrive. Do you have your magic password software with you?"

"Yes, it's on my laptop now."

Prado nodded, closed his eyes and was instantly asleep.

***

DI Campos met Prado and Phillip at Atocha station in an unmarked car. They parked in the Comisaría garage on Calle Legonitas and stopped off for a coffee at the café opposite. They took a seat at a pavement table and ordered up.

"Be careful what you say," said Campos leaning forward and speaking quietly despite the noise of passing traffic. "Zambrano's lawyers are inside the café. They're the best money can buy, so I wouldn't be surprised if the bastards can lip read. Your evidence better be solid."

"We're confident of a conviction with what we have already," said Prado. "But we want to ensure that Bosque's machine doesn't hold any surprises."

A black Bentley with a golden coat of arms painted on the rear door stopped directly outside the Comisaría ignoring the double red lines and huge police no parking signs. They watched as a young, handsome, liveried driver grabbed something from the passenger seat, opened the door and ran into the front entrance. Seconds later, he was back in the car and drove off.

"I think that we can safely conclude that was Bosque's computer," said Campos gulping down the rest of his drink. "Shall we go and see what gems we can find?"

Prado paid the bill and they stood up to leave.

As they crossed the road, three very smartly dressed men and an elegant woman regarded them carefully through the café window. Their conversation paused for a moment.

Once Campos had settled them into his tiny office on the top floor with marvelous views over terracotta-tiled rooftops, it took Phillip ten minutes to link Bosque's laptop to his and discover the password. It was *duquesa*.

"Should have tried that in the first place," said Phillip. "Now, what do we have?"

There wasn't much on the old, slow laptop. Bosque had not used it for communications, only to store reports and various sets of accounts from his hotel chain. There were two main folders that piqued Phillip's interest.

One was entitled Sociedad which contained were several sub-folders, among them one named Zambrano and another Fredo Ordoñez.

The other main folder was CVS.

Inside the Zambrano folder was a report from a firm of private detectives based in Madrid. Phillip read it aloud to the others.

"Don Pablo Bosque expressed concerns to our chief investigator that Joshua Zambrano was not pulling his weight as a member of the Royal Taurino Society Committee. He stands accused of being absent more than what was acceptable to other members, who had complained about his lack of contribution. As there were no obvious excuses such as illness, business problems or pressure of work, Bosque decided that a full analysis of Zambrano's life was required to learn if anything was wrong prior to taking any action.

"Our investigators were instructed to keep a discreet eye on Zambrano's movements, evaluate his background, monitor his communications and report our findings with a list and description of any of the target's contacts that could be of concern to the Society.

"We researched the target and learned that his main residence is an apartment in the historical Madrid neighborhood of Chamberí. He also has a wine estate in La Rioja and a black-foot pig farm on the outskirts of Huelva in Andalucía. His primary business interests are wind turbine manufacturing with a large factory based near Tarragona in Catalonia.

"Joshua Alejandro Zambrano Rojas was born in 1944 in Barcelona to an impoverished family. At school, he showed a keen interest in engineering and was offered a free scholarship to Barcelona University, where he designed the technology to make wind turbines more efficient.

"In the late 1960s, under Dictator Franco, raising money to form a new company in Spain to manufacture them proved impossible, so Joshua took his ideas to Germany, where he was employed by a large concern. He learned German and English and returned to Spain in the 1980s with enough capital to start Spain's first wind turbine company. When Spain joined the EU in 1984, he applied and received grant money to expand his company across the EU to assist in their policy of switching to alternative energy.

"As far as our inquiries can uncover there are no

reasons to be concerned about the target's business life which appears to be above board. However, we quickly established that his personal life was completely the opposite.

"The target is unmarried, lives on his own, and is a homosexual. He has a Polish driver and staff who attend to his daily requirements and domestic chores. He eats out all the time and, on at least three occasions a week attends a nightclub where he meets young men, some of whom he takes home for the night.

"The target is also a heavy gambler often losing excessively enough to seriously interfere with his wealth. His main interest is Blackjack, which he plays daily at the Casino on Gran Via. We also discovered that he is a subscriber to several online betting sites some legal, others not. One illegal site that concerned us greatly was Dabblers, a gambling platform for high net worth individuals who prefer to tailor their own wagers on bullfights. We discovered that Dabblers has a registered office at lawyers Martin & Bayne, Main Street, Gibraltar along with an account in an adjacent bank. Full details of directors and shareholders are shown on an attached report, but we suspect that these are front men nominees. Our technician was unable to bypass the bank security systems so we could not access the Dabblers account transactions.

"Zambrano also has a bank account in Gibraltar at a different bank on Main Street. Here our technician was able to access the transactions, which showed that he pays far more to Dabblers than he wins. In our professional opinion, we are concerned that Zambrano, as the main shareholder in a public quoted company, could be a likely candidate for blackmail. Several recent phone calls, (recordings on enclosed

DVD) with a man called Patrick confirm that is the case.

"Patrick has threatened to expose Zambrano's gambling debts to the Financial Media and to the Royal Taurino Society. This would be a disaster for Zambrano, effectively damaging his company's ability to negotiate future government contracts, which are his main source of revenue. His share price would tumble which in turn would affect his borrowing arrangements. His membership of the Society would also be terminated, which would be a huge personal blow, and would cut him out of the business community.

"In effect, he would lose control of his life's work and be wiped out financially.

"At this stage, we should mention the results of our research into Patrick. In short, not much. He speaks only English with a heavy southern Irish accent. He communicates by WhatsApp, and the only way we could record his conversations was by bugging Zambrano's phone. Our technician was unable to trace Patrick's full name, nationality or an address. To all intents and purposes, Patrick is a ghost, a person operating completely off the radar. We would consider him highly dangerous and any dealings with him should be treated with extreme caution.

"To deter Patrick from exposing him to the markets, Zambrano has agreed to collaborate with Patrick in a conspiracy against the famous bullfighter Diego Romero. Zambrano's role is to brief another indebted Dabblers subscriber, Fredo Ordoñez, who is the adviser to the Society on veterinary matters. Fredo's eldest sister Maria is Diego's mother and the two men have a close relationship.

"Zambrano', pretending that he was representing the Society, briefed Fredo to personally deliver a message to Diego saying that he must win a pardon with his first bull at La Goyesca. If he succeeded, Diego would be a hero of the Society. However, under no circumstances was Fredo to explain to Diego what would happen to him if he failed to achieve a pardon.

"If he failed, then Diego was to be killed by Fredo. Zambrano would give a silenced pistol to Fredo, just in case Diego failed. Fredo was to return the pistol afterward via Zambrano.

"In the final conversation between Patrick and Zambrano, Patrick was clearly offering fantastic odds on Diego winning the third pardon and strongly recommending that Zambrano place a large bet that would substantially reduce his indebtedness to Patrick.

"Initially, we were mystified as to why Patrick would offer such attractive odds on Diego winning a pardon and then want him killed if he failed. Surely if Diego failed then Patrick wouldn't have to pay out. But then, we concluded that win or lose, perhaps Patrick has no intention of paying out at all and will keep all the stake money. Perhaps as a final fling before retirement. We assume that Patrick knows that whatever the Society might do to save bullfighting, it was bound not to work. In addition, Diego's new style would likely decimate his betting business almost overnight. Hence his dramatic solution to extract one last giant wedge of cash before hanging up his calculator for good.

"Again, this is pure speculation but might go some way to explaining why Patrick would want Diego dead if he did fail to win a pardon. We presume that Diego's murder is a double-edged sword. On one side, it's an act of deterrent to those that lost money. Scaring them to write off their winnings, rather than chase Patrick for payment. On the other side, it would remind those that still owed Patrick to pay up or risk dire consequences.

"All the conversations between Patrick, Zambrano, and Fredo were recorded on the enclosed DVD and presented along with our report typed to Señor Bosque on the Thursday prior to La Goyesca."

"As the report says," said Prado. "It's a shot at explaining what Patrick is up to, which I find extremely poignant."

"Me too," said Phillip. "Before we go talk to Zambrano, shall we have a quick look at these other files?"

Phillip clicked on a sound file in the folder and played back one of the video recordings between Fredo and Zambrano. It was from a different angle and the sound wasn't as good, but it was the same as the videos they found on Fredo's pen drive of the conversations between Zambrano and Patrick.

Prado rubbed his ear and said, "If Bosque had read this the day before La Goyesca, why didn't he warn Diego that he was in danger from Fredo?"

"Perhaps Bosque also wanted Diego dead?" said Phillip.

"Possibly, we're never going to know for sure," said Prado. "However, this report underpins everything we've learned so far and points to Fredo still being our main suspect except for one tiny fact, Diego was stabbed, not shot. So, did Fredo use the sword instead of the pistol, or did someone else kill Diego? What's in Fredo's file?"

Phillip clicked on the word document, skimmed through the single page of text and said. "Basically,

Bosque appointed these detectives to hack our servers, upload a cartoon, disrupt our filming and inform him of any developments. They briefed Fredo on his role but when we took down their cartoon so quickly decided to stop any further action against. Apparently, the panicked that we might be able to trace and identify them.

***

The three male lawyers from the café were sitting on chairs outside the interview room. Prado and his team nodded at them then entered. Zambrano was sitting down on one side of the table next to his lawyer. They ceased chatting as their interviewers sat down.

"Inspector, would you please confirm the charges against my client," said the elegant and attractive lawyer who had introduced herself as Cristiana Montero.

"Señora Montero, we can play this two ways," said Prado. "We can treat this meeting as just a little chat about a police murder suspect linked to your client. If he answers our questions honestly and fully, I doubt that there will be any charges and your client will be free to go. However, if he lies or refuses to respond to our inquiries then I can assure you that we have enough evidence to bring conspiracy to murder charges against him. I'm sure you can advise your client on the consequences of those charges."

Cristiana turned to Zambrano and nodded.

"Fair enough, inspector," said Zambrano. "How can I help you?"

"Señor Zambrano. We understand that you have substantial gambling debts with a company called Dabblers and have been in conversations with their representative, a man known as Patrick."

Zambrano nodded.

"Please speak your reply, Señor Zambrano. It's for the recorder," said Campos.

"Sorry, yes I have substantial debts with Dabblers and Patrick is about to expose those facts to the financial media."

"I'm going to show you a screenshot from a video," said Prado. Phillip turned his laptop around and showed Zambrano a picture of Patrick. "Is that Patrick?" said Prado.

"Yes," said Zambrano.

"What can you tell us about him?" said Prado.

"He's Irish," said Zambrano in a steady voice. "And runs Dabblers, a Gibraltar based dark web Internet company. He's devious, fearless and an absolute brute. He sucks you in with Irish charm, encourages you to increase your exposure, finds your weakness and exploits that to get what he wants."

"Has Patrick mentioned a man called Donald MacKinnon?" said Prado.

"Yes, he made no secret that he killed MacKinnon some four years ago. He would mention his name if I was dithering over payment terms and imply the same would happen to me."

"Did Patrick give you any instructions concerning Fredo Ordoñez?" said Prado.

"Yes, I was to pretend to be acting on behalf of the society and give Fredo some instructions."

"Were any other members of the Society aware of this?"

"No, I was acting purely for Patrick."

"What were the instructions?"

"Fredo was to tell Diego that the society demanded a third pardon at La Goyesca."

"Was the society offering any incentive for Diego, to obtain such a pardon?"

"None, other than that the Society would think him a hero."

"Was there to be any punishment should Diego fail?"

"Yes, I was to say that the Society would not renew his bullfighting license."

"What were Patrick's actual instructions?"

"Should Diego fail to obtain a pardon, Fredo was to shoot him."

"Can you confirm that you personally gave Fredo the pistol and silencer that was to be used to kill Diego?"

"Yes, I met Patrick the day before La Goyesca at Atocha Station. He gave it to me in a black velvet bag tied with a drawstring. I presented this package to Fredo in the society's office later that day with his final instructions that he was to use it only should Diego fail to win a pardon."

"What was Fredo to do with the weapon after he had killed Diego?"

"Return it to me, and I would pass it back to Patrick."

"When was the last contact you had with Fredo?" said Phillip.

"Shortly before Diego's death. He called me to confirm that Diego had killed his bull and to ask should he go ahead shoot him. I told him yes."

"When did you learn how Diego died?" said Phillip.

"I read it in the Sunday papers. I was shocked that he'd been stabbed with a bullfighter's sword, not shot."

"What conclusion did you draw from that?" said Campos.

"I was confused. Fredo was meant to shoot him not use a knife or whatever it was."

"Has Patrick been in contact with you since Diego's death?"

"No, and he hasn't returned my calls."

"Who do you think killed Diego?" said Prado.

"It must have been Patrick," said Zambrano.

"Why?" said Prado.

"Diego was killed in the same way as MacKinnon. Fredo wasn't strong enough to do that."

"If Patrick had ordered Fredo to kill Diego, why did he then do it himself?" said Prado.

"Patrick's style is to create chaos," said Zambrano. "His aim is to confuse everyone with a range of potential culprits, motivations and conflicting evidence, then he slips in and does the job himself. Look. Patrick knows that Fredo and I are not killers. I have enough trouble treading on a spider and Fredo's whole career has been about saving animals. Patrick only used us, to divert attention away from himself. He would have wanted to make sure that Diego died, and he'd want his debtors and stable of bent bullfighters to know that it was him that did it. It's a control thing."

"How did you draw that conclusion?" said Campos.

"Part of Patrick's job is to persuade, tough fearless bullfighters to bend to his will. It ensures they follow his instructions in the ring and are gored on time and in the right part of their body. Patrick must make them more afraid of him than they are of the bull. On the other side he needs to collect substantial debts from strong-minded, capable, wealthy people normally desensitized to threats. For both groups, Patrick is masterful at projecting an aura of terror. His victims' quake whenever he contacts them. The man is a monster."

"Is that how he made you feel?" said Prado.

"Yes, and until I know where he is, will continue to do so."

"Can't you contact him?"

"For the last few years, we communicated at least twice a day. Since Friday he hasn't called me and hasn't answered mine."

"Why such regular contact?" said Campos.

"I'm a gambling addict, I had to place bets with him daily plus we'd discuss payment terms and we'd chat generally. I felt I was actually getting to know him."

"What language did you use?" said Phillip.

"English, always English. Although I found it difficult to understand his Irish dialect at times."

"Do you have any ideas about how to locate Patrick's address?" said Prado.

"That's a huge problem," said Zambrano. "I've had private detectives searching high and low for him but he's an expert at covering his tracks and we've learned practically nothing about him. We don't even know if Patrick is his real name, or if he is actually Irish."

"What have you learned?" said Prado.

"During the many conversations I've had with him about betting on the outcome of bullfights, he's impressed me with substantial knowledge of bulls, bullfighting, and bullfighters. For example, he knows which bullfighters are more susceptible to be gored, which ranches produce the fiercest animals and the degree of efficiency of each arena management team."

"Any ideas as to where he came by this knowledge?" said Campos.

"It's not something you can read in a book or study at university," said Zambrano looking more confident now. "You learn about bullfighting by doing it or living closely among bullfighters."

"Would you say his limp is genuine?" said Prado.

"Yes, his expressions of pain seem authentic to me," said Zambrano. "Perhaps it's an old bullfighting injury. Maybe he was an apprentice that never made it, but it is clear to me that this in-depth knowledge can only have been accrued in and around bullfighters."

"How do you communicate with him?" said Prado.

"I text and when he's ready, he replies depending on the degree of urgency."

"Is that channel still open?"

"No," said Zambrano. "As of two days ago; the number has been disconnected."

"OK, Señor Zambrano," said Prado. "Thank you for your assistance in this matter. I'm going to drop the charges and you may go home. However, we still have evidence to prove your involvement in a conspiracy against Diego and I reserve the right to charge you with further offenses. If Patrick does contact you, please let us know immediately."

"With pleasure, inspector. Gracias"

38

It was dark by the time Prado arrived at the Guardia Civil in Ronda. Captain Mendez was waiting for him by the reception desk. They had a quick update then Prado went through to the interview room. Tobalo was sitting on one side of the table, a solitary and somber figure. Prado sat down opposite but didn't turn on the recorder.

"Tobalo, we've known each other for at least ten years, right?" said Prado.

"More like twelve," said Tobalo with a quizzical expression.

"And how long have you been acquainted with Patrick?"

"Er, I'm sorry."

"You heard," said Prado tersely. "Patrick. Tell me about him."

"But I don't know any..."

"Tobalo," said Prado. "The only chance in the world that you have of keeping your job, saving your marriage and ever seeing your children again is to stop fucking with me. How long have you known Patrick?"

"About three years, but I call him Patricio."

"Oh. I see," said Prado. "We'll explore how you met him later. What I need first, is to tidy up a couple of loose ends." Prado dug out his phone, swiped up the image taken by the drone of the red-haired animal protester from outside Ronda bullring standing next to Tobalo.

"Is this Patrick, sorry Patricio?" said Prado showing him the image

Tears rolled down Tobalo's face. "Yes."

"And what is he giving you?"

"Nothing," said Tobalo. "I'm passing him the key to the bullfighters changing rooms."

"Did you assist in Diego's murder in any other way?"

"I didn't know that Patricio was going to kill Diego," said Tobalo. "I was as shocked as everybody else. Patricio told me that he just wanted a quiet word with Diego."

"Did he say what about?"

"No, and it wasn't my business to ask, but I assumed that it was a gambling matter. Why else would Patricio want to talk to him?"

"Then I'll rephrase my question. Did you perform any other small tasks for Patricio on the day of Diego's death?"

"I provided him with two sets of bandoleros clothing which I left in a plastic bag under the hedge opposite the main bullring entrance. Afterward, Patricio put the bag back under the hedge and I disposed of it later. I also followed Fredo when he left the arena."

"How did you manage that?"

"I went out via the staff entrance and came back in the same way."

"I'd given instructions for it to be locked."

"It was, but other than a fingerprint scan there is also a code pad. I had the master code."

"Was it you that collected the pistol from where Fredo dumped it in the car park?"

"It was."

"What did you do with it?"

"I still have it at home. I'm due to return it to Patricio the next time we meet."

"When is that?"

"Don't know yet, but he'll call me. He always does."

"I'll need our forensics people to inspect it before you give it back."

"You'll need to be quick. If I don't have it with me when Patricio wants a meet, he'll suspect that the police are involved. Then he'll be gone, and you'll never find him."

"When we've finished, a forensics officer will accompany you to your house to collect it. Does your wife know where it is?"

"My wife is er… not there. She and the kids have gone to stay with the in-laws."

"Until you stop gambling, right?"

"We will see."

"Sebastian told me that you fainted when Diego killed the bull?"

"That's an exaggeration. Yes, I was shocked, but I overplayed my reaction as a ruse to fool Seb. Then he wouldn't question my absence."

"How did you meet Patricio?"

"A fellow gambler introduced me to the Dabbler's

site. I joined and gradually started betting in increasingly higher amounts. I was winning more than I was losing. Patricio requested a meet where he offered me a more personal service with higher stakes and a credit limit."

"I wasn't aware that you could speak English."

"I can't, we always spoke in Spanish."

"How is his Spanish?"

"Like mine and yours, I would say that he is Spanish or at least of mixed parentage."

"English and Spanish you mean?"

"Or Irish."

"What collateral did you have to provide, to be extended the credit?"

"The equity of my house, and a life insurance policy that I signed over to him."

"Was that enough to cover your debt?"

"No. I was obliged to perform tasks for him."

"Such as?"

"I was to meet some of his other clients and collect cash payments on his behalf."

"Where?"

"All over Andalucía."

"What did you do with the money?"

"I delivered it to Patricio personally."

"Where?"

"Wherever was convenient. Motorway services, bus stations, cafés."

"What vehicle was he driving?"

"It varied between a powerful motorbike and a plain white van."

"Did you take a registration number?"

"No. I was just relieved that he turned up and took the money before I was tempted to gamble it on something."

"Did he pay you for these collection services?"

"Yes. He reduced my debt by two hundred Euros for each delivery."

"How many per month?"

"It varied from five to twenty."

"Did you learn the names of these other gamblers?"

"Yes."

"Could you write me a list?"

"Of course, but I can't remember all of them, only the regulars."

"Were there many regulars?"

"Forty or so."

"OK," said Prado extracting his notebook from his inner jacket pocket. "Write them down in here while I go and fetch us some water."

Prado left Tobalo to it, closed the interview room door behind him and walked to the water dispenser. He filled a couple of plastic cups and thought about Patrick speaking Spanish. Could it be possible? He took out his phone and called Juan.

"Any progress?" said Juan.

"Some, especially with some new information that's just come in about Patrick. We've been assuming that he's an Irishman, who only spoke English, but Tobalo tells me he speaks Spanish like a Spaniard. He could be of mixed parentage as apparently, his English is also mother-tongue quality."

"How does that information change matters?"

"Hold on, there's more. Zambrano was most impressed with Patrick's incredible knowledge of bullfighting, so much so, that he thinks Patrick must have studied or lived among bullfighters for quite a while. Add to that what appears to be a genuine limp and it's painting me a picture of an injured bullfighter or apprentice. Now I'm sure the Society keeps impeccable records. Is there some way that we could obtain a list of wounded bullfighters going back twenty to thirty years?"

"That would make Patrick around fifty?"

"Late forties, certainly."

"The Society's records are renowned for their accuracy, but mainly about the pedigree of the bulls, not bullfighters. However, it would do no harm to look. Slight problem though. Given our current relationship with the Society, I can't see them opening up their archives to the likes of me."

"Nonsense," said Prado. "You could say you've been asked by the police to find an injured apprentice bullfighter who could help with the inquiries into Diego's death. Then use it as a bridge to open a dialogue with them on joining forces for a managed transition from old bullfighting to new."

"Mmm…," said Juan. "Good idea, I wonder which committee member would be the best to approach?"

"Try Escobedo. Of all them, he seems to be the most favorable towards merging their and your interests."

"How do you know that?"

"I overheard Bosque and the committee members talking in Ronda Bullring. Just after Diego's announcement. Escobedo was suggesting a merger as the best way forward."

"Brilliant. I'll call him. Anything else?"

"Yes. As you know, Patrick has blank stock transfers signed by Fredo. Cesar should have canceled them by now, but if we are to flush out this Patrick, and find his real identity, we need to tempt him with something. Would you consider making him an offer to buy them back?"

"I'd be happy to, but it's an expenditure that would need shareholder agreement, and as we have already canceled the transfers and no longer need them, I can't see them voting for it?"

"I understand. I'm just trying to find a way to tempt Patrick to come to us."

"Sorry, my friend but you'll have to use public funds."

"El jefe wouldn't support that."

"Then it will have to be old-fashioned policing."

"I know, thanks anyway."

"Thank you, Leon."

Prado poured two waters from the dispenser and carried them to the interview room. Tobalo had finished his list and was pacing around the room.

Prado studied the list. Some of the names shocked him. He glared hard at Tobalo.

"Are you serious?" he said. Tobalo sipped his water, returned his gaze and nodded. "So, if I'm reading these correctly, there's a bank manager, a mayor's assistant, a priest, and a judge?"

"That's right, and what's worse, Patricio has some of them running around providing him with favors."

"Such as what?"

"I'm not familiar with the details," said Tobalo. "But I've always wondered who Patricio is. I don't know his full name and he must have an address somewhere, otherwise, he couldn't open a bank account, procure a phone, hire a car let alone get a driving license and he appears to have all those."

"Sounds logical. Are you suggesting these gentlemen are providing them?"

"Yes, but my suspicions are not based on guesswork. Sometimes, when I collect the money for Patricio, it's accompanied by a separate envelope. There's nothing on the envelope to indicate its contents but I could feel what's inside. Once, it was a passport, another vehicle documents and several times they were credit cards or sets of keys."

"Here," said Prado handing his notebook over. "Mark the names who sent the passport, various cards, and keys."

Tobalo thought for a bit, pulled the book toward him, picked up the pen, made four ticks and passed it back.

Prado picked it up and read the names again then looked at Tobalo. "Ok Tobalo, you are in enough of a mess without me adding to it with an arrest. Frankly, I want you out there, in case Patricio calls and needs you for anything. However, this time, you'll be doing it with me. Understand?"

"Yes, sir. Thank you."

"When I have Patricio behind bars, you can thank me. Until then you remain under suspicion. You can go now but you are not to discuss this with anyone, not even Seb."

"You can rely on me, sir."

"Mmm," mumbled Prado skeptically as Tobalo closed the door behind him on the way out. "Gamblers and reliability are about as compatible as chalk and cheese."

39

Phillip and Amanda were lying in bed at Phillip's villa contemplating getting up when his phone rang. It was Juan.

"Inma mentioned your suggestion about filming Diego's funeral tomorrow morning," said Juan. "Do you still have time to set up?"

"Where are you holding the service?"

"In the Iglesia de Nuestra Señora de la Merced Ronda, and then after at the family church at the ranch. However, we only want you to film in Ronda."

"Do you want us to sell the footage to the other networks?" said Phillip.

"No, give it to them," said Juan. "We want Diego's death plastered all over the place. It should help feed the growing international pressure on politicians and the Taurino Society to change bullfighting."

"When can we have access to the church?"

"Any time today," said Juan. "The flowers have been ordered. A giant TV screen is being mounted outside and the invitations have been sent. One of the King's daughters is attending along with the deputy Prime minister."

"Impressive," said Phillip.

"The Condesa is well connected. However, it will be a short service, not too heavy on the religious bit as Diego wasn't into all that. Oh, I nearly forgot, the Condesa will be giving a Eulogy. Make sure you help her prepare for it and film her face real close as she talks."

"OK. What do you prefer for the emphasis of the film?" said Phillip. "Light-hearted, dramatic or emotional?"

"A mix of light, but emotional. It won't do any harm to tug at a few heartstrings. Diego was well-loved among all generations of Spaniards and today's youngsters are into honest feelings, so let's give them some. It can only help our cause."

"OK, we'll prepare our kit and head up there."

"Thanks, Phillip. See you tomorrow. Love to Amanda."

"Say hi to Maribel."

***

Later that afternoon, with the help of the film crew, they were ready. Despite several battles with truculent flower ladies and Father Ignacio who insisted on knowing the best camera angles.

Early evening, the Condesa appeared to practice her Eulogy. Phillip gave her a cable-free microphone and listened to her tearful rehearsal. He filmed her discreetly and when she'd finished approached her as she sat on the altar steps sobbing quietly.

"Would you like to see how it sounded, ma'am?" said Phillip.

She looked up at him with her soulful brown eyes, smiled wanly and said. "That bad?"

They watched the film together. Phillip made a few suggestions and she parted seeming happier.

Finally, everything was ready.

Phillip and Amanda adjourned to their room at the Parador. Seated in the lounge overlooking the gorge were several members of the Romero and Ordoñez families who were also staying there. They agreed to dine together in the hotel restaurant.

It was a casual affair muted by the sadness of the occasion.

Amanda sat next to the Condesa and they chatted intensely until everyone else had gone to bed.

Phillip mingled with several currently active toreros and discussed the new style against the old. While all were enthusiastic about the future, some were skeptical. They were worried about the entertainment value and its sustainability but would give it their best shot. Phillip reckoned that they were just wary of change.

***

The next morning, as the bell tolled, hundreds of mourners slowly drifted into the church. Many glamorous couples, the women clad in an impressive array of black outfits and hats milled about outside beforehand posing for photographs.

Highly polished black cars came and went dropping off the mayor and other local dignitaries. Finally, an elegant Rolls Royce flying the Royal and National Flags on its front wings stopped at the bottom of the steps. A security man in plain clothes opened the rear door and the Condesa, Royal Princess and Deputy Prime minister climbed out.

They mounted the steps, turned briefly and waved to the swelling crowd and went inside.

Just before eleven, all the seats were taken, and a massive crowd had gathered outside in front of the giant screen.

The hearse followed by several limousines arrived bang on time. The immediate family went inside. The pallbearers mainly toreros such as Sammi and Macca but also including Juan and Prado gathered around the hearse, heaved out the impressive oak coffin and lifted it onto their shoulders and swayed in unison after Father Ignacio. They placed it on a stand in front of the altar steps where flower ladies arranged masses of wreaths, and bouquets around its base and on top.

Father Ignacio, a short rotund man with wispy gray hair stood between the coffin and the altar. He took a deep breath and spoke.

"In the midst of life, we are in death," he began in a clear booming voice that echoed around the church. "From whom can we seek help? From you alone, O Lord, who by our sins are justly angered.

"Diego Maximilian Romero lies before us today in the coffin that will take him to his final resting place at the family church. There, he will join his many illustrious ancestors, several of whom like him were taken from us at an early age.

"That such a revered young man has departed this earth in the prime of life with his proud and exciting agenda unfulfilled, is a tragedy. Yet, I am sure that his friends, family, and supporters will continue his good work to modify our National Tradition, just as his forebears did centuries ago. Once again the name Romero will be carved into the history books of bullfighting."

Father Ignacio, turned to face the altar, made the sigh of the cross, and withdrew to his seat in the choir stall.

The Condesa was seated in the front pew, she stood and walked the short distance to the coffin, nodded to the cross behind the altar, turned and faced the congregation. With one hand resting on the coffin stroking it gently, she turned the microphone on, waited for the coughing and shuffling to die down and raised the device to her mouth.

"Thank you," she said. "For sharing with me this precious and final farewell to my beloved fiancée, Diego Romero. I'll be brief and won't dwell on the tragedy and sadness we all feel. Furthermore, I won't make a fuss about the unfairness of such a popular and kind man losing his life at such a tender age. Father Ignacio has covered that quite beautifully. What I will say, is that because of Diego's passing, a giant hole has opened in my life.

"We met at Salamanca University when we were both in our late teens and I can honestly say that it was love at first sight. However, that was before I knew he was an apprentice bullfighter. It soon became clear to me that he was committed to a career in the bullring. There was no way that even I could stand in the way of centuries of Romero family tradition.

"I can tell you that having been vehemently anti-blood sports all my life that was extremely difficult for me to accept. Especially being a stuck-up brat with a fancy title and hereditary obligations of what I was to do with my life. Nevertheless, I loved him, and love conquers all, so I agreed to his marriage proposal, but with certain terms and conditions. My darling Diego reluctantly accepted them, he loved me so.

"I know that he was a wild man, and had certain needs, especially after surviving another session in the bullring. I accepted that. I didn't demand anything from him, just that he loved me unconditionally, stay alive, eventually quit the ring, and then marry me.

"What a fool I was. All those wasted years. Now here I stand, a virgin in my mid-twenties, alone and miserable. Oh God, why didn't I just get on with having lots of sex and babies with my gorgeous man? At least then, I'd have some amazing memories and some mini versions of him to stand by me in this giant hole and share the unbearable pain.

"Again, thank you for coming."

The whole church stood as one and applauded as the Condesa returned to her seat, sobbing uncontrollably, handkerchief to her mouth. Three aging tenors from the local choir then sang *Nessum Dorma* followed by a final blessing from Father Ignacio.

Afterward, everyone filed out slowly. Juan and the bullfighters assembled on the steps outside the church in a show of strength and unity.

The camera zoomed in on Juan surrounded by his supporters. Phillip passed him a microphone. The crowd applauded.

"Thank you for your support this morning," said Juan fighting back a tear, as the crowd stilled. "Whatever journey Diego may now be starting; his memory will always be with us. It will continue to drive me," Juan paused to indicate the other bullfighters.

"And all of us, to finish what he started. First, we have decided to change the name of bullfighting to reflect more accurately our intentions. No longer will we fight bulls, we will join with them in a demonstration of mutual respect at a Festival de Toros, Bull Festival."

The crowd mimicked the words among themselves and generally nodded their approval.

"We welcome anybody," Juan continued. "To join with us including the Royal Taurino Society. We invite them to build a program together with us that fades out the old and brings in the new. Today, I can confirm that our first event will take place, as announced by Diego, here in Ronda in two weeks' time. It will be on national TV, free to view, available for everyone to watch, enjoy, and make comments or suggestions. Your support will ensure that the Festival de Toros will successfully evolve into being Spain's new national tradition and ensure Diego's death would not have been in vain. Thank you."

40

Prado skipped Diego's wake in the bullring café, his deadline to solve the case was rapidly approaching, and he needed to move the investigation forward. He headed down to Málaga to meet with el jefe to discuss the latest developments and plead for an extension of time. Ninety minutes later, he was approaching the Comisaría when his phone rang. He pressed the hands-free.

"Buenos tardes," said Juan.

"Hola hombre, I assumed that you'd be occupied with all the freeloaders?"

"I am, but I wanted to tell you that I did as you suggested and called Escobedo last night."

"And?"

"You were right, he was most cooperative, and we've begun a discussion on how we might come together, but more importantly, he instructed the archives manager to go look for a wounded bullfighter."

"Any luck?"

"I've just received an email. Leon, he found one from the 1989 intake to the apprentice school in Madrid who was seriously gored in the right thigh by a cow in the practice ring."

"There for the grace of God, go I," said Prado, laughing. "I still owe you for that."

"Nonsense," said Juan.

"What's his name?"

"Nicolas Patricio O'Reilly Santana. According to his application papers, he had a Spanish father from Marbella and an Irish mother originally from Killarney."

"Any photos?"

"One. It's definitely a younger version of Patrick."

"Do you have his fiscal number?"

"It's on the application, I'll forward everything through."

"Is there an address?"

"Central Marbella, an apartment block I think, probably his parents."

"Well, that's something. All we need now is to find him. Thanks, my friend."

Prado pulled into the Comisaría and went quickly up to his office. He turned on his laptop and read Patrick's application.

He'd attended a private international school in Marbella but had left before taking any exams to follow his dream of becoming a bullfighter. His father was a property developer; his mother hadn't worked.

Prado then looked at the photo. Patrick's eyes haven't changed a bit, he thought.

Prado forwarded the email to el jefe and requested a search on the current residents in the parent's apartment. Patrick's fiscal number was to be checked to see if he was registered on any state databases.

El jefe would need some time to process the information about Patrick, so Prado popped out for a late lunch. He was starving.

After a tasty bowl of Salmorejo, some crusty baguette and a couple of beers at Cortijo de Pepe, Prado returned to the office and went up to see his boss. He knocked on his door and entered. How his confidence had changed since Angelika's kidnapping, he thought. El jefe was on the phone, he waved him in and pointed to the chair opposite.

El jefe finished his conversation, reached over and picked up some reports.

"Before we start on your intriguing list of names," he said. "I've managed to obtain; don't inquire how, a report on the bank accounts of Peepers, Dabblers and CVS Ltd."

"That is good news, sir?"

"Not really. All three accounts are, or should I say were, in the same bank, but have been closed and their substantial balances transferred out of Gibraltar to CVS Holdings Ltd., in the Turks and Caicos Islands, where we may as well say goodbye to any further information."

"CVS Holdings? Now that is a coincidence, sir. Phillip told me that his server was hacked via a data center based in Mumbai, India. Guess who the owners were?"

"Tell me."

"CVS Holdings Ltd."

"What does that signify?" said el jefe.

"A link between Crown, O'Reilly, CVS and possibly Pablo Bosque or someone in the Royal Taurino

Society. What is also interesting is that the Gibraltar based lawyers, nominee directors, and shareholders for the three companies are, or were the same. They've been wound up now."

"Martin and Bayne?"

"Correct."

"So, are we assuming that Peepers, Dabblers and CVS have, or had some kind of relationship?"

"It would appear so, but a personal connection between Crown and O'Reilly would clinch it and I think we have that, sir," said Prado.

"How?"

"They are both forty-seven years old. In O'Reilly's application to the bullfighting school, he had to include his education details. We already had Crown's school report, and when I compared the two documents it all became clear. Sir, they both attended the same international school in Marbella at the same time."

"And with the same age it was likely they were in in the same class," said el jefe.

"So, childhood friends working together thirty years later in separate crime categories. What's that all about?"

"It must be a strong bond, to have lasted that long."

"You're right, sir, but I can't see them telling us why. Anything on O'Reilly's parents?"

"The father died a few years back, but the mother is still alive and living in the same apartment," said el jefe. "I've sent a local officer to knock on the door, but he hasn't reported back yet. Now let me tell you about O'Reilly's fiscal number."

"It's not been used since 1991?" said Prado.

"How did you know that?"

"That was when he was injured at the bullfighting

school. I'm surmising that when he came out of the hospital, his torero dreams shattered, he was forced to start again from scratch. However, he had no qualifications and all he had to offer was knowledge of bullfighting. I think that he joined the black economy and since then has made a living taking bets under the radar. As his enterprise expanded, he used his debtors to apply for official documents and bank cards on his behalf."

"So like Crown, he was also off the radar?"

"It appears so."

"Then perhaps they've joined together in some form of conspiracy?"

"Could be but we could speculate about that all night," said Prado.

"You're right. Let's concentrate on what we have. The four names you sent me last night. Tobalo identified the bank manager, Trujillo as the one with the passport envelope so I've issued a warrant for his arrest. Thankfully, the local officers found him still working late at the bank in Fuengirola. He'll be delivered here in about twenty minutes."

"Could we discuss my time limit on the case, sir? I believe that we're almost there but will need a day or two more to locate Patrick."

"Time limit, Prado? What time limit?"

"Fine, sir."

"Anyway, we've traced the Albanians and Scandinavians who are now under lock and key awaiting deportation.

"Excellent work, sir. What worries me most about Patrick, is that none of his usual contacts have heard from him since last Friday, and the last time he was seen was leaving the bullring on Saturday. I think that he has gone to ground or is in the process of doing so. All the signs are there. His phone has been disconnected, the website taken down, and as you said, the money has been moved."

"Then all we need is Patrick's passport details from Señor Trujillo and we should be able to find him or prevent him from leaving the country."

El jefe's phone rang, he turned on the speakerphone.

"It's Officer Cano, sir, I've just come out of O'Reilly's mother's apartment."

"Did she let you in?"

"Er... no, sir, there was no answer, but a neighbor had a key and accompanied me inside. The mother is suffering from Dementia and has recently moved into a private care home here in Marbella. I found a paid invoice dated ten days ago on the dining room table. It covers five years of fees. The spare bedroom has obviously been in use. There are a few items of male clothing in the wardrobe and a red wig on the desk but nothing else of interest."

"Has the neighbor seen anything of Patrick?"

"Occasionally, but not for a couple of weeks."

"Thank you, Officer Cano. Good work. Ask the neighbor to lock up and call you if Patrick turns up."

"Right, sir."

"Five years of care home fees," said Prado. "That must be a lump sum in advance. A definite sign of going to ground."

"Sounds like it," said el jefe. "Where would he go?"

"No idea," said Prado.

Someone knocked on the door and entered. It was Isabel, el jefe's assistant, a well-rounded, but stylishly dressed woman in her late thirties with dyed blond-highlighted hair. "The Fuengirola police have delivered Señor Trujillo with lightning speed, sir," she said. "I've put him in the downstairs interview room."

"Thank you, Isabel," said el jefe

Prado and el jefe went down to the room adjoining the interview room to look through the one-way mirror at Señor Alfonso Trujillo. Trujillo was pacing about muttering to himself.

He was in his late thirties, of average height, short-cropped dark hair, brown eyes, thin oval face sporting gold-rimmed half-moon spectacles perched on the end of his nose.

He wore a dark blue blazer, grey flannels with a white shirt and garish tie.

His black shoes were spotless, noticed Prado. However, his hands were shaking, and his nose was speckled with blue veins.

"Whiskey drinker, wouldn't you say?" said el jefe.

"Or brandy. First impressions are dapper, but look at those shifty eyes," said Prado.

"A devious type," said el jefe.

"Then I suggest a full-frontal attack."

"The warrant included a full search of his property and devices, sirs," said Sergeant Santamaria coming in to join them. "I found this on his phone."

Prado looked at the screen to see a Spanish passport. The photo was of Patrick with cropped hair but using the name, Geraldo Jimenez Bueno.

"Well done detective," said el jefe. "I'll go and put out an all-points bulletin for Señor Jimenez Bueno while you have a little chat with Señor Trujillo."

Prado entered the interview room.

Trujillo stopped pacing and sat down tapping his fingers on the grey laminate desk. "Why have I been arrested, and I demand the return of my phone," said Trujillo.

"The phone will be useful to call your solicitor," said Prado. "Because Señor Trujillo, you are going to need one."

"What have I done?"

"To start with, you have fraudulently obtained a passport in the name of Geraldo Jimenez Bueno."

Trujillo's shoulders slumped and his eyes watered. "This will finish me," he said.

"Probably," said Prado. "However, now my main concern is finding Señor Jimenez Bueno or should I refer to him by his proper name Nicolas Patricio O'Reilly Santana.

"We suspect that Patricio has committed at least two murders and is about to go underground. Your cooperation in catching him would be most appreciated."

"Right, then, I'll come clean," said Trujillo. "Also, on my phone is a photo of the campervan I purchased and insured for Patrick's girlfriend last week. However, I have no idea where they might be going, but she is Moroccan."

"Name?"

"Jamila Harrack. There's also a copy of her Moroccan passport. I had to present it to insure the vehicle and put it in her name."

41

"We're approaching Tarifa Ferry Terminal," said Jamila in Spanish, a young woman in her late twenties with brown eyes, medium-length dark hair and a pretty face. "I should drive from here."

"You're right," said Patrick also in Spanish. "I'll stop at that rest area on the top of the next hill. Let's fill up the tank and you take over. Have you got all the papers ready?"

"Yes."

"And what will you say if they ask you why we are visiting Tangiers?"

"Attending a family wedding, returning next week."

"Don't forget to take both passports and buy return tickets?"

"I won't."

They stopped, filled the tank and grabbed a coffee to go. Jamila drove. Patrick strapped himself into the passenger seat, pulled the peak of his baseball hat downwards and put on a pair of large sunglasses.

They parked the camper van outside the ferry terminal. Jamila went inside, joined a short queue and purchased two return tickets with cash. She then drove the van to join the back of the vehicle queue. The ferry was due to leave in thirty-five minutes. With fifteen to go, they drove on to the ferry, parked as directed by the deckhand, locked up, climbed the steps to the lounge and sat down in a corner seat where they could see over the terminal.

At last, the ship's rear hatch closed, and the sailors responsible for the mooring ropes were preparing to cast off. The minute hand reached twelve on Patrick's watch.

Two black cars with blue lights flashing pulled up outside the terminal building. Six men in plain clothes leaped out and ran for the ferry. Patrick looked at Jamila, smiled and shook his head.

"Fuck. It looks like the cops found Trujillo," he said. "Sorry love, but this is it. Remember, no comment is all you say. Your crimes aren't serious, so you won't be inside for long, and there's plenty of money for you when you're released. Don't forget the code numbers?"

***

Prado and Phillip took their seats opposite Patrick in the Málaga Comisaría interview room. A bulky uniformed officer stood behind Patrick. Prado turned on the recording device, announced the obligatory data and the two murders that Patrick had been charged with.

Then Prado stared at Patrick saying nothing.

Up close, Patrick was a mean-looking man, with a

dour expression. His grey eyes were cold and hard. He had a small scar running down the side of his lip and his nose was crooked as if it had been left alone to mend after being rearranged. There was a hint of grey in his cropped black hair and stubble covered his face.

"Please confirm," said Prado. "That you are Nicolas Patricio O'Reilly Santana."

"I will be confirming nothing nor answering any fucking questions," said Patrick gruffly in English with a broad southern Irish accent. "So why don't you just lock me up? It'll save us all a hell of a lot of time."

Phillip translated for Prado, who nodded, turned off the recorder, stood and left the room.

"Shall I inform your mother of your current status?" said Phillip in English. Patrick continued to glare at him. "I'll take that as a no then," said Phillip. "In that case, I'm going to paint a picture of what is likely to happen to you when you leave here for Alhaurin Prison to await trial. There are many avid bullfighting fans inhabiting your imminent accommodation. They won't be too fondly disposed towards the murderer of Diego Romero and Donald MacKinnon. What I'm saying is that we can ensure that you are kept separately from them providing that you cooperate with us now."

Silence.

"We have plenty of evidence to secure a life sentence. To be frank, you will be dying in that prison."

No reaction.

"It's only a question of time before we obtain access to Dabbler's bank accounts in Turks and Caicos. All the money you have stashed there will be recovered and there won't even be a cent to cover your funeral expenses. Furthermore, your mother's advance private care home payment will be recovered, her apartment sold, and the money used to pay for accommodation in a basic state institution."

Phillip paused to gauge any reaction.

Nothing.

"Very well, two more questions. We note that Dabblers shared the same bank and lawyers as a company called CVS Ltd., in Gibraltar. Funds from both companies were transferred to the identical bank in Turks and Caicos. What is your relationship with CVS Ltd.?"

No reply.

"We note that you attended the same school as Malcolm Crown."

O'Reilly's eyes snapped up to stare hard at Phillip, but then quickly reverted to their bored, indolent stare.

"Do you know him?"

"No comment," said O'Reilly.

"And finally, Jamila has been most cooperative. We know where you lived, and officers are on their way to search the premises. Is there anything you can tell me that may help your case?"

Patrick shrugged but remained silent.

Phillip gathered his papers, stood and left the room.

Prado was waiting in the corridor. He put his arm around Phillip's shoulder and whispered to him as they headed back to Prado's office. "Due to the scale of O'Reilly's crimes and his potential link to Crown, el jefe has obtained a special order to monitor them both in prison. I've arranged for Patrick to share accommodation with Crown in a cell fitted with listening devices and a camera. Their conversations should prove interesting."

42

Phillip set light to the kindling in his Weber Barbecue parked in a brick recess to the side of his pot plant lined terrace. At the top of the recess was a chimney that sucked the smoke up and away from the villa. He preferred charcoal to gas and used newspapers and canes from the old terrace shading to avoid tainting the grill with chemicals. Today's offering was to be butterfly king prawns followed by Toro de Lidia Steaks shipped to him from the Romero restaurant in Madrid. He'd prepared them in a spicy paprika rub. The invited guests would provide salads, wine, cheese, and desserts.

Amanda stood by the terrace bar near the table laid stylishly for ten people with plain white plates, silver cutlery, and tulip-shaped wine glasses. She poured two glasses of chilled Verdejo, brought them over, handed one to him and put an arm around his waist. He bent his head to kiss her then they chinked glasses, took a sip and watched the flames take hold.

"Remember last time we did this?" she said.

"How could I forget our first kiss?" he said.

"Seems like a lifetime ago now."

"Just over four months actually."

"What time are our guests due?"

"Richard and Ingrid will be bang on time, in about five minutes. Prado, Inma, Juan, and Maribel no idea, my sister Glenda and Jose in about ten minutes."

"No nieces?"

"On a school trip to Galicia apparently."

"Then we can let our hair down after they've all gone."

"Little tart," said Phillip hugging her tight.

"We're all right, aren't we?" she said smiling.

"Not too shabby," he grinned shifting a few coals with the tongs.

A large Mercedes pulled up and parked in the drive. They went out to greet their business partners, Richard and Ingrid. Richard was American. A chunky, congenial man from Boston, Massachusetts, in his early sixties with a ruddy complexion, thinning gray hair, twinkling hazel eyes, and a deep throaty voice. He was wearing his usual leather sandals, khaki shorts, and a light pink Lacoste polo shirt. His wife Ingrid was German. A petite, graceful, woman in her late fifties, oozing confidence, with fair curly hair and gray eyes. She was dressed in blue jeans, a loose white blouse, and blue framed sunglasses.

Richard grabbed a cloth bag from the back seat and handed over the customary entrance fee of two bottles of Arzuaga Crianza.

"Can someone take the potato salad?" said Ingrid from the passenger seat holding it up from her lap.

Then a tall, slim pretty woman in her late thirties

with long curly blond hair and striking blue eyes arrived at the gate carrying a salad bowl under one arm and holding hands with a slender man of the same height. He had dark hair and a full beard. It was Phillip's sister Glenda and her husband Jose who lived on the farm next door.

Another Mercedes parked behind Richard. Juan was driving with Prado in the passenger seat. Inma and Maribel were in the back. They all climbed out and closed the car doors behind them.

Amanda introduced everyone and led them in the front door, through the modern kitchen and out onto the spacious terrace at the rear where she served drinks. They all sat down at the table and raised their glasses.

"Before we eat," said Prado putting his glass back on the table. "I want to bring you up to date with the Darkness in Ronda case."

"How are Crown and Patrick getting on?" said Amanda.

"Other than the occasional greeting, they don't talk with each other at all," said Prado. "Nevertheless, there have been a couple of incidents that lead me to suspect that they do know each other."

"Such as?" said Richard.

"As you know sex offenders are usually kept in solitary confinement. Now that Crown is in the general prison, there have been several attempts to attack him. On each occasion, Patrick has defended Crown. Patrick may have a damaged leg, but the man is brutally violent, and the attackers ended up in hospital; now they are left alone. One would have thought that Crown would at least have thanked Patrick for his help, but they both sustained their silence routine. It makes me think that Patrick is in some way subservient to

Crown."

"You mean Crown is his boss?" said Phillip.

"Exactly," said Prado.

"So, what now?" said Phillip.

"We'll keep them in the same cell until their trials are due, which with the current overloading in the courts, could be at least a year. We'll continue to monitor them, but I don't hold out much hope unless they have a falling out or decide to confess. Meanwhile, we have begun proceedings to gain access to the offshore bank accounts."

"What about the Moroccan girl?" said Amanda.

"She'll be deported back to Tangiers next week."

"So, we'll just have to be satisfied," said Phillip. "That at least we have the perpetrators behind bars with sufficient evidence to keep them there for the remainder of their lives."

"Yes, but all the unresolved loose ends leave a sour taste in my mouth," said Prado.

"Such as what?" said Juan.

"Thanks to Tobalo, we have the pistol that was given by Patrick to Zambrano who passed it on to Fredo. The weapon was relatively new but has no markings or history of use in other crimes. It does have Fredo's prints all over it, so confirms that he dumped it in the trash can at the Ronda car park."

"Does that mean Fredo didn't kill Diego?" said Inma with tears in her eyes.

"Almost my love, but we have more recent forensics that exonerate Fredo completely. Fredo was not involved with the Mackinnon murder, he was in Mexico at the time. Furthermore, forensics have deduced that for the sword to have penetrated Diego's back at the angle it did, it must have been delivered by a tall person, Fredo was simply too small. The killer had to reach over the back of the pew, raise the sword high enough for the required leverage and correct angle, then using two hands, thrust downwards vertically enough to miss bone and directly pierce the heart. Patrick, even with his bad leg could have easily managed it, Fredo never. Add the red hairs at both crime scenes, and that Tobalo gave Patrick the key to the bullfighters changing rooms in Ronda, and we have a cast-iron case against Patrick."

Inma smiled, breathed a sigh of relief and wiped her eyes with her serviette.

"Did you find anything on the second Bandolero?" said Phillip.

"Nothing," said Prado.

"Could he have been the killer?" said Phillip.

"Unlikely, one of them would have stayed outside the chapel door, and the red hairs place Patrick inside the chapel."

"So how come Fredo didn't see Patrick in the chapel?" said Juan. "They must have been there at about the same time."

"As was I," said Prado. "But before both. It's amazing we didn't cross anywhere. We're assuming that Patrick hid in the confession booth with the curtain closed until Diego arrived. When Diego was concentrating on his mental preparation, he then crept up behind and stabbed him. He then received a signal, a quick tap on the door maybe, that someone was coming. So, slipped back into the booth, closed the curtain then wiped the blood from his hands onto the priest's robe.

"He must have nerves of steel. Those few minutes in the booth while Fredo was there must have been terrifying knowing Fredo had a pistol. Patrick then rejoined his fellow bandolero and hobbled out passing me coming in the other way. They rejoined his fake protestors who swarmed around so they could slip out of their disguises. One of them then stashed the clothing under a hedge, and they dispersed."

"What about Patrick's mother," said Phillip. "Couldn't she confirm that Patrick and Crown knew each other at school?

"Sadly, she's in the advanced stages of dementia and can't recall she has a son, let alone his childhood."

"Did Patrick own any property?" said Juan.

"Patrick owned nothing, in either of his names," said Prado. "That was the secret of his success. No traceable responsibilities and everything he needed was paid for by others."

"Did you recover any money?" said Richard.

"One of Patrick's debtors was a man named Trujillo, a bank manager in Benalmadena. He'd arranged a genuine passport for Patrick in a false name and purchased the campervan for their escape to Morocco. All the money Patrick collected in cash, such as from Fredo and Zambrano, was paid into a secret account in Fuengirola. It was then transferred offshore. We managed to stop the last payment and recovered sixty thousand Euros, so at least that's something."

"Talking of loose ends," said Phillip. "Did Ana develop that roll of film we found at Cortijo Infierno?"

"Not yet," said Prado. "However, she has found a Lab in the USA that is prepared to try? It will take a month before we can see what secrets it contains."

***

The convivial afternoon passed and as the sunset to a glorious kaleidoscope of pinks, oranges, and reds, the guests took their leave. When the final car lights disappeared around the corner, Phillip and Amanda stood watching them go, hugging. They turned and looked into each other's eyes.

"Well my darling, what are you thinking?" said Amanda.

"Other than being totally in love with you and wanting to know what the fuck is in that film we found up at Cortijo Infierno, I was wondering what you were discussing so intensely with the Condesa on the night before the funeral."

"Oh that. It was nothing really."

"It must have been something because her eulogy the next day was totally different from what she was blabbering on about during rehearsal. Much better I thought."

"I may have influenced her a little bit, but we talked about other stuff too."

"Such as?"

"The protests in Madrid. It was her that dreamed up the scheme and made all the arrangements with the people, but Diego had financed it. He called it a pardon guarantee fund."

"That was a hell of a risk. Getting one pardon, let alone two is a complete lottery."

"She said he was confident and was prepared to lose the money rather than let the Society have their way uncontested."

"And that conversation took all evening?"

"No, the rest was girlie stuff."

"I'd love to hear about it."

"Wow you are a one-off, but if you insist. We were

discussing the conflict of love, having a family and being a smart successful career woman."

"So that's where lots of sex and babies came from."

"Yes," she whispered holding him tighter.

"And do you feel the same?" he said lifting her chin and stroking her cheek. She nodded and buried her head in his chest.

"Then, there's only one thing for it," he said getting down on his knees, taking her hand and kissing it.

"Will you marry me?" he said.

She looked up at him and giggled. "Of course. I thought you'd never pluck up the courage to ask."

The Author

Paul S Bradley, originally from London, England, has lived in Nerja, Spain since 1992 where he established a marketing agency to help Spanish businesses sharpen their communications to the rapidly growing number of foreign visitors. He's traveled extensively around the Iberian Peninsula, visiting most of the ancient cities and countless wine bodegas. In the early years, he published lifestyle and property magazines, guidebooks and travelogues in English, German and Spanish. More recently, groups of discerning Alumni of Americans and Canadians have enjoyed his tour director services. He's lectured about Living in Spain, bullfighting and has appeared on local radio and TV. The Andalusian Mystery Series draws on his own experiences as a voluntary translator in hospitals and police stations.

What did you think?

Reviews, good or bad fuel this independent author's continuous efforts to improve. If you enjoyed this book, please leave a comment on my blog, Amazon or Goodreads, or follow me on Facebook or Twitter. See website for more details. Thank you

www.paulbradley.eu